a weekend away from conception ridge

chloe maine

father of the bride

an age gap romance

FATHER OF THE BRIDE

She's the maid of honor. He's the father of the bride.

Thanks to a snowstorm on the East Coast, I'm the only member of my best friend's wedding party to actually arrive in Vegas as planned. But she has a plan. . . her father will pick me up at the airport, and we'll take care of any last-minute wedding details together. Not in the plan is the unexpected sizzling chemistry with an older, off-limits man and being talked into sharing his suite.

What happens in Vegas, stays in Vegas? Not if the father of the bride claims you as his own.

1
rosie

I STARE at the arrivals board, a sinking feeling of despair growing in my belly. Melanie's flight out of New York has been canceled—and it looks like a lot of others have, too.

Digging out my phone, I turn it off airplane mode and send the bride-to-be a quick message.

I just landed. . . your flight was canceled? I'm so sorry.

I'm sorry for myself, too, but I don't let that bleed into my text message. This weekend is all about her.

She replies immediately.

It's a mess! Major storm, so many flights need to be rebooked. I'm hoping we can get out tomorrow, but my dad is already on top of it.

I flush at the reminder that Melanie's dad will be here. Is already here in Vegas, apparently.

Okay, my dad is on his way to pick you up.

What? No. Oh *no*. Hot embarrassment fills my chest. The last time I saw him. . .

I need you to help him, Rosie.

The texts keep pinging on my screen, a laundry list of wedding tasks. A meeting with the catering staff, a check-in with the florist, and picking up our dresses from the dress shop.

He doesn't care about the details the way I do. Promise me you'll stick by his side, okay?

She has no idea what she's asking—or how awkward it will be. Not that Mel would care. Nothing phases her.

We're a strange pair of best friends. She's two years older than me and runs in a very different social circle now that we're adults. But once upon a time, she was my next-door neighbor, back when her dad was a struggling construction worker. Before he worked his way up the business, then built his own firm and became a big-shot zero energy home developer.

Now he's one of the richest men in Conception Ridge. And the most eligible bachelor because he never re-married after Melanie's mom left him.

Growing up, Melanie would come to dinner at our townhouse when her dad was working late. By the time they moved when she was a teenager, we had a friendship bond that was more like sisters.

We love like sisters. Sometimes fight like sisters. But at the end of the day, we're always there for each other.

Even if she wants me to spend twenty-four hours doing non-stop, wedding-related activities with her dad, all because of a storm.

Why didn't she get married in New York???

I guess for the same reason she didn't get married in Conception Ridge. Vegas is easy and different and exciting.

It's only easy and exciting because someone else—me—will be running around like crazy with her—

"Rosie?"

I jerk my head up and gasp at the shot of aroused need that runs through me. Mr. Burke is as hot as ever.

Usually, I see him in T-shirts and jeans, not a suit. And today, he's wearing a perfectly tailored black suit, looking like money and power and sex all rolled into one.

How have I never seen him in a suit?

And why is he dressed up like this? I'm wearing yoga pants and an anime T-shirt, dressed for flying on the most budget-friendly ticket possible, squished in the middle of a row.

Mr. Burke looks like a high roller, his usual laidback dad vibe replaced with shiver-inducing intense energy that makes me do a double-take.

"Hi," I stammer. "You didn't need to pick me up."

He raises his eyebrows and holds up his phone. "Express orders from the bride. Yes, I did."

Oh. Right.

"She wants us to do some of the last-minute appointments?" For some reason, it comes out sounding like a question.

"I saw that, too." He flicks a gaze down to my suitcase, then drags his attention over my outfit. "Do you want to go straight to the hotel? Are you tired from the flight?"

"I. . . uh, no?" Fuck, I sound like a brainless idiot. I sigh. "No," I say more definitively. "I'm fine. If you want to drop me off, if you have somewhere to be, I can take care of the wedding stuff myself."

He frowns. "That was not my instruction. And I don't have anywhere to be."

"You're all dressed up."

He looks at me like I'm an idiot. "I'm in Vegas."

It's not the first time he's given me that look, like I'm a little girl who doesn't understand grown-up things. It fills me with righteous indignation. I spread my arms wide. "I'm in Vegas, too, and I don't have anything that looks like that."

He laughs and leans in. "Are you wearing a cute T-shirt like that to the wedding, then? Was that approved by the bride?"

Heat swarms my face. "No. I'm picking up my dress here because the store closest to Conception Ridge didn't have my size."

"Is that on our to-do list for today?"

"Tomorrow."

"Ah." His grin slowly fades to a serious expression. "We have our work cut out for us, don't we?"

Our. We.

I cannot spend the next thirty-six hours with this man. I swallow hard. "I guess so."

"So much for my plan to hit the casino." He winks. "But we can do that after we finish our assigned tasks."

I shake my head. "I can't."

"Why not?" He gives me a playful look, one I vaguely remember from my childhood.

"I'm not old enough," I whisper.

His face tenses, and he steps back. Suddenly, the people are all around us, and airport noises come rushing back. For a moment there, we'd slipped into a private back and forth, and I'd forgotten my place. "Right," he says tightly. "My bad. . . I—"

"It's fine. I don't want to gamble anyway." It's a lie. I wish I was old enough to go to the casino. It feels exciting and magical, and when am I ever going to be back here?

Never, that's when.

"I thought you just had your birthday." His gaze is so hard to read. Is he mad at me for not being twenty-one yet? "After. . ."

After he caught me at The Roadhouse back in Conception Ridge, trying not to get carded. It was one of the few times I'd gone out with friends from college, but what is the point in a town that small?

If you try to order a cocktail with rum and pineapple juice, there is a better than one hundred percent chance your best friend's dad will be there to furiously drag you away from the table and remind you that you're not quite legal.

And not old enough to have grown-up fun yet.

Even though I'm twenty years old—technically an adult for two years already—Mr. Burke will always see me as a little girl.

But apparently, he forgot it that night. One of the most

embarrassing nights of my life—and the hottest too, although that's a secret I'll take to my grave—and he's acting like it meant nothing to him.

Because I'm nobody to him. Whew, well, I guess I needed that reminder.

"Time flies," I say lightly. "But not that fast. My birthday is on Sunday, actually."

The day after the wedding.

It was another reason I was thrilled when Melanie asked me to be her maid of honor. I'm going to turn twenty-one in Vegas, and I have big plans to celebrate properly.

But first, I need to work with Mr. Burke to make Melanie's wedding perfect. Which means letting go of past embarrassment and showing him I'm mature.

He nods slowly. "Well, happy early birthday. We'll make sure to carve some time out for you—"

"Shall we go to the florist?" I know I'm interrupting him, which is rude, but I'd rather focus on the wedding tasks. "And then, if you want, you can drop me at my hotel, or I can make my own way from the flower shop. You really didn't need to pick me up."

"You aren't staying at the Babylon?"

"Nope." I point outside. "Are you parked that way?"

He frowns but accepts my change of subject.

He picks it up again as soon as my suitcase is stowed in the trunk of his high-end rental car, and I'm in the passenger seat—his captive to lecture, apparently. "And *why* aren't you staying at the same hotel as us? All the wedding events are there."

My face goes hot. "I, uh. . . can't afford it."

He slows the car to a stop at a red light. Ahead of us are the lights of the main strip.

I sneak a glance at his profile. His jaw is tight with tension, the muscles of his cheek in starker relief than before.

"You shouldn't have to—" He clears his throat. "I'll get you a room."

"No, please don't—I think I can catch a bus or a shuttle—"

His eyebrows jolt up, and he turns his head, pinning me with a furious gaze.

I press back into the lush leather seat. "It's fine."

His eyes go wide, and he stares ahead again. "Fuck, Rosie. Sure, it's *fine*, but it's not *good enough*. Do you think I'm mad at you?"

I nod, my head wobbly with uncertain nerves. "A little. I didn't think I needed to check my hotel booking with Melanie. I don't think she cares where I stay."

"But I care. And I'm not angry at you. The idea of you taking a shuttle back and forth. . . It won't do. Understand? I want you close." He swallows hard enough that it's visible, and the muscle in his cheek twitches again. "For the planning."

2
daniel

WE CROSS LAS VEGAS BOULEVARD, and the built-in GPS in the rental tells me how to find the flower shop.

Beside me, I catch Rosie sneaking glances at my profile. I can feel her confusing, burning gaze, but I can't look back at her.

The plan was simple. Pick up the girl, deliver her to the hotel, and head out for the night.

Because it's not often I get a weekend in Vegas, but when I do, I like to play cards. High-stakes games. Real money. The kind of money I didn't always have. The kind I worked hard to earn. Life-changing money.

There aren't many things in life that give me that kind of rush. I'm a tightly controlled man. A father, although after this weekend, my daughter will officially be a married woman herself, and my responsibilities there will ease a little.

I'm feeling some kind of way about that because being a father has been my single driving force for the last twenty-two years.

And now my child has decided to have a Vegas wedding to a man fifteen years older than her?

Leaving me more time to unwind at a card table, in theory.

And maybe find someone to take back to my suite—an indulgence I haven't allowed myself in all the years I was being a father. Because a long time ago, I made a reckless choice and knew far too well what the consequences could be.

That was the plan, anyway.

But when I stalked into the airport arrivals area, I found little Rosie, all grown up. It was a painful reminder that what I wanted *in theory* and what I *actually wanted* with every fiber of my being were two very different things.

For months now since I dragged her out of The Roadhouse, pressed her against the wall, and demanded to know why she was drinking alcohol, I've wanted this girl to be mine.

And since she hissed up at me that she was almost legal, that it didn't make a difference, and that I was embarrassing her in front of her friends, I have wanted to drag her home and show her all the difference it makes.

But there are lines one does not cross.

That night took me by surprise. When I saw her at The Roadhouse, it had been a few years since I'd last seen her. A few very important years. The kind that takes a girl and turns her into a woman. Years that can change the relationship between a young woman and an old guy who should know better than to want her in nothing but her nerdy little T-shirt.

Straddling my face as I lick her sweet little cunt until she cries out my name.

I'd managed to convince myself it had all been a fantasy. That she hadn't been everything I ever wanted that night outside the bar back in Conception Ridge. That it didn't matter if she hated me for being an overbearing, prudish old man because she was never going to be mine.

But as soon as I saw her tonight, curves spilling out of yoga pants, making yet another cartoon T-shirt stretch in all the right ways, I knew those few years hadn't been an illusion. This was not the Rosie I once knew.

This young woman was ripe and breedable, and I needed to be very fucking careful that I didn't ruin the tenuous relationship we still had.

Father of the bride and maid of honor.

We had two days of wedding-related tasks ahead of us when all I wanted to do was drive out to the desert, drop my right hand to the curve of her thigh, and tell her I knew exactly how to celebrate her birthday.

My face between her thighs, my apology for past mistakes given in the form of slow, firm licks against her clit.

"The flower shop is. . ." She twists her head to the right. "Back there."

The GPS unit tells me the same thing in a cool, detached tone. I had fully tuned out, apparently.

Fuck. Me.

I shove down the dark fantasies I shouldn't have and circle the block.

Once we're inside, both Rosie and I try to introduce ourselves at the same time.

"We're here about—"

"I'd like to speak to your manager."

Rosie turns and gives me a *what the fuck* expression. Then she looks back at the clerk. "The Burke Ruiz wedding on Saturday?"

"My daughter's wedding," I bark.

The clerk's wide eyes soften, and she smiles at Rosie. "Your dad's nervous, huh?"

"She's not—" I start to protest.

Rosie waves her hand in the air. "Oh, you know how they get. Can't bear to see their little girls all grown up."

There's a dig somewhere in there, a punishment for treating her like a little kid a few months ago.

But she's got it all wrong. I'm deeply fucking pleased she's all grown up. Sarcastically referring to herself as my little girl makes my cock—already heavy and aware of her—twitch in delight.

"Okay, I have all your details here. We spoke on the phone, right?"

Rosie pauses before answering, and I wonder how far she'll take the ruse of pretending to be Melanie. Then she sighs and shakes her head. "I'm not actually the bride. I'm the maid of honor. But this is her dad! We. . ."

She gives the entire story, including showing the clerk the text messages from my daughter.

Way too much information.

But it endears her to the florist, who tells us how nice it is that we could stop in. She says she'll show us the flowers they're going to use and finally reassures us that everything will be just perfect on Saturday.

All in all, it's way more talking than was necessary, but it gets the job done.

Rosie takes a few pictures of the orchids, texts them to Melanie, and thanks the clerk for her time.

Back outside, I follow her to the car but set my hand on the passenger door before she can open it. "I think we need to clear the air," I say firmly.

I need to tread carefully. But I won't have her stewing over a misunderstanding, either.

She blinks up at me, the sassy control she exhibited in the flower shop gone.

She may not be a little girl anymore, but she is still too damn young.

It's a punch in the gut.

"I know you're a grown woman," I finally manage to say. "I won't repeat the same. . . I won't. . ."

Her lips part as if to reply, then she pauses, and the tip of her tongue swipes out. Wet, pink. *Little.*

"You won't push me against a wall and demand to know if I've been drinking?"

"I didn't push."

"You pinned me against it, just like you're pinning me to the side of your car right now." Her words are breathless now. Less smooth.

Her gaze is full of fire. A warning that she might be young and innocent, but she is on a mission this weekend to make Melanie's wedding perfect, and my bossiness will not get in the way of that.

I lift my hand and stroke my knuckles over her cheek.

My goal is to be softer than before. I didn't want to pin

her to the car—just like I didn't mean to pin her to the wall of The Roadhouse.

I tried to make her look at me both times without touching her too much.

I fix that now by touching her cheek, and now I can't stop because the soft press of her cheek under my fingers is doing fucked up things to my sense of right and wrong.

Her breath hitches as I drag my fingers down the side of her throat.

Fucking hell.

I force myself to step back. "It won't happen again."

It's a short drive to the hotel. A short, tense drive, but the unspoken conflict between us fade as soon as I hand the keys to the valet and Rosie hops out of the passenger side.

I get her suitcase from the trunk, then meet her at the passenger door. She's gazing up at the glittering lights of the hotel soaring above us.

"This is nothing like Conception Ridge," she breathes. Her eyes are wide with wonder, and a smile plays at the corners of her soft mouth. "Wow."

"Not a bad start to your birthday weekend?"

She laughs gleefully. "I'll say."

"Good." I gently place my hand on her elbow and steer her inside, painfully aware that this is the second time in a short span of minutes that I've touched her.

But now that I know what her skin feels like under my fingers, I can't stop. All I can do is keep it on this side of *I'm your best friend's dad*.

Unfortunately, my plan to get her a room hits a snag at the counter when the clerk shakes her head. "I'm terribly sorry, sir. There are no other rooms available tonight. There's a conference until tomorrow, but we might be able to arrange for a room at another hotel."

"I have—"

"No, that's fine." I'm careful not to look at Rosie after I cut her off because I don't want to see her protest. "Ms. Johnson can be added as a guest in my suite."

3
rosie

I JERK IN SURPRISE, but Mr. Burke pretends not to notice. My heart pounds as I think about sharing a space with him—but of course, I'm not going to.

I have my own room reserved at another hotel on the outskirts of town. I'll go there after we finish our errands for the day. And if he wants me to have a room and use his suite for wedding-related tasks, that's fine.

It's fine.

So why is my pulse slamming in my neck, making a dull roar in my ears?

I can't breathe properly as he settles his hand in the small of my back and turns me, pointing us toward the elevators.

"What's next on our agenda?" he asks like this is completely normal.

He's taking me upstairs to his hotel room. It's just the two of us alone together in Vegas. Nothing about this is normal.

"Oh, um. . ." I fumble for my phone. "Menu tasting dinner tonight. And picking up our dresses tomorrow."

"Explain to me how your dresses are here? Isn't that something that you'd need to try on?"

"We ordered them through a chain. I went to Portland to try mine on, and Melanie went to the store in New York. The final fitting will be done tomorrow, and they apparently have a seamstress on site who can make any necessary adjustments."

It seemed like a great idea, especially for Melanie, because a wedding dress would take up an entire suitcase. Her canceled flight now makes this all a little more stressful, but it'll work out. *It has to.*

"Anything else?"

I scan through the messages. "Oh, she wants us to time how long it takes to go from the chapel to the rooftop pool area because that's where they're taking pictures."

"We can do that after dinner. I was up there last night; they have a nice hot tub." He skims his hand up my back and rubs the tense spot between my shoulder blades as the elevator doors open. "You had a lot of things added to your plate today, Rosie. You deserve a bit of relaxation tonight, too."

"It's fine," I insist under my breath as we step into the crowded car.

He doesn't reply.

His suite is at the top of the tower, so we have to keep shifting to let people out of the elevator. With each departure, I'm moved a little closer to Mr. Burke. By the time we reach his floor, his arm is all the way around my shoulders, and I'm leaning into his heavy warmth.

As soon as the doors open, we jump apart. I'm probably

blushing as I scurry ahead of him, which is silly—I don't know which way his room is.

So I stop, suddenly.

And he plows into me from behind, his hands catching me by the hips.

"Sorry," I squeak.

He rubs my side for a moment then steps around me. And he holds out his hand. "This way, Rosie."

All of the little touches so far have been *very* nice. The way he stroked my face outside the flower shop? The casual way his fingers traced on my upper arm in the elevator?

So freaking nice.

But sliding my fingers into his so he can tug me along to his hotel room?

There is no way I'm going to survive a weekend with Mr. Burke without revealing that he's the only person I've ever fantasized about.

The door to his suite is halfway down the hall—and I realize with a start that it's the last door on this side.

Which means his room—suite—is massive.

Inside he takes me through a central living room space with floor-to-ceiling windows overlooking The Strip to a bedroom with an untouched king-sized bed.

"This is the second bedroom," he says, setting my suitcase on the bed. "It's all yours."

I turn in a slow circle. It's gorgeously decorated in luxurious cream fabrics with gold accents. The windows here are covered in thick curtains, and it's so much bigger than my bedroom back home. Bigger, quieter, and prettier.

"Can I really stay here?"

"Of course. I want you to."

"Because I have a reservation, but. . ." I've already lost the money for tonight's stay. But if I can save the money I would spend on the other four nights, I might be able to do something really special on my birthday.

"Rosie, it's fine. I *want* you to stay here with me."

I lick my lips. "Melanie might wonder—"

"Tell her you're staying next door." He steps closer and lowers his voice, even though it's just the two of us in the suite. "This can be our secret. And she's not going to be in until tomorrow anyway, so don't worry about it for tonight."

I nod, a smile spreading across my face. "Okay."

He grins back at me. "Yeah?"

"Yep."

"Then I'll leave you to unpack and get ready for dinner." He glances at my suitcase. "It's Vegas. Don't worry too much about what you wear."

"I have a couple of dresses," I say in a rush. "They're not fancy. More like sundresses."

His gaze snaps back to my face. "Whatever you wear will be perfect, Rosie. I promise you that."

Once he's gone, I skip to the bathroom and groan in delight at the giant soaker tub and separate shower with a complicated multi-head system. So many choices.

I have time for a good long bath, so I start that, then go back to the bed and open my suitcase.

The first thing I do is put the dress I want to wear tonight on a hanger so the few wrinkles collected on the flight can fall out. Then I put away the rest of my clothes and take my makeup bag and toiletry kit to the bathroom.

There's a bag on the back of the door with a tag

explaining the suite has complimentary laundry service, so I strip out of my clothes and put them in the laundry bag.

So this is what it's like to be rich. I twirl naked and scoop up my toothbrush, then dance into the bedroom again to get my phone so I can listen to music in the tub.

I'm halfway across the room when there's a knock at the door.

4
daniel

IT TAKES her a minute to come to the door, and when she does, she only opens it a crack, but it's enough for me to see that she's wrapped in a towel. Soft, white cotton tugged around her torso and bare limbs. . .

"Hi." She's blushing.

Whatever I was going to say dies on my tongue. "You—"

My cock thickens at the thought of her naked and just a few inches from my hungry grasp.

"I'm going to take a bath," she says breathlessly.

"Good."

"Did you need something?" She eases the door open another few inches, and now I can see her bare legs and the curve of her shoulder.

I *need* to plant my palm on the door, spread my fingers wide, and push it open. I *need* her on the bed, legs spread wide so I can taste her tight little pussy.

Instead, I brace my hands on the doorframe—which I probably can't push in—and ask the damn question. "Just wanted to double-check what time the food tasting is at."

"Seven."

"Lots of time, then." This was a mistake, having her in my suite. Pretending I can make small talk with her.

"I won't be long in the bath."

I exhale roughly. "Take all the time you want."

She searches my face, her expression uncertain. On top of all the depraved thoughts spiraling through my mind, what I want most of all is to gather her in my arms and reassure her I won't do anything she doesn't like.

I only want to do what she wants. Whatever will make her moan and sigh and swoon.

I push off the doorframe and step back.

The corner of her mouth quirks up. "This is a little weird, right?"

I laugh. "Maybe a little. I wasn't expecting a guest."

"I can go to the other—"

"No," I bark out. An order. "I'm happy you're here. It's good to have some company. I promise. Have a good bath. Relax. Come find me when you're done."

"This place is massive; that might be hard." She says it straight, but there's a teasing look in her eye.

I like it. "We can play Marco Polo."

She giggles, and fuck, that takes my cock from hard to throbbing.

After she closes the door, I palm myself and groan, then drag myself to my end of the suite.

I wrench open my pants and roughly fist my cock. It takes three strokes and a very clear mental image of her soft thighs rubbing together for me to come harder than any time in recent memory.

——————

After I clean myself up and pour a stiff drink, I log in to my virtual workspace and check my messages. I run a construction firm back home in Conception Ridge, and we break ground next week on the new town hall. It's our biggest project for the spring and over the summer, but we also have an ongoing housing development project that is multi-year in scope and some individual renovation projects happening in our residential division.

This is the longest vacation I'll have ever taken from the firm, but I won't let some downtime stop me from checking in.

My best friend and co-owner must have noticed that my profile shows me as active because he opens a message thread.

```
Heath: It's a quiet Wednesday at the
office, nothing to worry about.
Daniel: I'm not worried.
Heath: Why aren't you out on the town?
Daniel: I'm waiting for my dinner date to
be ready.
```

As soon as I type it out, I second guess the words—even though they feel disturbingly accurate. But Heath doesn't know *who* my dinner date is, and strictly speaking, that's who Rosie is tonight. We're going to share a meal. I get to take her to a restaurant.

```
Heath: Fuck off. Are pigs flying?
```

Daniel: Cool your jets. It's just dinner.
Heath: Go wild, man. What happens in
Vegas, stays in Vegas.
Daniel: That is not my experience.
Heath: Fuck, I walked right into that one.
Daniel: Maybe less swearing on the company
intranet?
Heath: You're no fucking fun.
Daniel: You tell me that daily.
Heath: And I'm always right. Oh, gotta go,
something's on fire.
Daniel: Now you're the one who can
fuck off.

He leaves a string of laughing emojis before his icon goes gray. He's off-line, the fucker.

It's true. I am the more straight-laced of the two of us. But we're both rough construction workers at heart. I just learned to clean up my language because I had a little girl to raise all by myself.

If Heath knew the filthy fucking language that streamed through my head when I thought of taking Rosie on the floor, hunched over her like a rabid beast. . . well, he wouldn't believe me.

I don't believe myself. And yet here I am, with another hard-on. I try to push away that dark, delicious image, only for it to be replaced with a picture of Rosie in the bathtub, her towel pooled on the tile floor beside her.

I don't even need to picture her body. Just the soft lean of her head against the back of the tub, wet tendrils of hair plastered against her skin. A soapy hand, a splash of water. . .

What is about this girl? She's nothing like the women I've tried to date since Melanie left home. Is it that I've been alone for so long I'd rather focus my fantasies on someone totally off-limits? Am I more attracted to her innocence and youth than I should be?

I shake my head and try to think of literally anyone else. Another friend of Melanie's, or the summer students we hire from the college.

Nope. Gross. Fuck, I want to punch myself in the face for even trying.

Barking a laugh, I push away from my computer. The universe has some twisted sense of humor, waking my libido up in this very specific-to-one-girl kind of way.

I thought my reaction to her at The Roadhouse a few months ago had been an aberration. I've avoided the bar ever since, thinking it was too jarring to see little Rosie Johnson in such a grown-up setting.

I didn't think twice about seeing her at the wedding. Of course, she would be Mel's maid of honor. They were thick as thieves when they were little, and I was working all the time. Rosie's parents have four other kids, all younger than Rosie, so they were happy to have my daughter spend time with them after school until I got home from work.

How many weekend nights did the two girls babysit Rosie's siblings, with me just next door, so her parents could go out for date nights?

I've known Rosie almost her whole life and never thought about her like this. . . before now.

Today, it slammed into me like a freight train. *Mine.*

I hear her door open from across the suite, and I cross to my own bedroom door.

She doesn't see me at first, glancing around the living room, then goes to the floor-to-ceiling window and presses her nose against the glass.

I lean against the door frame and inhale at the vision in front of me. Curvy, bare legs disappearing underneath a red dress. Her hair is still damp and pinned up into a twist, revealing a deep V-cut down the back of the dress. All I can see is smooth skin.

She's wearing black heels and turns around as I approach, now closer in height to me than before.

Our gazes collide, and time stands still.

In this moment, she's a beautiful young woman I've just met, and all our history fades away. I want to know every-thing about her. I want to make her fall in love with *me*, a man who loves gambling and sailing and paperback thrillers. A man aching to know what she tastes like everywhere.

But then she laughs nervously. "Is this alright? I got it at Target, but the heels make it look more dressed up, right?"

And she's Rosie from Conception Ridge again. Not for me to touch because my touch will be a violation.

"You look absolutely beautiful," I say, meaning every word. But the way I say it is a lie. At the last minute, I hear the risk in the words and catch myself, making it sound fatherly. It sounds wrong and dismissive.

She puffs out her cheeks like I just called her a pretty little girl, and she doesn't like it.

Against my better judgment, I get pulled in. "Not what you wanted to hear?"

"No, I'm glad it works. Thanks. But I was hoping I managed to look like a real grown-up, you know?"

I make a choked, grunting sound, and she covers her face. Fuck, I'm the one who should be embarrassed, not her.

From behind her fingers, she mutters, "Ignore me. I don't know how to do this whole fancy thing. I literally was in charge of finding strippers, and I'm not even good at that!"

"What the hell?" The words come out sharper than I mean.

She drops her hands and gives me a wide-eyed look of panic. "Nothing."

"For the bachelorette party?"

"Nope. Nothing to see here, Mr—"

"Stop calling me that." It makes me want to see her on her knees, batting her eyelashes up at me in mock innocence. *Can I lick it, Mr. Burke?*

But there's nothing pretend about Rosie's innocence. She's on the cusp of adulthood, and a natural step is to call her best friend's father by his first name.

I soften my voice. "Call me Daniel. Or Dan, most people call me Dan."

She searches my face. "Who calls you Daniel?"

I shake my head. "Not many people."

She tips her head to the side. "Hmm."

"We're not skipping over the stripper conversation to focus on what people call me," I say as neutrally as I can, which isn't that fucking neutral.

The corners of her lips turn up. "I'm just Rosie. Did you know that? It's not short for anything. Or, long for Rose, I guess."

"Did Melanie specifically ask you to find strippers?

Because there are other ways to celebrate a bachelorette party."

She nods a little. "I think I'll call you Daniel."

I laugh. I can't help it.

She smiles, and we wordlessly agree to shelve the conversation about the bachelorette party until after dinner.

5

rosie

THE RESTAURANT for Melanie's wedding reception is at the top of the casino hotel. It has a panoramic view of the city and the dark, mountainous desert. The maître d' leads us to our table in a private tasting room and goes to pull out my chair for me but stops when Daniel clears his throat. He moves behind me, his hand ghosting over my hip, then holds my chair for me.

Like he's going out of his way to treat me like a grown-up after my confession in the suite.

We're hardly alone for a minute before two people arrive —a wedding coordinator for the hotel and one of the chefs— to go over the tapas-style tasting menu Melanie selected.

"I spoke with Ms. Burke this afternoon, and she explained that due to the storm in New York, you two would be enjoying the dinner preview that is a part of her wedding package."

Mr. Burke—Daniel—has a subtle reaction to the explanation. His whole face shifts ever so slightly. It's not quite an eyebrow raise, more of a sustained twitch, like a cross between being amused and trying very hard not to say something sarcastic in response.

Like the fact that he's paying for this dinner, I realize.

When the introduction is finished and we're alone, he slides a glance my way. "We need to work on your poker face," he murmurs.

"What?"

"The way you looked at me."

I blush. Was I checking him out? "I didn't mean—"

"You totally picked up on my reaction to her calling it Mel's wedding package like I'm not paying for it."

I exhale in relief. "Oh. Yes. I did guess that."

"And then you gave me big eyes across the table." He grins. "I liked it. But I'm not showing you my hand when we play cards later."

Has he already forgotten I'm not old enough to go on the casino floor? "I told you, I—"

"I've been thinking about that. There are private games where nobody checks ID. They're better than the casino floor, anyway. No tourists. If you want the full Vegas experience, I'd be happy to take you."

"I don't have that kind of money." I don't have much money at all. Every cent I've made working at Brewed Awakenings back home has been funneled into paying for this weekend.

"Consider it a birthday present. If that's what you want —I don't want to push my interests on you. And I'm rapidly coming to the realization that you are not the little girl I once knew."

I'm blushing again. Maybe still. "Thank you. That's very kind. And you aren't pushing anything. . . there's a reason I was so excited to come to Vegas *this* weekend. I'd love to learn how to have a better poker face. If you don't mind me tagging along?"

He shrugs. "I'm all alone. Thought I'd have time with Mel and her fiancé tonight, so you're keeping me company. And it is good to catch up. Other than that unfortunate incident"—he winks, making me laugh—"I haven't seen you since Melanie moved to New York."

I nod. "And then they moved to the Caribbean!"

Her fiancé works in finance and has an office in the Turks and Caicos. They go back and forth between there and New York City, living the absolute high life.

I will never in a million years understand why they opted for a Vegas wedding, not that I'm complaining. It's probably the only one I could have afforded to attend unless she went for a back home wedding in Conception Ridge.

Daniel makes a face, interrupting my thoughts.

I sigh. "You don't like that she's so far away, either."

His expression turns thoughtful. "I'm happy for her. But for a long time, it was just the two of us, and it's been an adjustment process." He takes a deep breath. "Learning to live by myself and all that. If you haven't figured it out yet, Rosie, I'm a very lonely man."

"There are plenty of people interested in becoming Mrs. Burke." I don't know why I say it.

It's definitely a mood killer. *Not that there's been a mood between us.* But he ignores it and turns the conversation to me. "How about you? Are you still living at home?"

I swallow my discomfort again at *why I said that* and answer the question. "Yep."

"You stayed in Conception Ridge for school."

I don't want to tell him it's the only thing I could afford. He could send Melanie to the best university, wherever she wanted to go. For me, my option was the college in town or nothing at all. "I like Ridge College."

"It's a good school. We always hire co-op students from the engineering program."

"That's amazing. Your company has grown so much. I remember when it was just you and your pick-up truck."

"It took me a while to find my groove."

I exhale. "That's what I'm afraid will be the case for me, too."

"I didn't say it like it's a bad thing." He takes a long sip of water. "I got to spend more time with Mel when she was little than I ever did when she was a teenager. I had your parents to help, and for that, I'm grateful. There's a time for the big professional push, and it doesn't need to be in your twenties. That's all I'm saying."

"Well, that's good because I still don't know what I'm going to do for any professional push. I don't see myself being a barista forever."

He chuckles. "You work at a coffee shop?"

"Yeah, Brewed Awakenings just off campus."

"And I always go to Wake Up Call downtown." He crooks a smile. "I'll have to change up my routine now that I know."

"Oh, please don't."

That makes him laugh. "You don't want to see your friend's dad while you're at work?"

"What? No! I mean, sure, I want to see you. That would be fine."

He sits up straighter and leans in, bracing his forearms on the table. "Then why shouldn't I change where I get my morning coffee? What if I want to see you more often?"

Before I can answer, the first course is delivered. If you can call it that. It's foam.

"We eat this?" I ask Daniel once we're alone again.

He shrugs and takes a spoonful of it. "Let's see what it tastes like."

I follow suit. While the foam is weird to look at it, it's *wow* on the tongue. I groan and take another scoop, which sadly is the last of it. So little foam, so much flavor. I lick the spoon again, then glance up at Daniel.

He's staring at my mouth.

"I liked it," I say a bit awkwardly. "I wish there was more? But I guess with ten courses. . ."

But each subsequent plate is just as small as the first. All the food is delicious, but it's more of a tease than a meal. By the sixth plate, Daniel is frowning at the menu card the chef gave us.

"Are you worried about the meal?" I ask him.

A muscle in his jaw twitches. "What do you think?"

It's a fancy, impressive event. "Melanie is going to love it."

His gaze softens. "And does *Rosie* love it?"

I fight a smile. "*Rosie* thinks it's more decoration than food and isn't sure which parts are edible."

He exhales. "Thank God. I was worried it was just me."

I laugh. "No."

And then my stomach rumbles.

He frowns. "We should probably add something to this menu, right?"

I tilt my head to the side. "Will most guests have already eaten earlier in the afternoon? There's a whole dessert buffet that we won't be tasting tonight."

"Oh, that's right." His eyebrows raise in disbelief. "How do you keep it all straight?"

"There's a Google Drive folder dedicated to the details. With subfolders." I pause for effect. "You've been added to it."

He pauses with his glass of beer halfway to his mouth. "Are you suggesting I'm not taking my duties as father of the bride seriously?"

Now I'm outright grinning at him. "Are you going to pay for the reception?"

"Of course."

"And are you going to walk your daughter down the aisle without growling too much at anyone?"

He winces. "Yes."

"Then your duties will be taken care of. *My* job is to worry about the little details. And a bachelorette party. And make sure the champagne brunch the morning of the wedding is heavy on the brunch, low on the champagne."

"That's a lot. And now apparently, tiny food assessment."

"It's *so* tiny, Mr. Burke—"

He holds up his hand.

I blush. "Daniel."

"Thank you. Don't make me feel like an old man too much, all right?"

"You're not old." *You're perfect*, I want to say.

But that might be the lightheadedness talking.

He relaxes back into his chair. "What do you say we go off script and order some burgers?"

"I would *love* that."

When the next course is delivered, he does exactly that.

6
daniel

THE ONLY THING better than the sight of Rosie licking foam off a spoon is the sound of her licking mustard off her thumb.

I know we're supposed to be giving the hotel the thumbs up on their fancy-ass meal, but all I care about is feeding this girl some real food.

Tomorrow. We can care about the wedding details tomorrow.

But my plans to take her gambling after dinner are no match for her determination to check another task off our to-do list.

"We need to do the time trial now," she insists when we leave the restaurant. "During the day tomorrow won't be an accurate representation of the traffic of people. It's the wrong time."

Melanie is having an evening wedding. The ceremony is at seven, followed by photos while her guests start the ten-course meal of almost nothing, and the bride and groom arriving. . . "Remind me of the schedule again?"

As we head to the floor where the on-site chapel is secreted away, Rosie patiently walks me through the plans for Saturday night one more time. Mel wants to arrive in the restaurant for the fourth course, so the timing—

I cut her off. "You know what? I'm not going to remember it all. I trust you that we need to do this dry run."

She glances sideways at me. "Don't you hold a lot of complex schedules in your head for work?"

I lean in, smiling at her. "Your point?"

"Maybe your reluctance to retain the details is about not wanting to fully accept that your daughter is all grown up?"

"Any chance you're studying psychology at Ridge College?"

"Maybe." She's smiling back.

"Tuition dollars well spent," I murmur. "But as I said in the restaurant, I'm proud of her for venturing out into the world and finding someone she loves. No growling this weekend, I promise."

Her eyes go soft.

That wasn't all I said over dinner.

I also told her—a sweet young girl of twenty, who doesn't need to know my drama—that I'm lonely.

Fuck me.

The elevator doors slide open, saving me from having that conversation again. I offer her my arm, ignoring the way my chest goes tight when she slides her little hand against my body. Her knuckles graze my torso, then her fingers wrap around my biceps. "How do you want to do this?"

The first thing she wants to do is look inside the chapel, which is unoccupied at the moment. Once she's texted Mel a few notes about whatever she sees, she sets her stopwatch, and we head back to the elevator to make our way upstairs.

The hotel has three towers, and at the top of each, there are terraced public spaces on one side and penthouse suites on the other. The pool is located on the shortest of the three towers, and the restaurant we left not that long ago is at the top of one of the other towers. My suite is in the final one, the tallest one.

The night view was stunning from the restaurant, but it's out of this world from the rooftop pool.

And definitely not like anything we have in Conception Ridge—or anywhere in the Pacific Northwest.

Rosie takes a moment to gawk again, then remembers her task.

"Seven and a half minutes," she reports as she simultaneously types a message to my daughter.

"Not bad. That leaves lots of time for photos because it's not far from here to the restaurant."

"Right." She does a slow circle, taking in more of the rooftop area. The area of the pool that we can see is a gradual walk-in wading area. But the best of it disappears behind built-up rock formations. "This is gorgeous. But it's a bit cold."

She shivers, and I shrug out of my jacket. "Here." I drape it over her shoulders, trying to ignore how good her skin feels against my fingertips as I adjust the collar around her neck.

"Thanks." She breathes the word, a mere whisper, but I hear it just fine because I have her inside the circle of my arms now.

She tips her head up to look at me, and a wave of profound need slams me in the chest. Her eyes are endless pools I want to get lost in, her mouth a lush playground.

That need tightens and swirls deeper, tugging at me.

I don't let go of the jacket. "What's next on our agenda?"

Her gaze turns mischievous. "I think we're off the clock until the morning. You said something about a card game?"

A white-hot current of possessive jealousy spikes through me. Why did I suggest that? If I take Rosie into a high roller game, the other players will want to play for *her*.

I would never in a million years let another man touch her.

"We need to work on your poker face first," I say, buying myself a bit of time.

Her brow dips in confusion. "How are we going to do that?"

I glance around. There's a bar on the other side of the pool, and they have outdoor heaters set up. "Can I buy you a drink?"

She follows my gaze, still looking confused, but a smile curls up her lips. "Sure."

We sit in a protected corner of the bar, in a booth built for two. I tell her to keep my jacket on, and I still sit right next to her. For warmth, I tell myself.

A lie.

After we have our drinks—scotch on the rocks for me and unsweetened iced tea for her—I take our paper coasters and set them aside from our drinks. "These are our poker chips."

"I only have one?"

"We're both down to our last chip."

"High stakes."

"The highest."

She licks her lips. A sweet tell. She's already nervous, my precious girl. "What's the game?"

"It can be anything. Two truths and a lie."

She cracks a smile, being brave. "Okay."

"Your choice, do you want to guess or be the dealer, so to speak?"

She takes a deep breath. "I'll guess."

I nod, thinking. "All right. I was once in the military, I'm afraid of heights, and my favorite ice cream is pistachio."

Her gaze is locked on my face as I rhyme them off. "You've played this before."

"Who hasn't?"

"Me." She licks her lips again. "I have an advantage here. I know you more than some random person at a card table."

"You think you know the lie?" There's no way.

"It's the ice cream," she says confidently.

I frown, not ready to admit she's right. "What's your reasoning?"

She raises one eyebrow. "Is that a part of the poker face lesson?"

"We haven't even gotten to that," I growl, leaning in. "But I want to know how you think you know me."

She leans in, too. "I *do* know you."

How is that possible? Sure, I've known her almost her whole life, but tonight has made me think that maybe I don't really know her at all. Not this newly bloomed woman. Not this confident vixen. "Or you guessed."

She raises one finger between us. "You have a couple of military storage boxes in your attic with your name stenciled on them." Another finger. "You always, always wear safety gear when you're on a roof, and you got kind of frantic when Mel and I figured out we could climb out her window." A third finger. "And pistachio ice cream has never once been in your freezer. Your favorite flavor is raspberry ripple."

Jesus. "Nobody knows I'm afraid of heights," I grind out.

She smiles, and it goes all the way to her pretty eyes. "Well, I do."

I exhale and give her my coaster. "You win."

She shakes her head. "That was a practice round. My turn."

I'm going to lose so badly.

Her tongue swipes against her lower lip again. I need her to stop licking the flesh that I want to lick before I lean in and catch her pink tongue with my teeth. "Okay. . ." she says slowly. "Uh, I'm going to get a tattoo for my birthday, I still don't know what I want to do when I grow up, and my favorite soup is chicken noodle."

As she finishes in a rush, I replay what she's just said in my mind. How she said it. Where she sounded nervous and where her voice got more confident.

Then I glance down at the coasters. Both are currently on her side of an imaginary line. She nudges one into the center. "Which is it, Mr. Burke?"

She's teasing. More confident now.

I drop my hand to cover hers, enjoying the way her breath hitches. I'm confident, too. "Your favorite soup is tomato," I say huskily. "You don't need to know what you want to do when you grow up, but you're genuinely worried about that. Which means you actually are planning to get a tattoo for your birthday, and I want to know where."

Her eyes go wide. "No."

"You have a lovely, expressive face, Rosie." I slide the coaster out from under her fingers and pull it back. "Now we're tied."

"Best of three?"

Best of infinity. I never want to stop playing this game with her. "My middle name is John, I've been skydiving three times, and my favorite movie is *Jaws*."

She whimpers. "I hate that movie."

I grin.

She gasps. "And you do, too! I'd forgotten about that night."

A memory swarms over me. Mel made us all watch it, and Rosie scampered off to make popcorn and stayed in the kitchen for fifteen minutes. I tracked her down and confessed I didn't like it, either. I exhale. "Same. I guess I gave you that one."

She rolls her eyes and yoinks the coaster back. "Please don't diminish my victory."

I lean back, immensely amused. "Your turn."

She smiles triumphantly. "So that means the skydiving is true? You've jumped out of a plane?"

"Surprised?"

"Very. You're afraid of heights."

"Sometimes you need to face your fears head on."

"Three times?"

"Turns out I'm not afraid of heights when I'm wearing a harness."

"Interesting." She purses her lips for a moment. "I don't

like coffee, I've always wanted a cat, and my name was supposed to be Angela."

I frown. That's three lies. "None of those are true."

"You're guessing," she says, her cheeks turning pink.

I shake my head. "One, you work at a coffee shop."

Her cheeks pink up. "So? That could still be true."

"It's not."

She dissolves into laughter. "No, it's not."

"Two, your parents always wanted to call you Rosie. And three, I know for a fact that you're a dog person."

"You win." She slides the coaster over, nudging my fingers with it. "I thought I could trick you. Maybe I'm not ready to play poker just yet."

Then she yawns.

"This was more fun than cards," I say, nudging her drink in her direction. "Want any more before I tuck you in for the night?"

"Making me go to bed early?" Her tease should make me feel awkward about the age gap between us.

It only gives me filthy ideas.

"We have a big day tomorrow." I lower my voice. "Are you going to be a good girl for me this weekend, Rosie?" The question is out before I can think twice about it. I regret the word choice immediately. It sounds inappropriate—because it is inappropriate.

Her eyes go wide, her lips part, and her cheeks flush. But then she nods vigorously, and something unexpected happens to her expression. It lights up like I've asked exactly the right thing in exactly the right way. "Yes."

I shouldn't read too much into a single breathless answer. One word. One syllable.

But in that moment, as I tell her she needs to be a good girl and she enthusiastically agrees, I realize she's willingly playing another kind of game with me.

One I've never played before, but I immediately want to win.

7

rosie

Thursday

I WAKE UP EARLY, dragged out of a delicious sleep by the most unlikely sound—the quiet click of a door.

Bolting upright, I grin as last night comes back to me. I wore Daniel's jacket all the way back to the suite. He only took it back when we stopped in front of my room. The last thing he did before telling me good night was to drag his gaze down my body, then back up again.

I crawled into bed and touched myself for a full hour, imagining it was his fingers between my legs instead of my own. His corded forearm, his heavily veined hand.

When I finally let myself come, his name was on my lips, a wordless plea.

I don't know if he'll act on whatever is humming like an electric current between us. He might not. Melanie and her fiancé are arriving later today. That could change everything.

But if he doesn't make the first move before the wedding, I'll. . .

I sag back against the pillows.

I'll do nothing.

The thought of humiliating myself is a buzzkill. I can't throw myself at him. What if he says no? I would die of embarrassment.

Wincing, I roll out of bed.

After pulling on a pair of shorts and a hoodie, I go into the living room and find him standing at the window, talking on the phone.

Room service breakfast is set out on the table.

He glances over his shoulder and points at it, indicating I should get started. I take a seat, but other than sipping at my orange juice, I wait for him to be done with his call. I can't guess who he's talking to from his short answers, but when he hangs up, he explains right away.

"That was Javier." Mel's fiancé. "They've been moved up to an earlier flight, and they're heading to the airport. Most of his family is on the same flight, so a limo will pick them up."

I should be thrilled they've managed to rescue most of their time in Vegas. Instead, my first thought is shamefully about how little time left I have with Daniel all to myself.

I force myself to look at my phone—the text updates from Mel and the Google Drive updates. "So they'll be here by mid-afternoon, which means you don't need to go to the dress shop anymore. Mel will be here in time for that."

Another text pops up on the screen from the bride-to-be.

Javi's sister wants to know how the stripper search is going.

I shoot a look at her father, now sitting across from me. He lifts the lid off one of the breakfast plates. "Toast?"

"Yes, please." My throat is dry. I take a long sip of orange juice before texting back.

Is that what you really want?

Did my dad find out? I'll call him. We have a few minutes before we board.

Before I can stop her, Daniel's phone rings. His face softens, and he grins. "Hi, Peanut. What? Uh. . ." He gives me a surprised look. "Yes, it came up. Look, I don't want to cramp your style, but—" He exhales roughly. "Yep. No, what the bride wants. I get it. If your husband-to-be doesn't—"

He holds the phone away from his ear, and I start giggling.

"Rosie's laughing at me because you're reading me the riot act," he growls at his daughter, but there's no heat. There never has been. He's the most doting father.

Which he knows and addresses as soon as he hangs up. "I've spoiled that one far too much."

Mel is willful, but as an adult, it's actually proven to mean that she has strong boundaries. "What did she say?"

"That she doesn't need her husband's permission and that Javi trusts her completely. Something about I should drag myself out of the nineteenth century, too."

"I didn't tell her to call you." I hold up my phone. "I just asked if that was what she really wanted for her bachelorette party."

"Are you uncomfortable planning it?" He looks uncomfortable asking me the question.

"We don't need to talk about this."

"But—"

"I should have done this weeks ago!" I burst out. "I got decision paralysis back home and thought I'd have time once I got here to figure out something amazing. But then you picked me up at the airport, and don't get me wrong, I had an amazing time last night. I'm glad I wasn't all alone at a seedy motel, Googling last-minute stripper options in Vegas. That sounds like a literal nightmare. But I'm in over my head, and I'm the wrong person to do this. So are you, by the way." I scan the table. "No vodka for my orange juice? Jeez Louise."

He chuckles as I sag back in my chair. "Good to get that off your chest?"

"A little."

"I know staying here will cramp your plans for the weekend. Mel said—" He cuts himself off.

I frown. "What?"

"Nothing."

My eyes go wide. "What did she say?"

"It's understandable that you want to have some experiences you can't have back home." But he says it tightly. Like it's not. Like he's judging me for wanting to have a wild weekend in Vegas when I don't. Not really.

"Uh. . ." I flush, hot and embarrassed. "She misunderstood. Or you did. I'm practically a virgin," I blurt out. "And if I said anything to your daughter about anything, it was only a foolish fantasy. Not what I really have planned. Not at all. You don't have anything to worry about."

His mouth falls open.

Silence fills the space between us.

I drop my gaze to the table. To the toast he offered me and the now almost empty glass of orange juice.

"I was thinking about that tattoo you wanted to get," he says quietly. "That's all."

"Oh."

He doesn't say anything for a while. I recognize it as a classic dad move, but it's different coming from him. Less annoying, and more like he's actually giving me some space to admit what's really wrong.

"I'm so embarrassed," I finally mutter. "I can't even throw a bachelorette party. How am I ever going to have some wild and crazy solo adventure after the wedding?"

He sighs, then stands up and comes around to my side of the table.

I still won't look at him.

He crouches down beside me, forcing me to make eye contact with him.

Why does he have to look at me like I'm some kid who needs help when all I can think about is how his stubble glints like silver in the morning light and how it would feel against my fingertips. My lips. My—

I twist my head away.

He smooths his hand over the back of my head, then slowly circles his fingers around to my chin. He turns my face so I'm looking at him. "You are a good, sweet friend." Oh God, no, I am *not*. "And I'm sorry I played any part in making you feel embarrassed about not knowing your way around Vegas. I know how you can plan this party—and it won't have anything to do with me."

He hesitates a beat, then stands and kisses me on the forehead before making a quick phone call. The kiss scalds my skin. Does he have any idea how he affects me?

Twenty minutes later, after he's gently but determinedly fed me breakfast, a woman from concierge services arrives in the suite.

Daniel excuses himself to go to the gym.

I immediately confess my lack of preparation to the woman, who is apparently fazed by nothing.

"People pull together last-minute bachelorette parties all the time," she reassures me. "I understand the bride wants her party to be a little more on the risqué side?"

I nod.

"There's a new mostly male burlesque show that's still in previews, so there isn't a ton of hype around it yet. But I can tell you it's going to be the hot ticket in a few months. It's upstairs from a dance club, so the party can move back and forth, and for a premium, the dancers upstairs can be hired for a private show."

I must look anxious because she gives me another reassuring look. "Your dad said everything would go on his room charge. If you want to arrange individual payment from the people attending, I can help with invoices."

"Sure." I exhale shakily, too nervous to correct her that Daniel isn't my father. "Thank you."

She hands over a business card. "This is a great store just off the Strip that sells matching tank tops for parties, helium balloons, that sort of thing. And I'll let you in on a secret. Most people are happy to be here, and the Strip is decoration enough. But a few *vino before vows* streamers can't hurt."

I take the card gratefully. "Awesome."

"It's normal to be nervous before a wedding, especially if it's your big sister."

I open my mouth to correct her, then stop.

Of course, she thinks I'm Mel's sister.

It's either I'm Daniel's mistress or his daughter, because why else would he have a twenty-year-old girl in his suite?

I've had enough embarrassment for one day, and it's not even nine in the morning. I snap my mouth shut and make a shopping plan.

daniel

"WHAT DO YOU THINK? Pink or gold?" Rosie holds up two identical except-for-color balloons.

"Both."

"That's been your answer to everything."

"My job is to pay for things, remember?"

"Sure, but we don't need to waste your money!" She gives me an exasperated look that makes me want to kiss her.

"Will Mel love it all?"

"Probably."

"Then it's money well spent." I shove my hands in my pockets to keep from touching her. I want to move her toward the door and hurry this stop along so we can fit in a late lunch at a nice restaurant before everyone else arrives.

It'll be the last meal I get alone with her until Sunday at the earliest.

Her confession from breakfast rings in my ears like the echo of a gong. *Practically a virgin. Wants an adventure.*

"All right, let's get it all." She sighs happily. "Now we

just need to get into her hotel room and decorate before she arrives!"

Back at the casino, we get a room key from the concierge for my daughter's suite.

She needs my height and reach to affix the top row of balloons to the wall. I relish every second of standing that close to her, working together. When we finish, and I ask her to join me for lunch, the glittering smile I get back is more than reward enough.

We go to a farm-to-table restaurant in the next hotel over, and we're seated at a community table after Rosie expresses delight at the concept to the hostess.

Any protest I might have over sharing her with a table of strangers ends when we're seated next to each other. The first thing Rosie does is lean in and whisper how good the menu looks.

I take a long, shuddering inhale of her sweet scent and agree that I'm ravenous.

Which she takes literally. "How hungry are you?"

Jesus, she's going to be the best kind of death for me. I slide my arm over the back of her chair. My fingers graze her far shoulder and her breath hitches. Her gaze doesn't waver, though. If anything, the way she's looking at me deepens, gets warmer. "Starving," I admit. "I didn't realize just how much."

"We should fix that." A slow blink. "Their flatbreads sound amazing."

Food isn't what I need. But it's all that's on offer. I squeeze her shoulder and turn to the menu.

We take our time and order a few rounds of small plates

and two refills of iced tea for Rosie before getting a group text message from Mel.

"They've landed," Rosie says, and I want to imagine that she sounds as bittersweet as I feel.

Which is ridiculous because we should both be relieved the East Coast guests have finally arrived, and the party can begin.

But when she twists around to look for the waiter, and her hand briefly falls to my thigh, all I want is to hit the pause button on our time.

To freeze us in this moment while I figure out how to tell her how much I want to be what she needs. To show her I can be that adventure she craves.

There's no way to do that without ruining my daughter's wedding, though, so I swallow it down and accept that I've run out of time.

It's a short walk back to the hotel, and as we walk up, a limo pulls up to the curb. The window rolls down, and my daughter gives us jazz hands. "We made it!"

Selfish time is over.

Rosie pulls away from me and darts ahead, throwing her arms around Mel as she spills out of the vehicle. They squeal and jump up and down.

I extend my right hand to Javier, greet his parents, then join Mel and Rosie.

My daughter launches herself at me, and I squeeze her lovingly.

"Are you all right?" Mel asks quietly into my ear.

It takes me a moment to remember why she would ask. I told her Vegas was more than fine as a wedding location, and I meant it. But the last day with Rosie has replaced all long-ago memories with much sweeter moments. "Yes," I tell her honestly. "Totally fine."

She lets out a relieved breath. "Rosie says you took good care of her."

I swallow hard and catch Rosie's curious gaze.

"I tried," I say thickly. "She made it easy."

9
rosie

AFTER THE OTHERS get checked in, and we take some group photos in the bridal suite with the decorations—which Mel *loves*, thank goodness—Daniel disappears with Javier and his father to have a drink.

I head to the dress shop with Javi's mother, Mel, and her two other bridesmaids, roommates from college. Leigh lives in Paris now, and Leesa flew in from Tulsa. We've been in a group chat for months, but this is our first time actually meeting.

They're nice.

I should be having fun. We pop a bottle of bubbly in the limo, and I take a few sips.

I'd rather be drinking an iced tea and laughing with Daniel. My gut twists at the betrayal of my best friend. It's her wedding weekend, and I'm falling desperately, pathetically in love with her father.

I should be mad at myself. Plunging headlong into a forbidden crush is a stupid way to celebrate your twenty-first birthday. But I can't be mad when I remember how it felt to have his arm draped over the back of my chair.

I surreptitiously open my phone and glance at the group text Mel sent when she arrived. It's the first message she sent to both Daniel and me.

It's the first time his phone number has been in my phone. *I could text him.*

I won't.

It would be weird.

I should be focused on the wedding stuff. I take another sip of champagne and try desperately to stop thinking about how warm his body was when he leaned in against me.

The relief I feel when we pull up at the dress store is weird and bittersweet. Inside, it's easier to get caught up in the excitement. Leigh hasn't tried the bridesmaid dress on at all, coming in from out of the country, so she goes first. Melanie picked a simple rose gold slip dress, cut on the bias, and the store has them in all of our sizes plus a few extra sizes just in case. The second one Leigh tries on is perfect and doesn't need any alterations, and we all cheer.

I go next. My dress has already been customized to allow more space for my boobs, which always need some management to fit into standard sizes. In the dressing room, I wiggle into the strapless bra I'll wear on Saturday, then slide the slip dress on over my head.

After twisting and turning to look in the mirror, I step outside, and the girls all clap. "Gorg," Mel says, toasting me.

The seamstress tells me to leave the dress on until the end, so we can see all of us lined up together. Then it's Leesa's turn. The seamstress makes a joke about their names being similar and their sizes being identical—both of them having standard-sized boobs that require no adjustments. Then it's Mel's turn in the fitting room.

She needs the seamstress to help her into her dress, so the three of us are left alone in the fancy sitting area.

"We *are* almost exactly the same," Leesa says to me, gesturing at Leigh. "Except for where we live. And our taste in men."

"Remember when you had that crush on our English Lit professor our second year?" Leigh makes a face. "He was so old."

I'm with Leigh. I'd never have a crush on any of my college instructors.

Leesa shrugged. "What can I say? I like 'em with experience."

"That's because you're a lazy bitch who doesn't want to train a twenty-five-year-old man to eat her out properly."

My cheeks heat up. Mel can come out of that change room any time now.

"Do you think that Mel isn't riding Javi's face every night?"

Too much information. I pull out my phone and think about texting Daniel again.

"Or Mel's dad," Leesa says, dropping her voice. "You know someone else is calling him Daddy in that big mansion of his now that she's moved to the opposite side of the country. Those hands? That fierce glare? I'd call him Daddy this weekend if he'd let me."

My phone slips out of my hand and hits the carpeted floor with a thud.

The screen lights up. Daniel's name is on it. Did I accidentally call him?

Leesa and Leigh glance my way as I pick it up, flustered. "Hi! Hello. What's up?"

"Just checking in," he says in my ear, his voice familiar and strong.

Someone is calling him Daddy.

My stomach flip-flops dangerously. "She's about to try her dress on. Do you want to talk to her?"

"No, just wanted to give you a quick update." I can hear him shift on the other end of the line, and when he speaks again, it sounds like he's smiling. "So you can update the spreadsheet. Javi's best man has arrived from L.A."

"Great."

He pauses. "Did you try your dress on?"

"Yep."

Another pause. "Are you okay?"

"Great. Yep."

"You keep saying those two words."

"Mmm."

"Should I ask for a proof of life photo?"

I laugh. "No. Maybe."

"It's full steam now. Nothing but wedding stuff all day, every day, for the next three days."

"Yeah."

A third pause. "Send me a picture."

Someone. Calls. Him. Daddy.

Wild, jealous heat swirls through me. And then I remember he means a picture of *Mel.* His daughter.

The bride.

I exhale. "I will. Oh, she's done. Talk later."

Hanging up, I switch to the camera app and snap a few pictures as Mel settles in front of the mirrors. As the seamstress works, I adjust the aperture in the app and try a few different angles. Being behind the lens feels good, like I've got something to do with my hands, and I can pretend I wasn't just thrown, *again*, by this weekend being just too much for me.

When I'm *doing* something, I can forget this feeling of being a kid playing dress-up, like I don't belong at this grown-up event, talking about things I can't relate to.

After the seamstress is finished, she offers to take my phone to snap some pictures, and we all crowd around Mel and ooh and aah over her dress. It's beautiful, and I tell her that repeatedly.

Leigh and Leesa go into the dressing rooms first, and Mel gives me a cringy look. "I heard what Leesa said about my dad," she murmured. "Can you run interference if she gets a little too mimosa happy and hits on him?"

"Official maid of honor task?" Easiest assignment yet.

I'll stab her in the heart with my high heels before letting her get her hands on Daniel.

And fingers crossed, Mel will never find out my glee at the idea of cockblocking the other bridesmaid comes from a deeply selfish, hypocritical place.

daniel

TWENTY MINUTES after my call with Rosie, I get a text message from her. No words, just a photo of Mel in her dress. It's official, my daughter is getting married in two days. And from the beaming smile on her face as the seamstress adjusts her train, she's beside herself with excitement.

My gaze slides to the woman taking the picture. Her reflection is captured in the mirror in front of the bride. Rosie's hip is cocked, and her head is tilted in the same direction. The pose exaggerates the tight nip of her waist, the roundness of her hips, and the youthful perkiness of her breasts in a slinky-looking dress seemingly made of molten metal. The overhead lights in the shop catch every plane of her curvy body, and my fingers itch to find out what she's wearing underneath that dress.

My pulse jacks up as I tap on the photo and save it.

"Everything all right?"

I put my phone away and glance up at Javier as he returns to our table. The banker is only six years younger than me. It's an adjustment to think of him as my son-in-law. In another setting, we'd be more believable as colleagues.

But I'd be the worst kind of hypocrite if I didn't embrace him as the man of Mel's dreams while I'm quietly lusting after Rosie.

"Everything's great." I put my phone back in my pocket. "Dresses all look good."

I spend the rest of the afternoon meeting wedding guests and being more social than I've had to be in years.

By the time afternoon drinks spill into pre-dinner cocktails, I've had enough. I excuse myself to go back to my suite, hoping I'll run into Rosie, but she's nowhere to be found.

I check my work email, call into the office, then head to the chapel for the "ten minute, super fast wedding rehearsal," as it's labeled in Rosie's calendar entry. Apparently, she invited me to it at some point.

Mel and Javi are waiting outside, having a quiet conversation. She sets her hand on his forearm as I approach, pausing whatever they're talking about.

"Dad," she says, reaching her other hand for mine. "Javi said you had a good afternoon."

"We had a *great* afternoon. But I had to hear from your fiancé that you have a new job?"

"It's been a busy few weeks." She gives me a sheepish grin. "But hopefully, we can find time to catch up at dinner."

Too many people will be around tonight. "Or over breakfast tomorrow?"

She nods vigorously. "Yes. Of course. Your suite?"

Nope, that won't do. My suite has a secret guest in it. "I'll come to yours. I imagine you'll have lots of last-minute things coming up."

She brightens. "Good point. And I can have my girls there, too."

So much for our father-daughter meal.

At this point, I'll have to fly to New York when this is all over to have any quality time with my daughter.

But I'm surprised to realize I'm not bitter about this realization. I've been in denial about her fully growing up and being a wholly independent adult. Her wedding weekend is as good a time as any to snap the fuck out of that delusion.

"Babe, your dad doesn't want to play second fiddle to your wedding excitement." Javier's tone is gentle, but Mel reacts to it immediately.

"Oh. Right. Sorry, Dad. I'll tell the girls to do their own thing until we're done with breakfast."

"It's fine, sweetheart." I kiss her on the cheek. "Really. Javi's right—I would like some quality time, just the two of us. But we have the rest of our lives for that. This weekend is all about the two of you getting married."

Inside the chapel, I finally see Rosie for the first time since lunch. She's talking to the other bridesmaids. They're all wearing matching tank tops now, one of three sets she bought earlier today, and her long brown hair is twisted up on top of her head in a big, messy bun. The sight of her is like a long, cool drink of water, and I'm a thirsty man who waited too long to take a sip.

She's the only person in this whole circus with whom I've had a real conversation. Of course, that was before everyone arrived.

As if she can feel the weight of someone's assessing gaze, she turns slightly, then smiles when her eyes meet mine.

Hi, she mouths.

I want to order the room cleared so I can kiss her until she's gasping with a need to match my own. Unzip her dark blue jean shorts and find out what she's wearing under them, if it's cotton or silk, and what it feels like against my nose as I breathe in the scent of her.

Practically a virgin.

How little experience does she have? I have twenty-five years of fantasies built up. More years of filthy desire than she's even been alive. Her innocent desire is no match for what my lizard brain wants.

That moment in the chapel will be as close as I get to her all evening. The rehearsal spills into a boisterous dinner, and then the girls (as Mel keeps referring to them) leave as a group.

I excuse myself as soon as is politely possible after that and retreat to my suite.

My quiet hotel room is a relief after a non-stop day. I throw myself into the shower, but I'm filled with an unfulfilled energy that won't be washed away.

Jerking off doesn't help, either.

So I pull on workout clothes for the second time in a day, and because I'm forty-three years old and know two workouts in one day will be hell on my body, I grab my swim trunks, too.

I'll soak in the hot tub I spied this morning after excising the demon who wants me to rut on top of my daughter's best friend.

I drop my gym bag on a lounge chair next to the pool and hot tub area an hour later. I'm on the far side of the roof from where Rosie and I had drinks last night. On this side, the fake rock formations create mini private pools, some heated more than others, according to the attendant in the gym.

I hop into the nearest one and settle in front of a jet. As my limbs slowly relax, I sink lower into the water.

And that's when I hear them. My daughter, her best friend, and her two bridesmaids laughing as they approach the pool. They didn't come from the same direction I did by the gym. They're walking along the rock formations from the bar.

I push off the wall and glide deeper into the covered cave I'm in until I can see them. Four young women, all in bathrobes. Giggling like they've had a bit to drink.

I narrow my eyes on reflex, then roll them at myself. That was the same reaction that got me into trouble with Rosie in the first place.

Better if they don't know that I'm here. And as long as they don't swim in this direction, they won't. If they do, I'll take advantage of the cover of darkness and disappear out another pool entrance.

As a group, they disrobe, but I only have eyes for one of them. Rosie turns her back to me as she shrugs out of the robe.

I silently lift my fist to my mouth, biting down on my knuckle as a strapless bikini is revealed. Bright yellow strips of material wrap low on her luscious hips and in a hypnotic twist around her breasts.

The same curves that looked so innocent and sweet in a T-shirt and yoga pants, that transformed into pure beauty in a red dress, and proved effortlessly touchable today in a tank top and shorts, now look like utter sin in that bikini.

Above the low waistband, her belly slopes in a sexy

round bump before curving into her waist. She has to hold on to the top as she jumps into the pool, giggling delightfully as the water splashes around her.

Below the water, my cock strains for release.

I want to paint every inch of her sweet body with come. Splatter her tits and belly and inner thighs with my seed.

I swallow against the rough vision. Her, sprawled on a bed. On the floor. My cock swinging above her, dripping post-climax. Her fingers trailing through it, marveling at how it feels against her skin.

Mr. Burke. . .

Call me Daniel.

A wicked smile. *Is this how Daniel behaves with other girls? Or is this Mr. Burke being very, very bad?*

Rosie would never be that saucy. That's a fucking fantasy right there, one I shouldn't entertain while she's a guest in my suite.

I entertain it anyway.

Squeezing my erection hard beneath the dark surface of the water, I quietly slip further away from them. But it doesn't matter how deep into the caves I move. I can still hear them. Her, particularly. The throaty laugh, the light gasps. She's such a gorgeous contradiction of a woman. Knowing and innocent at the same time. Forceful and unsure. *Fuck, do I like that combination in a lover.*

A fantasy of a lover, anyway.

At least half an hour passes, and then one of the bridesmaids announces that she's beat. "Time for bed."

"Me, too," my daughter says. There's splashing, and I swim closer to get another glimpse of Rosie in that bikini as she gets out.

But then the God of Perverted Old Men grants me an absolute blessing because Rosie waves them on ahead of her.

"I'm going to swim a little longer," she says. "I'll see you in the morning."

A gift of stolen time with her that I will not waste.

From my seat in the shadows, I watch as the other girls climb out of the pool and towel off, then wrap themselves in their robes.

I wait until they're out of sight before pushing off the wall and gliding closer to Rosie.

"This is a coincidence," I murmur from behind her.

She jumps and gasps, spinning around. "Daniel!"

"Fuck, sorry." I reach for her. "I scared you."

She giggles nervously, steadying herself, her hands wrapping around my shoulders. "Yeah."

Once she's treading water again, I let go of her, but I don't move away.

"Where did you come from?"

"There are hotter mini pools in the cave. I was having a soak after going to the gym."

She gives me a curious look. "Again?"

Not that it did any good. I track a water droplet curling its way down her cheek, gliding past the corner of her mouth. "It helps me sleep."

"That's why I wanted to swim a bit. I'm all. . ." She churns her hands in the water. "Ramped up, I guess. It was a lot today."

"I highly recommend the jets." I point, and she nods, then slices her arm through the water, starting to swim in that direction.

I hang back for a beat and tip my head up to the cool,

dark sky. *I won't do anything*, I think, but it's not much of a vow. It's almost guaranteed to be a lie.

I will do whatever she wants.

When I catch up to her, she's navigating her way around a couple locked in an embrace. She glances at me with a secret smile. Inside the cave, there are dim lights in nooks and crannies, creating lots of secret shadows—but there's enough light to see someone up close.

I catch her hand and tug her into the next hot tub. For now, we have it all to ourselves.

She sighs in happiness as she leans back against a jet. I sit across from her and drink in the sight of her bare shoulders and plump breasts.

"Finally alone," she whispers, then giggles.

"What's so funny?"

"I shouldn't tell you."

"I think that means you should."

She groans and covers her face with her hands. "It's kind of awkward."

"I love awkward."

She peeks between two of her fingers. "Really?"

"It's a very human feeling. Usually relatable, not that most people want to admit that."

Her hands splash down into the water. "That's true!"

"I know." I crook my fingers. "Out with it."

"One of the bridesmaids is on the prowl for you."

That was not what I was expecting her to say. "Oh?"

"Mel made me promise to run interference." Her voice goes up at the end, as if asking a question but actually making a statement in disbelief.

My chest tightens. If she's happy to run interference on

behalf of my daughter, then she's hardly going to share my darkest fantasies.

Talk about fucking awkward.

And now I've dragged her into a goddamn water cave so I can, what? Molest her?

I need therapy. And a drink. And a willing woman in my bed.

But the only woman I want to be willing is sitting across from me, waiting for me to say something.

Interference.

I clear my throat. "Consider me fair warned. If it comes up, you can assure my daughter that I am a monk."

"Well, that's too bad," Rosie says. The words rush out of her.

I don't think I've heard her properly. I crook my head to the side.

She makes a strangled humming sound. "For Leesa, I mean. *Leesa* will be bitterly disappointed."

"Rosie?"

The sound she's making turns into a little unsure, "Uh-huh?"

I move across the hot tub to float in front of her. Under the water, her bright yellow bikini calls to me. I want to trace the edges of it with my fingertips. Dip under the fabric here and there. "I'm not interested in Leesa. At all."

"That's good," she whispers. "I don't know why I brought it up."

I do. With blinding clarity, I suddenly see that the chemistry I've been mainlining since yesterday is definitely reciprocal. A two-way lust street between my daughter's best friend and me.

I have no doubt about it now, but I need to choose my next move carefully, or she'll spook.

I don't want to spook her. I want to love her. Every sweet inch.

"My daughter worries about me because I've never dated anyone. And she thinks I can be trapped by some overly aggressive younger millennial."

That makes Rosie laugh. Good. "Yes," she says huskily. "I think there's definitely some of that worry beneath it all. She's very protective of you when she's not wrapped up in wedding stuff. She doesn't want you to be hurt."

I stroke a wet strand of hair off her cheek. "What do you know about that?"

She worries her bottom lip. "Just what Mel has said over the years. That you don't like to talk about. . . her mother. That you've vowed never to marry again."

"The first part is true. The second, though. . . I don't know about that anymore."

Her lips twist. "The ladies of Conception Ridge will be delighted to hear you're back on the market."

"I didn't say that." I can't stop touching her. My hand drops to her shoulder, and my thumb strokes over the curve of her flesh before I pull back. In my veins, my pulse is heavy and needy. "It would have to be the right woman. Just one. But that's not why Mel is worried about me this weekend."

11
rosie

DANIEL'S FACE TIGHTENS UP, the dimple in his chin deepening as he nods slowly, as if to himself more than me. "I met my ex-wife here. It was a whirlwind weekend that ended up with me putting a ring on her finger. She was from Montana, born and raised on a ranch. Came here to escape that and got a job as a waitress. I was stationed in California with the Army and came here for a leave weekend. She thought we'd travel the world and live in interesting places. Six months later, she got pregnant. When Mel was one, she told me she needed out of our life. It wasn't what she wanted."

His voice grates on the last sentence, and the roughness of it sends a shiver through me despite the warm water.

"She never told me those details."

"I've always made it clear to her that we all need to follow our hearts. I don't blame her mother anymore. I wanted to be a parent. She didn't. I wanted to settle down in a small town. She didn't. But I couldn't ever risk someone else breaking my daughter's heart."

"Or your own?"

He raises an eyebrow at my question. "You think I'm that fragile?"

"Just human."

He smiles. "Maybe."

I chew that over. Growing up, I did think of him as a superhero. Big and strong, never upset. What had it taken for him to stay that contained?

"Why do you come back here?" I shake my head. "Why did Mel pick *this* city of all places to get married?"

"To show me that it doesn't always turn out the way it did for me." He leans his head back against the rock wall and exhales. "A ham-handed message, but an effective one. All of that was a long time ago. I'm not nursing a broken heart, Rosie. I haven't been for a very long time."

"Good." I swish my legs in the water, and my calf brushes against his. Another shiver runs through me at the contact, and this one lingers in my core. A profound aware-ness of his body in front of me, shielding me from the rest of the pool. We're all alone in this little hot tub nook.

"But to answer your first question—why do I come back here?" He pushes his arms through the water, a lazy treading motion, and his fingers brush against my thigh.

An involuntary whimper slides out of my mouth.

He groans my name. "Rosie. . ."

A loud splash nearby is followed by a cacophony of masculine voices. A group of young men has waded into the hot tub area.

No. Not now. *Go away*, I want to shout. But since they have every right to be here, it can be us who leave.

"Let's go," I whisper, pushing past Daniel.

I stand up, and he catches my wrist as the boys swim into view.

The first young man leers at me, giving my tits a once over. That's all he gets to see before Daniel pulls me back behind him and growls at them to keep moving.

"Sorry, sir, didn't realize you were here with your hot daughter," one of them says.

I wince. How many times this weekend is that going to be assumed about us? I poke my head around Daniel's rigid body. "He's not my dad," I say hotly.

"We get that all the time, boys," Daniel rasps. "One day, you'll understand."

I gasp, then giggle as they move on as ordered. As I laugh, he turns around catches me in his arms. The giggle fades fast. "Daniel?"

"Am I too old for you?"

"What?" I blink in surprise.

"Tell me to leave you alone."

"I don't want to do that." My heart is beating extra fast now.

"I'm not a gentle man. It's been a long time since I've explored—"

"I'm not that innocent." I lick my lips. "I have dirty thoughts about you, and you're never gentle in any of them."

He sinks into the water again, pulling me against him. Our legs brush again, and I want more of him against me. His hands glide up my back, one settling at the nape of my neck, the other drifting lower again, to my hips. He murmurs my name.

I bring my fingertips to his jaw. To that silver stubble I've thought so much about.

No, he can't leave me alone. Not tonight.

I close the gap between us, pressing my mouth against his. I feel his groan more than I hear it. His lips are firm and warm, and as soon as I make contact with them, he takes over.

Heat swirls in my belly, licking higher and lower as he drags his lips back and forth, then parts them, letting me taste him for the first time. I lick against the seam of his mouth, all the way to a corner, and as I return, his tongue thrusts against mine.

My turn to gasp. To groan. To cry out, but he swallows that.

His name is a drumbeat in my veins.

My legs go around his waist because he's pulling me to him. His hands are on my ass, fingers grazing the bare skin above and below the band of my bikini bottoms like hot, perfect brands. Thumbprints I want to wear forever on my body.

Then between my legs, up against the snug nothing of my bathing suit bottoms, I realize he's hard. Really hard.

Really big, and solid, and long. He drags me up and down his body, nestling us together until there's no space left. Until we're fused at the mouth and chest and belly and below, where his cock is riding against my clit and oh, *God*—

The hand on the back of my neck squeezes hard, and the other curves around to find my breasts. "Fuck, Rosie."

Yes, I want to say. He should fuck Rosie. He should fuck her here in a public pool before he thinks twice about it.

I can't say it, though, because his mouth is on mine again,

and I'm desperately climbing him, my hands splaying wide against his muscled back.

He's so big. Thicker in my embrace than I imagined. I can't wrap my arms all the way around him, but I try anyway. I cling to him as he tugs my bathing suit top down enough to slide his fingers inside and find my nipple.

I moan out loud.

"Shhh," he whispers as I pant against his cheek. "Remember you said you'd be a good girl for me?"

Fuck, someone just might call him Daddy after all, and that someone might just be me. I nod feverishly and clamp my lips together.

"So good," he murmurs. "So quiet. Ride me. I'm going to kiss you again. Whatever happens, happens. You're okay. I've got you."

People were all around us. Not close at the moment, but that could change at any time.

That wasn't going to stop me.

Nobody has ever kissed me to orgasm before. Nobody has ever really *gotten* me to orgasm before, other than myself. This may be a once-in-a-lifetime opportunity, and I am not wasting it.

I kiss him now, hungry for more of those almost silent groans that I feel through his entire body. I lick the other corner of his mouth, delighted that it's just as sensitive. And when he licks back, I catch his tongue in my mouth and suck on the tip.

His hands flex hard against my body. He grinds us together, pinches my nipple, and it makes me so wet, so absolutely achingly mad that we're not all the way naked. I want to suck on more of his body. Lick him everywhere and see how he tastes.

His mouth tastes amazing. His lips, too. His neck. . . yes. Oh, *yes*. He has the faintest stubble here, and we both shudder as I swipe my tongue against it. Down, then up to his ear.

"Please," I whisper. I'm panting. I don't even know what I'm asking for. Harder? Slower?

He does both, reading my mind.

Then he dips his head and catches my nipple in his mouth, and that's game over for my soul.

I slap my own hand over my mouth as I come, a shuddering, slow quake of a climax.

He nestles me into his body, letting me ride out the aftershocks before restoring my bikini top to its proper location.

My breath catches as he straightens his head after that and cups my cheek, his thumb brushing against the corner of my mouth. "Your mouth, Rosie. . ."

It's yours. "Yes?"

"I should confess that I've thought about nothing but these lips and everything I want to do to you since the moment you stepped off that airplane." He doesn't look like it's a confession at all. His eyes glitter in the dim light.

I bite my lip, but it doesn't stop a smile from spreading across my face. "Really?"

"Goddamn it, girl, yes. Since that day at The Roadhouse, if I'm being honest. Little Rosie Johnson, with a beer in her hand, made me see red. Flirting with grown men?"

"I wasn't really." My feelings are in free-fall now. For months he's had these thoughts? My stomach flips with delight that this might be more than one night, more than one magical secret kiss. "I was happy to see you that day. Only disappointed that you treated me. . ."

"Like a kid." He grunts. "I know you're not that anymore."

I smile again and kiss the corner of his mouth. "Good."

"It was just a shock. Because I'd missed the memo, baby girl. I didn't know you were all grown up yourself."

He loops back to that a lot. Maybe there's something to that? A little grown-up fun to be had. *Someone calls him Daddy.*

Only me, if I have anything to say about it.

"I'm not quite legal for *everything*," I whisper. Gambling and alcohol, but who's counting the technicalities? "My birthday is on Sunday."

Daniel takes the bait. "You're legal enough for me to want to claim you," he growls. "And if it were any other weekend, I'd already have you naked in my bed, proving to you just how much I want you to be mine."

"Yours?"

"Mine." His grip tightens on my neck, and my thighs tremble at the effect his possessiveness has on my body. I'm soft and pulsing for him.

But then I hear the other part of what he just said. *If it were any other weekend.*

Which means this weekend, he feels like he can't.

Of course not. Of course, he can't. His daughter is getting married in two days, and I'm the maid of honor.

12
daniel

ROSIE EASES OFF MY LAP, her gaze wary. "We should go back to the suite."

I catch her around the waist and pull her back, this time sitting the other way. Her round little ass is all I've ever wanted, apparently. I am a deeply satisfied man.

But I must also be a patient man, and she needs to be a patient girl. "This isn't over. It's just the beginning. You know that, right?"

She nods.

"Good." I squeeze her hips, then run my hands up her belly and maul her tits for a second. God, she feels good, and I tell her that.

Then I pat her bum. "It's bedtime, though."

She rolls her eyes at me and smiles, mollified a little.

I see you, Rosie. She can't quite believe this is happening.

But I saw an opening, and I took it. I'm not a man who is afraid to go after what I want. I follow her out of the water, guarding her as she puts on her robe and slides her delicate little feet into her flip-flops.

I take her hand and walk around the long pool area to where I left my gym bag. I pull on a T-shirt then point to the entrance I used near the gym.

"This place is massive," she says as we wait for the elevator. We need to go down to the mezzanine level, then up to the other tower to get to my suite.

Too fucking far away. I want her in my arms again.

When the elevator arrives, we have it all to ourselves. I press her against the wall and kiss her again. She's fucking little, a soft, curvy plaything I want to toy with for hours.

The ding indicating we've arrived on the main concourse level means I only had twenty seconds.

Not nearly long enough.

The doors slide open—

"Dad!" Melanie squeals and throws her arms in the air. "We're going for nachos, do you—Oh! Rosie! I texted you. . ." Mel trails off, taking in the fact that we're both fresh from the pool.

"Look who I found at the pool," Rosie says with a confident gush. "Your old man."

She's going to pay for that.

I grunt.

"Do you want to come with us? We can come to your room while you get changed," Mel offers.

My ears start to burn.

"Nah, I'm good." Rosie slips past me. "Night, everyone. I'm exhausted from my swim."

Leaving me standing with an erection to cover up with my gym bag.

"Don't forget to moisturize!" Mel calls after her. Then she turns her gaze to me. "Dad? How about it?"

"Nachos sound great," I hear myself saying. No, they don't. Fucking hell. "But I'm. . . I don't have anything to wear. So I'll pass, too."

She frowns. "Okay."

"Don't forget our breakfast date, sweetheart. Bright and early."

"Yep."

By the time I get to the other elevators, Rosie's long gone. I call another one and exhale in relief.

That was close.

There will be a time for me to sit Mel down and tell her how I feel about Rosie. Tonight is *not* that time.

Upstairs, the hallway is quiet. So is the suite, when I let myself in. But after a moment, I hear a shower on. Two steps inside, I realize it's *my* shower.

And the erection is back.

I drop my gym bag and peel out of my damp clothes in the doorway of my room. The bathroom door is ajar, and I hear singing.

Singing.

In my shower.

I nudge the door open and lean against the frame, then wrap my hand around my cock. She's gorgeous.

Not that the bikini left a lot to the imagination, but her curves are more obvious when she's all the way naked. Even with steam in between us.

Her belly curves down to dark curls. When she turns around, the roundness of her plump, perfect ass makes me grit my teeth to keep from moaning. Her thick thighs taper down to those delicate calves she wrapped around my back, and her feet are dancing around in a circle—

"Daniel," she gasps.

I just keep stroking. "Invited yourself in?"

"I wasn't sure if you'd think to join me in mine. . ." She crooks her finger. "And we need to wash off the chlorine."

I join her. "And then moisturize, apparently."

She laughs. "Bridesmaid rule #74: no dry skin in photos."

"Her *old man* wasn't given that same instruction." I haul her up against me and kiss her mouth hard. She tastes like joy. Like youthful freedom.

"Sorry about that. I was thinking on the fly," she pants when I let her go.

"Something tells me you're not going to stop making the old man jokes any time soon."

"They give me a certain thrill."

"I'll give you a certain thrill." I haul her up onto my thigh, rubbing my cock against her hip at the same time.

"Mmm. . ." She grinds her pussy against me but then wriggles out of my grasp.

And slides to her knees in front of me.

I groan. "No, Rosie. Let me make you feel good again, first."

She pouts up at me. "But I've never given someone a blow job before."

This is a dream. I'm going to wake up and be all the fuck alone.

She leans in and presses her forehead to my hip. "Please, Daniel. Let me taste you."

Her gaze locks on my cock. To where I'm hard for her, and as she continues to stare, I get harder. My cock has never been this thick. The veins are pulsing, the skin stretched to the limit as my whole body throbs, churning seed for her. It beads at the crown, a pearly first taste.

I stroke her jaw, guiding her to open her mouth. "Then who am I to deny you?"

I feel her breath first, then her tongue. An inquisitive, eager swipe, then a slower slurp. Both make me rock forward on my feet, and I have to catch myself.

First time.

Wrapping my fingers around the base, I milk more of that seed for her. "This is all for you."

"It tastes good." She licks her lip. "Better than I imagined."

"You thought about this?"

She blushes and ducks her face.

"Uh uh." I catch her chin and lift her head again. "No hiding. I like that."

She licks her lips then resumes her exploration of my cock. Her mouth goes all the way around the head, then back to lick. Another test of taking a mouthful, then a lick.

Pre-come is flowing freely for her now. I'm slick enough I could haul her up and fuck her into the wall. There would be no stopping me as I thrust into her.

My body is primed to flood her with my seed.

A feeling I never thought I'd have again.

My Rosie.

She's getting the hang of it now, taking more of me and not pulling all the way off after each eager bob.

I make sure she knows I like everything she's doing because it's barreling in the right direction. "God, your mouth. So hot and slick. Lick me again, baby. Show me your tongue. Show me where you want my come."

Her eyes go wide, and she swallows half of me again, her lips stretched wide around my fat length. It's fucking crude, the look of my ruddy erection jammed in her mouth and making her throat bulge.

And she loves it. She's moaning around me now, her tongue working. Her hands brace on my hips for balance, and she blinks up at me.

Like this?

I nod. Yes, baby girl. Just like that.

It's a smile that undoes me. She tries to smile around my cock and gags a little, then catches my cock with a hand and finds her pace again.

So fucking happy.

I brush my thumb against the corner of her mouth and let my eyelids hood, let the heat of the shower and erotic display of Rosie on her knees sweep me over the edge. "Is this where you want it? You want to taste what you do to me?"

She bobs her head. *Yes.*

"Fuck, your face is just so—*Uhhh*—I'm coming. Coming down your fucking throat. Jesus."

I bite my lip as my cock pulses against her teeth and the top of her throat, my balls churning heavy spurts for her. Too much for her to handle, and she slides off, covering her mouth with her hand.

My come slides between her fingers as she stares up at me.

I stroke her cheek, run my touch over her throat, then peel her hand away. "Good girl," I mutter, feeling utterly spent. "You sucked my fucking soul out, didn't you? Show me."

She shudders and opens her mouth. Then sticks out her tongue.

I crush her to my body, stroking her hair as she laughs into my hip.

We rinse off, then get out of the shower and towel off. Rosie dutifully gets the moisturizer when I remind her about it, and she lets me apply it to every inch of her.

When I finish, I lay a lazy spank on her little bottom. Her round peach of an ass, firm with a bit of jiggle.

Mouthwatering.

I bring my hand down again and, this time, take hold of her, my fingers sinking into the warm space between her cheeks. She's smooth and slick, and, as I push my fingers lower, toward her front, absolutely wet for me.

I stroke the soft pout of her pussy lips, the off-limits baby-soft skin, and listen to the way my touch changes her breathing.

"On the bed," I order, and she jumps to obey.

I love how she looks stretched out for me. Her tits are round and jiggly, more so than her ass, and her curves spill down to a V of dark curls on her mound. I press my nose to them and breathe her in, then nudge her legs apart so I can stroke her bare pussy lips.

She's so fucking soft, impossibly soft. For a little thing, she's lush and warm and solid, all flesh and slick perfection.

Her body is begging to be violated.

I duck my head to her breast and suck one nipple deep into my mouth. The sounds she makes as she tightens her fingers in my hair are unholy.

Nnhhh. It's a whiny sound, a begging noise. It makes my

hands tighten on her ass, my fingers shoving deeper between her legs.

She's so fucking wet.

I strain with the need to shove her down and mount her. To slap my fat cock against her near-virgin cunt, then press into her as I watch her face.

It would be brutal.

Her sweet little innocent expression would fall away as I sear her from the inside out.

I shouldn't fuck her. Third base is violation enough.

But as soon as I think that, I'm filled with a vicious rage. The thought of another between her legs drives me mad.

No fumbling boy should ever have this chance again. He wouldn't do right by her. And another grown man?

My Rosie?

I couldn't handle that.

She's mine. I just need to tame my urges long enough to make it sweet for her.

Hard to remember when she tastes like me, the way I marked her mouth.

She whimpers after I kiss her, after I lick her tongue and groan at the flavor. Her gaze is loaded with a question when I pull away.

"What?" I shove her thighs open and climb on top of her.

Danger. We're both naked, and we haven't talked about protection or limits or anything else, but I'm so fucking happy I just want to spread her legs open and fuck her until she screams.

"Rosie," I growl. "Say whatever you were wondering there. I don't want any secrets between us."

"You really liked it? My mouth on you?"

"I want it again already. It's been a long time for me."

She lets out a clearly relieved exhale.

"Was that your worry? I told you, you're all I've wanted for months."

"Okay."

She makes a jealous face. "So there's nobody back home calling you Daddy?"

My cock pulses, demanding I fill her immediately. Pre-come slicks the tip once again as I stare down at her. "What?"

Her eyes flare. Her tongue darts out. "Just wondering."

It's fucked up. We're already in a precarious position. I should be doing everything to make her feel normal and more like my equal.

But that's not what I want. I want to shield her from the world, not push her out into it. I want to wrap her in my arms and never let go. Of course, she's my equal. But she's also a good girl—the best and sweetest girl—and if I can't use my decades of experience to put myself between her and everything rocky that might come next, what am I even doing?

"Where did that come from?" My voice rasps quietly between us.

She wriggles beneath me, spreading her legs. "Wild speculation from a certain bridesmaid." Her ankles hook around my waist, and her sweet, wet cunt finds my cock. "Forget I mentioned it. I just want to make you feel good again."

I curl my hand over her shoulder, pressing her into the mattress. "That's not how this works. You don't just make me feel good. For every orgasm you give me, I need to give you at least two."

"What?" She laughs. "No."

"I'm serious."

"That sounds unnecessarily rigid."

"Have you met me?"

She inhales sharply. "I've known you my whole life," she whispers.

Against my cock, she's getting wetter. Slick like warm honey. *She likes that part a lot.* All the old man jokes. Leesa's comments getting under her skin.

She has nothing to worry about. Rosie is stunning, effortlessly sexy. Utterly captivating to me and all I can see when I walk into a room. And she has no idea.

You're everything I would ever want. It's on the tip of my tongue. Instead, I grab her wrists and pin them over her head. "What if I told you I just want to take care of you? Make my sweet girl feel good? Is that less rigid enough?"

She squirms against my grip, and I immediately let go— only to grab her again when she grins. "Yes," she pants.

"And what if I want to show you things you haven't done before?"

"Like what?"

"Mmm. . " I graze my nose along her neck, breathing her in. "That depends."

My heart hammers in my chest. I catch her ear lobe between my teeth, grazing her flesh.

She's humping me shamelessly now, coating me in her essence. Her cunt flows for *me* because of this wild connection we have.

I owe it to her to bare my soul.

Exhaling slowly, I lower my voice to a dark whisper. "Why don't you tell Daddy what you want to learn?"

She cries out.

"Is that what you want to do?"

A nod. A desperate, sexy, out-of-control jerk of her head, and I claim her mouth again. Curious little girl. Sexy little slut. My fucking girl, all mine.

It makes me dizzy. I thrust against her, jizz threatening to spill out of me, all over her belly.

"Please," she begs.

"Tell me what you need."

"I want you inside me." She catches my face in her hands, slowing me down. Our breath syncs up as she holds my gaze. "Show me how it can be good, Daddy."

I hate what that implies. That she's tried before, and it wasn't everything she wanted. But I fucking love that I'll make it better for her. "I don't have any condoms." I brace myself on one arm and smooth my hand over her tummy. "I can pull out if it's a safe time. Do you know your cycle?"

"Just like that? So matter of fact?" She laughs slightly. "I'm on the pill. It's okay."

I slide my fingers lower, tracing through her curls to the bare lips of her pussy. They're slick with need, swollen and ready to stretch around my cock.

And now that I know there's no chance I'll accidentally knock her up. . . I frown and duck my head to her breast, licking a hungry swirl around her hard nipple.

Am I disappointed she's on the pill?

Am I that much of a caveman?

I suck harder and slide my fingers around her clit. Two of them rock into her tight channel. Finger fucking her cunt helps shake that thought away. Yes, I am a caveman. Now is not the time to worry about what the fuck that means for tomorrow and the day after.

She's safe from my desire to breed her, at least for tonight. One kink tamped down, another rising in a fast and furious way.

"You're so tight," I murmur against her neck as I lift her hips up and notch my cock against her slit. "Hold on to me, baby. Don't let go, even if it hurts."

"Why will it—" Rosie gasps as I use her slick, ready pussy, sinking all the way into her body in one unbelievable thrust.

Tight doesn't begin to describe it.

As ready as her body was in theory, in practice, she's never had a cock as fat as mine in her innocent pussy. If I'd wondered just how inexperienced she was, now I know.

I've stretched her to limits she's never felt before. My inner caveman roars in savage delight.

And my sweet girl clings to me, as instructed, panting unevenly in my ear.

I pulse my hips, just a little, and the panicky gasps increase.

"Shhh," I whisper, fucking enjoying every little sound she makes and the wide-eyed looks she's giving me. "You're okay. You're good. So good."

"No, wait."

I press my hips into her again. "Take all the time you need. Breathe through it."

"I thought it would be easier. . ." She throws her head back as if arching her body might help find some extra room for the erection I've shoved inside her. "Daniel!"

"I've got you."

"You've impaled me." She squirms, her pants turning to lusty moans as she finds a wriggly rhythm. "Oh, God."

"Ready for me to show you how good it can be?" I whisper as I kiss her mouth. My heart is hammering in my chest.

She shakes her head. *No.*

"But this is what you wanted." I sound cajoling now.

She smiles. "I take it back. I want to play the poker face game again."

I grin right back. "We can do that right now. Show me that this isn't affecting you."

"I can't." She squirms again, clearly ready for me to take over. She's searching for a feeling she can't quite make happen on her own.

"Rosie."

"Yes?"

"Do you trust me?"

Her breath hitches. "Yes."

I sweep my hand down her body, relishing how she feels in my arms. Shaking with need and ready to explode. I squeeze her hip, her ass, and then I start to move.

I watch her face as I drag my length out of her, inch by inch. I see the moment her brows furrow because she suddenly feels empty, and then I give it back to her.

Her lips part in a silent gasp.

I do it again.

Watching the whole time. Memorizing where she likes it the most. Halfway in on the third thrust, I slow down, then pulse there.

"Look down," I bite out. "See how you can take me."

She's stretched wide, but her skin glistens with the slick she's made. And as I fuck her—in and out, in and out, the flared head of my cock rocks against her G spot—she makes even more.

Within minutes, she's taking me all the way in with ease.

And still, she clings to me.

"What else do you want Daddy to show you?" I ask as I peel her arms from around my neck and press them over her head. Her back arches, and I latch on to her breasts.

Still fucking her. Slow and steady.

I can do this all night.

She cries out my name and tangles her fingers in my hair.

"What's that?" I grin against her chest. "You want to be on top?"

She laughs and then shrieks as I flip us over. She slides off my cock, and I drag her up to my face, diving into her cunt for another taste of her swollen goodness.

"Ride my face," I order her as I lap between her folds.

"I don't know what I'm doing."

"Whatever feels good."

She braces herself on the headboard and gazes down at me. "So all those TikToks about *if I die, I die happy* weren't kidding?"

I roll my eyes. "Grown men know how to breathe and suck pussy at the same time, baby. Leave that part to me. But if you killed me in the next five minutes, it would be the best death ever, yes."

"So just. . ." She wiggles her hips, and her plump pussy lips graze my mouth. "Like that?"

I growl and yank her onto my face.

Yes, like that.

Never fucking stop, like that.

I don't let her go until she shatters. Then I spin her around on top of me and use her again, my favorite person, the only one I've ever shared anything half this filthy with.

Daddy's little girl, his grown-up vixen. My secret lover. I work my erection into her again, and she takes every inch this time. I stroke in and out of her, eager to finish now.

"I'm going to come in you," I whisper as I hold her on top of me.

She smiles. "Good."

"Fill you up."

"Mmm."

"Make you all—" I cut myself off as my vision dims and my orgasm crashes over me. *Sticky.*

Thud. Thud. Thud. My pulse is a monster, stomping through my body. Heavy. Loud. My cock twitches, still spending inside her.

And on top of me, little Rosie Johnson giggles.

"I didn't know sex could be like *that*," she says after we get cleaned up.

"It isn't. Ever. With anyone else. The only person who is that good at sex in the whole world is me when I'm with you, so don't get any—"

She kisses me softly, her little lips sipping at my mouth. And she's smiling. "Good to know, old man."

I tangle my fingers in her hair and hold her still. Kiss her properly. And then I press my forehead against hers and tell her the truth. "It is like that when it's right. And it should always be that good. If it's not, you kick the asshole out of bed because he doesn't deserve you."

She nips at me, snapping her teeth. "I want to do it again." She climbs on top of me. "When can we do it again?"

I slap her ass lazily. "You want to ride Daddy's face?"

She grins. "Yes, please."

"Let me tell you about the first thought I had when I saw you in the airport. . ."

13
rosie

Friday

I WAKE up in Daniel's bed.

Naked.

I hear him talking in the other room, and my pulse ratchets up. But when he pauses, I realize he's on the phone.

Blinking away the sleep in my eyes, I look for a clock. Can't find one. I quickly go to the bathroom, then pull on the bathrobe I hung up last night before I helped myself to his shower.

And then his body.

And then his bed.

Daniel catches me around the waist in the living room as he listens to whoever he is talking to and gives me a not-that-quick good morning kiss.

I press my fingers to my lips as I dance past him and go to my room to grab today's bridesmaid uniform.

"Sorry, that was Heath," he calls. "I thought you might sleep a little longer."

"What time is it?"

"Almost seven-thirty."

Half an hour until breakfast in Mel's suite. I flush as I realize it's only taken me two days to get used to this life-style. Staying in *suites*. Anything we want, ordered or arranged with a wave of the hand.

Going back to motel life is going to be rough.

I set down the clothes I was about to put on. I have thirty minutes. One of only a handful of thirty-minute windows I'm going to have over the next two days to climb that big man out there and share some secret kisses.

Getting dressed can wait.

He's sprawled in a chair at the table when I return to the living room, looking at my door. Like he's waiting for me to come out.

"Did you change your mind about getting dressed?"

I brush my fingertips over my lower lip. "I thought that might be a bit hasty. Since we might not have another quiet moment today..."

He spreads his legs a little wider and pats one thigh. "Come here."

I crawl onto his lap. His hands go under the robe, and he hisses when he finds my naked flesh.

"And here I spent far too long thinking you were innocent..."

"I am," I tease.

He cups my ass, returning to it over and over again like he can't believe it. That makes two of us, but now that I know he likes my butt, I'll use that to my advantage. "There's nothing innocent about crawling on me with nothing on."

"I'm wearing a robe. It's *big*."

He tugs the belt open. "And utterly useless at protecting you from my hungry gaze."

"Speaking of hunger," I pant as he lifts me up and puts me on the table in front of him. "You have a breakfast date."

"That will be my second breakfast." He dips his head and licks his tongue in a slow, tantalizing swipe between my pussy lips. "I need to have you first."

———

I'm still thinking about how that felt when I arrive in Mel's suite an hour later.

I sent Daniel on ahead of me so we didn't have another "you two? Together again?" moment.

Too many of those, and Mel will figure it out.

She has to find out at some point. Because I'm not giving Daniel up. One night together, and I'm hooked hard.

I was hooked even before our first kiss.

But she's not going to find out today.

Leigh is already there, and Leesa arrives at basically the same time as me. Mel and Daniel are talking about baseball spring training, so I take this opportunity to review the plan for this afternoon and evening with the other two. The bachelorette party, which will start with a spa afternoon, then a limo ride to dinner for "just the girls" overlooking a lake. . . somewhere. . . *Thank you, Concierge team.* Finally, we'll head back to the hotel for a cocktail hour where the wedding guests will decide which evening party they want to go to—the three-level club and burlesque hall for some dancing and titillation or the private poker game Daniel is hosting.

A.k.a., the bachelorette and bachelor parties, although the only people bound to the separate events will be Mel and Javi and their respective attendants.

"What needs to be done before we head to the spa?" Leigh asks.

From across the room, Mel raises her voice. "First, you guys all need to eat some of this. My dad ordered way too much."

"I had three solid workouts yesterday," Daniel says, not looking at me.

I frown ever so slightly. He only went to the gym twice. Once— Oh.

He's counting sex with me as a workout. I see. And now it's a test of my poker face.

"Impressive for an old guy," I murmur as I load up a plate with French toast and fruit.

This feels like a solid point scored until Leesa giggles her way to the table. "Who are you calling old? Mr. Burke, you're in the prime of your life, aren't you?"

Which is true, but not something to say in front of Melanie.

Also, does she want me to yank out her extensions?

He frowns, doing a very good job of looking unimpressed. "Eat some toast, Leesa. I think your blood sugar might be out of whack."

She giggles again.

Mel gives her a WTF look, at least.

I move around the table and sit between Leigh and Mel. Is being irrationally cranky a sign of low blood sugar, too? I shove a bite of food into my mouth. Mmm. That helps.

"Coffee, anyone?" Daniel lifts the carafe.

"Yes, please." I hold out my mug.

He fills it for me, then stands up and comes around the table. "You've got a little. . ." And in front of everyone, he wipes the corner of my mouth with his thumb. "Syrup."

And he licks it off.

His gaze is hot, his intent clear—to me, at least. I don't have anything to worry about.

Poker face. "Thanks," I say coolly.

Because he can't do things like that in front of Mel. Not that she was looking. My pulse chills out when I realize she's deep in her text messages with Javi.

"You're his favorite," Leesa sighs after Daniel leaves. Mel has gone outside with him, walking him to the elevator. The three of us are sprawled on the couches, slightly full from all the delicious brunch food.

I ignore her. Of course, I'm his favorite. I let him come in my mouth and then showed it to him. And I know his favorite ice cream and the secret fact that he's afraid of heights. "We can't order that much breakfast tomorrow. We'll be slugs all day."

Leigh shakes her head. "Not at all. A big breakfast is important on a wedding day. My sister skipped it and then fainted just before she walked down the aisle. Once we get going, we probably won't eat again until dinner, both today and tomorrow."

I pull out my phone and make a quick note to schedule some micro-snacking moments to avoid that kind of disaster. "Good point."

"Hey, Rosie, do you hang out with Mr. Burke back in Conception—"

"What is your deal, honey?" Leigh snapped at Leesa. "Seriously. You have never been this obtuse before. He's not bang-able. Mr. Burke is a handsome man, but like, he's definitely a square. Right, Rosie?"

No comment.

Mel returns just in time to save me from that conversation with no good out. "Ready for a day at the spa, girls?"

I brought a bag with everything I'll need for the rest of the day. It seemed like smart packing earlier so I don't risk going back to Daniel's suite and Mel asking me where my room was. Now I have a weird ache in my chest at the thought of not seeing him again for hours.

It doesn't go away until we get to the spa. As I'm putting my phone away in the locker they provide, the screen lights up.

Having fun?

The way seeing Daniel's name on the screen changes my entire mood is startling. I grin like an idiot and text him back.

Perfect timing. I was about to put my phone in a locker. I'm off to get a hot stone treatment in five minutes.

He replies immediately, in two back-to-back texts.

Nice. Enjoy.
Can't wait to see you tonight.

I like his last reply, then type out **Same, old man**, just to keep it light. But it doesn't feel right, so I erase that. **Counting the hours**, I send him instead. It's true.

———————

Our afternoon is non-stop pampering, and by the time we get to our dinner, we're all relaxed and vibing hard on the fact that Mel is getting married. Tomorrow.

"To the most beautiful bride ever," I toast.

Mel lifts her glass in my direction. "And the sweetest maid of honor."

I only feel a small shiver of guilt, and it doesn't last long.

I didn't text Daniel all afternoon. I haven't even looked at my phone since we left the spa. I can do this. She's my whole focus for the next thirty hours.

That resolve lasts exactly two hours.

When we get back to the hotel, Mel and Leigh go up to the bridal suite to redo Mel's hair for tonight. Leesa and I go to the private dining room where the cocktail reception will be. A rehearsal dinner, deconstructed, Javi called tonight. Finger food, drinks, and no rehearsal because we did that yesterday. Just a chance for all the guests to mingle and get to know each other before the wedding.

Leesa and I are supposed to act as hostesses, making sure everything runs smoothly before Mel makes her grand entrance.

Something I never want to do at my own wedding, I think to myself.

And that's when I catch sight of Daniel. He's wearing a

suit without a tie, his shirt open at the top button, and he has a glass of something that looks expensive in his hand.

He looks every inch the father of the bride. Distinguished. Commanding. Not filthy at all.

Imagine him waiting at the end of a trail of rose petals. . .

I press my lips together. No, not his style.

His head tilts away from the person he's talking to and then turns in my direction.

Would you ever marry a girl like me?

His expression is so hard to read, his jaw tight. He excuses himself and strides in our direction without looking away from me.

"Hi, Mr.—" Leesa doesn't get to finish the greeting.

"Rosie, there's a small issue we need to take care of."

"Oh, okay, sure, I'm all yours."

He sets his hand in the small of my back.

Leesa raises an eyebrow.

"*Favorite,*" she mouths at me as he firmly guides me out the door.

"What's the problem?" I ask as we cross the wide corridor.

He pulls open a door, revealing a boardroom. "I may have lied about that."

"That there's an issue?"

He closes the door firmly and presses me against the wall just inside the room, kissing me as he guides my hand to his erection. "No. About it being small."

"Oh." I laugh and kiss him back.

His gaze rakes down my body. I'm wearing my favorite outfit that never gets to see the light of day in Conception Ridge, a tight black minidress with cap sleeves and a little white collar. It's fun and Vegas-approved: short, sexy, and a little naughty.

I'm waiting for him to tell me I can't go out like this, that I have to put on something more appropriate.

But he doesn't. Instead, he licks his lips, his gaze feral. "That dress is dangerous, Rosie."

"I'll be good tonight."

"I'm sure you will." He strokes his fingers across the inside of one thigh, then over to the other one.

I can feel the phantom brush against my pussy. If he goes an inch higher and buries his hand in the shadow between my legs, he'll find me soaking wet and ready.

"How am I supposed to control myself when you're wearing this?" He brushes his mouth against my ear. "What are you trying to do to Daddy?"

Make you fall in love with me. "I didn't. . . it wasn't. . ." I gasp as his mouth latches on to my neck. "I swear, I brought this from home. It was always going to be my outfit tonight."

He groans. "I need you. I can't let you go out tonight without marking you as mine."

I shiver. Yes. I need that, too. "We need to be quick."

He lifts me up and carries me to the far end of the room. He works my panties off, then spins me around and bends me over the table.

I cover my mouth as he trails his fingers through my wetness.

"We need to talk," he growls in my ear, bending over me. He unbuckles his pants, and I feel his cock behind me. Nudging my thighs.

"There's no time."

"I know." He thrusts into me. "We'll have all the time in the world when we get home. I'm going to be so sweet to you then."

I laugh desperately. "Okay."

"Fuck, Rosie." He growls. "Arch your back. Yes, baby. That's it. Fuck, you're so pretty. You're so wet for me. Taking me so good. That sweet little pussy needed to be filled, didn't it? You needed Daddy inside you. I've got you. It's okay."

It's a low string of filth and is exactly what I need. His words, goading me to come on his cock. I shove my hand between my body and the table and find my clit. His cock and my fingers send me flying so fast it would be embarrassing if he wasn't going to come just as fast himself.

"Jesus, Rosie. You're milking me. I should pull out, baby, but I can't."

"Don't pull out," I whisper.

"You want it? My mess inside you all night?"

I whimper.

He takes that as the yes that it is. "Fuck, here it comes. Nothing between us, my perfect girl. I'm gonna breed you."

His fingers tighten on my hips.

Breed me.

He smooths his hand over my hip as he shudders on top of me. "Fuck, we shouldn't do this. I could have you pregnant by the time we fly home."

As far as life plans go, it's fucked up and perfect at the same time. I'm ridiculously full of his thick cock. Can't breathe kind of full, and it's better than I could have imagined. My pussy is *still* clenching around him, delicious aftershocks rippling through me. Is this the right time to ask him if he's serious?

No.

Later.

When he pulls out, he presses something between my legs before turning me around. He kisses me carefully this time. Gently.

"There's a washroom out that door," he murmurs, pointing to the side exit of the room.

"You planned this!"

"I had my options laid out." He kisses my forehead again. "Such a good girl, my god."

By the time I get back to the cocktail reception, he has another drink in his hand, and he's chuckling along to someone's story. Calm, cool, and collected. Nothing about his demeanor betrays the fact he just bent me over an empty boardroom desk and filled me raw.

I can still feel his come slicking down my thighs, and he's drinking and joking with guests, completely at ease. Until he makes eye contact with me, anyway. Then he swallows, his Adam's apple bobbing once, and his gaze darkens as if to say, *I want to do it again. I want to do it here, in front of everyone.*

I would let him, too. We would ruin his daughter's wedding, but it wouldn't matter because nothing matters beyond Daniel losing himself inside me.

Filling me up. Breeding me.

I could have you pregnant by the time we fly home. I think he meant it. If I wasn't on the pill, I probably would go home from this trip with a baby in my belly.

14
daniel

BEFORE THE GIRLS leave for the bachelorette party, I make them promise to stay together and stay safe.

Mel rolls her eyes. "Yes, Dad."

Rosie's expression is. . .well, she's working on her poker face. I feel a savage pleasure at the thought that she's going out full of my seed. I want her thinking of me as she dances.

I want her to come back to me as soon as possible so I can fill her all over again.

Ten minutes after they leave, my phone dings. A text from Rosie.

Your stern Daddy routine is hot.

I'm glad I'm leaning against the bar, so nobody can see how I get an instant erection from her message.

I have so many rules for you to follow, little girl.

Like what?

Have fun tonight, Rosie. Send photos.

I want to know what the rules are!

And I want to make you wait.

Instead of replying again, she sends a selfie from the limo. I save it to my phone.

Six hours later, I'm with Javi and his friends at a private poker table, a stack of chips in front of me, when we're joined by a group of very tipsy young women.

Rosie slides into the chair next to me.

"How did you get in here?" I ask her as she tries to look at my cards. "And how much have you had to drink?"

"I threw the best party," she says happily, not answering either of my questions.

"It looks like it." I glance at my watch. "Time for bed?"

On the other side of Javi, Mel is nuzzling her face into his neck. "I'm going to miss you tonight," she murmurs.

Way too much information.

Rosie pats my arm. "I'll get her to her suite."

I give her a look that says, *I'll be along soon.*

I hate that I can't wrap my arm around her and publicly claim her. Not until after the wedding.

So instead of immediately following her, which is all I want to do—six hours apart is six hours too many—I play two more hands.

I lose both after winning all night.

My attention is now elsewhere. Bidding Javi and his friends a good night, I excuse myself.

When I get to the suite, I find Rosie sprawled on the couch, legs akimbo.

She gives me a naughty, happy smile. "Hello, you."

I shrug off my suit jacket. "Nice panties."

"They're wet," she whispers. "Because you filled me with come earlier."

I prowl over, catching her closest ankle and hauling her to the edge of the couch. Kneeling, I tug the damp cotton to the side.

Her pretty pink pussy is slick and swollen.

I swirl my fingers through the sticky mess I left behind hours ago. "Do you know how hot this is?"

She blushes. "I've been on edge all night."

Her clit throbs against as I stroke it with my thumb. "I might keep you there a little longer."

"Fuck me," she breathes.

"No." I grin. "How much did you have to drink?"

"Officially? *Nothing*."

"Unofficially?"

She presses her finger to her lips. "Shhhh."

I tease her entrance with a fingertip. "Did you have fun tonight?"

"Yes."

"Miss me?"

"Yesss."

"Were you a good girl?"

She bites her lips and rolls her hips, wanting more than just the tip of a finger.

"Rosie?"

"Yes," she whispers. "Didn't dance that much. Just a little."

I look up at her and catch a mischievous look on her face.

"Or a lot?"

"Only the fast songs. No slow songs with boys." The sing-song voice makes my balls tighten up with forbidden thoughts.

Daddy, being ever so gentle with his girl after a dance. Rewarding her for saving all her dances for her favorite man. A much older, secret lover.

I lean in and kiss the inside of her thigh. "I want to dance with you tomorrow night at the wedding."

"We're playing a risky game," she murmurs as I bite the soft skin just beside her cunt.

"Let me worry about that." I let her panties fall back into place, then open my mouth and gently press my teeth into her cloth-covered mound.

She rocks her hips into the sensation.

We need more space. "Bed. Now."

"What?" She protests but lets me help her up. I walk her into my bedroom and kneel in front of her to take off her strappy sandals. "You danced in these all night long?"

"I did miss you," she whispers again. "Do you like to go dancing?"

"I don't know. Haven't tried in a long time." I push her dress up her hips. What I want now is her naked and in my bed.

She reaches behind her head and unzips the dress, and together we pull it off her body. She's left in a damp pair of white panties and a matching white bralette that barely covers her breasts.

Twenty-year-old tits don't need that much support, apparently—a thought that makes me painfully aware that

I'm a filthy old man. I cup her swells in my hands, pressing them together.

Fuck, her sweet skin looks so good under my flexing hands.

I picture my cock between her round, bouncing tits, bumping into her slick mouth. Her deep cleavage is perfect for fucking. My erection strains and throbs as she sways in front of me.

This is all wrong. I should be licking her to sleep and tucking her in because she's had a few drinks.

We should take things slow.

I shouldn't touch her at all.

And yet I see myself unbuckle my belt and slide my zipper down, revealing the heavy press of my erection against my boxer briefs. "I need your mouth, baby."

She gasps, and it's a delighted sound. Pure happiness at seeing the outline of my fat cock.

"Just like you did in the shower," I tell her. "Take me deep."

She sits on the edge of the bed and circles me in her hand, first licking around the crown—which makes me twitch with need—then swallowing half my length on the first try.

I spread my legs wider, getting at just the right height for what I want next, then I cup her tits and squeeze them together. It's the wrong angle, but the sight of her breasts as a shelf beneath my cock, shiny with her spit, gives me another idea.

"Suck me until I'm close," I growl. "I want to come on your tits."

Her eyes go wide at my crude demands.

What am I doing?

Showing her who I really am. A dirty man. She's unlocked needs in me I didn't know existed.

Her eyelashes flutter shut, then she pulls off with a wet slurp.

"You want to come on me?" She blinks up at me. "Not in me?"

I grunt. "Already did that today."

She licks her lips. "Not in my mouth."

That makes me grin. "You like the taste of Daddy's seed, little girl?"

Her pupils go dark. "Yes."

"I do like seeing it in your pretty mouth." I wipe my mouth. "Lie down."

"You're bossy tonight." She scrambles back, stretching out as I strip. "I didn't really have too much to drink, you know. Just enough to be a little happy. I'm definitely sober enough to consent to you gagging me with your—"

I grab one of her ankles and lift her foot to my mouth, cutting her off. "Noted."

I kiss the sole of her foot, then her toes, and work my way up, tonguing the whole inside of her thigh until I get back to the pussy I've been neglecting for my own needs. She's right, I'm being brusque and bossy, and I don't know why.

Six hours apart from my newfound sex kitten, maybe.

She's slick again, fresh, clear arousal begging for something even better than her lips stretched around my shaft.

Stripping away her panties, I slap my cock against her glistening slit.

"I had plans to fuck your mouth." I fall on top of her,

shoving the bralette out of the way. I suck one of her nipples, then the other, and the sound she makes matches how I feel.

Like the more of her I consume, the more right it is.

"Please," she gasps.

I rise up and hitch one of her legs over my arm, opening her all the way for me.

With a single thrust, I seat myself in her cunt. Slick and hot and perfectly familiar now.

Yes, this.

I need this.

"I was going to fuck your tits," I growl, rolling my hips. "And then you spread out on my bed. Such a good girl for Daddy, listening to every word I tell you, and suddenly, using your hot little body isn't enough. Do you feel that? Feel how big I am for you? It's never been like this, Rosie. Not ever. What have you done to me?"

She cries out, and I hunch over her, fucking her faster now. I pin her wrists to the mattress and bury my face in her neck.

She's made me fall in love with her, that's what. She's branded my heart and soul.

Now, I can't just get off with her.

I need to fucking mate her like my life depends on it. Stroke into her deep enough that I make her see stars, slow enough that I light up her nerve endings in a way that guarantees she'll come first.

And she does, with my mouth swallowing half of one of her tits and clit pinched between my fingers. I get her there like it's my solitary mission in life, and then I shatter, my whole body pumping a full load into her already-bred cunt.

Twice a day is just enough to take the edge off this wild need, I guess.

When I finish pulsing inside her, I roll off her, pick her up, and carry her into the bathroom.

We both need to wash off the day before bed, and her poor, battered pussy needs some tender care.

"I've been practicing my poker face," she says as I wash her hair. "I think I'm ready to join you at the card table."

"I noticed. Is that what we're going to do for your birthday?"

"That would be fun." She sighs happily.

I rub my fingers over her scalp again, enjoying the sounds she makes.

"What else do you want to do? You mentioned a tattoo." I tug her back against me. "And you still haven't told me where you want to get it."

"Oh, that."

"Yes, that."

She glances over her shoulder, frowning. "Do you not like tattoos?"

I don't have any. From the outside looking in, I'm a relatively straight-laced, middle-aged dad. *Straight-laced when I'm not thinking of the depraved ways I want to fuck her brains out.* "I don't have an opinion on them in general. On you, though? It sounds hot. But I find myself getting a bit growly at the thought of a tattoo artist putting his hands on certain parts of your body."

"My foot," she giggles. "That's where. And the what is a sun and moon twisted together. It's a design I've gotten a few times at the county fair in temporary spray-on ink, and I really like it."

Her pretty little foot, all decorated for Daddy. "I want to take you to get it done."

"Okay." She twists fully in my arms, kissing me languidly. "I'd love that."

Once we dry off, we crawl back into bed. I tuck her into my side. She traces her fingers down my torso, and my abs flex against her touch. My cock thickens again, but it's a lazy arousal now. The kind that promises to wake her in the middle of the night but doesn't need to be sated immediately.

I just want her in my arms, her soft words murmuring against my skin.

"You mentioned rules earlier. Bossy Daddy rules."

"Mmm."

"That was hot."

"I was serious, though."

She smiles. "Okay. Like. . .what?"

I stroke her hair, gathering it into a loose ponytail to hold on to. "I want you to always be honest with me. If I'm asking for too much or pushing you too hard, you need to tell me to stop."

"That's not hot!" She pushes up, her face flush with indignation. "That's. . ."

"Bossy Daddy stuff," I say dryly. "I can't turn it off, Rosie. I'm almost twenty-five years older than you. I've lived a whole lifetime. Raised a daughter who is older than you. *I want the best for you, even if that's not me.*"

"Why wouldn't it be you?"

"You might not want a family with me, for example." It hurts to grate those words out, but they have to be said.

"I. . ." Her mouth drops open, then snaps shut. Her eyes shimmer and then spark. "I would."

"It's okay to just play with the idea because it's hot." Those words hurt, too, in an unexpected way. "You're protected. I can breed you over and over again without any consequences."

She bites her lip.

I stroke her mouth gently until she releases the worried flesh. "It's all right—"

"I don't just want it to be pretend," she says in a rush. "If we. . .if this turns into something, I *will* want your babies. Of course, I would want a family with you."

I had a whole list of things that a twenty-year-old girl might want instead of a life with me, but it goes fuzzy in my head now, with the way she's looking at me.

Indignant. Turned on. Powerful.

I haul her on top of me. "It's not a deal-breaker for me if you didn't. I will want you no matter what."

She straddles me, her wet sex finding my heavy shaft. "But you want to knock me up, too."

I growl and grip her hips, guiding her against me.

Maybe three times a day.

"It's crossed my mind." Hourly. I smooth one palm around to cover her soft belly. "You're fucking ripe, Rosie. Like nobody else has ever been for me."

"Then pluck me from the tree," she whispers. "Make me yours in every way."

I intend to.

She lifts up enough to ease the come-slicked tip of my cock into her pussy, then sinks down on me. There's no finesse to how we fuck now. It's raw and slow, me gripping her like my life depends on it, her thighs shaking from the very start.

I tangle my fingers in her hair and tug, holding her still on top of me. My orgasm churns inside me already. "Rosie."

She grinds against me.

"You're going to milk me, little girl."

"Good," she pants.

"You want me to fill you up? Tuck you in with a full belly?"

She makes a desperate sound that I take as a yes.

Yes, Daddy, breed me.

I cup her ass, my fingers sinking between her cheeks to tease her tight hole there. She shudders, and her pussy flutters around my thickness. I tease the smooth pucker again, and she bears down against me.

"Let me in. Good girl." I'm throbbing inside her now, my cock leaking right against her cervix. A few more twists of her hips, and I'll be knocking her up before she comes. "Let me play with your ass a little. It'll feel good for you, and the way your body trembles? That feels real good for Daddy, too."

"Oh my *God.*" Her thighs shake against my sides. "Daniel. . ."

"I know. I've got you."

"That feels. . ." She arches her back in my tight hold. "So full."

She's spasming around me now. Desperate in every way. I pulse my finger in and out of her, just the tip, and she rolls her hips, figuring out the rhythm.

"That's it." I kiss her as I urge her on. "You're so good for me. Fuck yourself on my cock as you take my finger, too.

Both holes are full now. You're so good to take me like this. Feel that? You're going to come for me, aren't you? Your tight little pussy is going to take me with you. I'm going to feel it in your ass, too. Every part of you is going to demand that I come in you, and I'll do it. I'll fill you up, baby. You just gotta come for me, first. You gotta get there."

She whines and shakes her head, but then she rolls her hips and sinks down on my cock again, taking me all the way to the root, and it feels so good, so goddamn good, that I can't stop myself, and the climax rips from me.

Her eyes go wide above me, and then she cries out. As that first spurt soaks her walls, her own orgasm hits, and her cunt seizes me in a vicious grip I fucking love.

It doesn't matter that she's on the pill. It doesn't matter that she's only been mine for a matter of days, and nobody knows yet.

All that matters is this wild, perfect connection. This beautiful second chance.

So I kiss her with everything I have and show her exactly how I feel about this gift she's giving me.

15
rosie

Saturday

THERE ISN'T enough space for all of us in the bridal suite at the same time. There should be, but the army of hair and makeup people who have arrived take up more room than we anticipated.

The brunch spread is competing for real estate, too.

And then there's Daniel, looming larger than life, officially here to watch over his daughter. Unofficially eye-fucking me every chance he gets.

So maybe it's just me who needs a break.

When it becomes clear that each of us will take about an hour with the beauty team, and we have a few hours until the photographer arrives, I excuse. I tell myself I need to fetch my dress from Daniel's suite, but clearly, I left it up there in the morning so I'd have this excuse to return.

Daniel follows ten minutes later, and for a change of pace, we fuck on my bed.

After, as he traces the lines of my naked body, he asks me when I'm going to put on my bridesmaid dress.

"Not until after my makeup, I think," I say, looking at the dress hanging on the wall. "Why?"

"I've been thinking about you in it ever since you sent me that photo."

I frown. "What photo?"

"From the dress shop." He finds his pants, abandoned beside the bed, and pulls out his phone to show me. "This one. God, you're so fucking sexy."

I'm in the background, and my face is obscured by the fact I'm holding my phone, taking a picture of Mel.

But I still flush with pleased heat that he so obviously wants me—and only me.

"That might be the nicest thing anyone has ever said to me."

"I'll make it my mission to say a hundred nicer things by the end of your birthday tomorrow." He looks at the time. "All right. Think we can last twelve hours this time?"

"What?"

"Before I can be inside you again."

I giggle.

He frowns. "I'm serious."

"Wow." I catch his face in my hands and kiss him full on the mouth. "That's another very nice compliment."

He holds me against him. "You're irresistible."

At this rate, he'd hit a hundred compliments before the wedding was over.

I love you. It's on the tip of my tongue but now isn't the time. "I have to go."

"I'll be down soon."

"Maybe wait a while so Leesa doesn't get suspicious at our conveniently timed absences."

He doesn't respond to that, and I kick myself for letting that thread of jealousy burst into this sweet moment.

Instead of pulling away, I burrow closer, soaking up the warmth of his skin and the comforting strength of the muscles beneath it. He's so rock-solid that I just want to cling to him forever.

"You have to go," he reminded me.

"I know. I just said that."

Now it's his turn to chuckle.

"I'm going." I smooth my hands down his bare chest. "Right. . .now."

I'm still grinning like an idiot when I stroll into the bridal suite with my dress bag over my shoulder.

The grin disappears when I find Leesa in tears, Leigh drinking deeply from a bottle of champagne, and Mel locked in her bedroom.

"What happened?" I turn in a slow circle.

The hair and makeup people are ignoring us.

Leigh waved the bottle. "Just pre-wedding drama."

"Mel?" I must look horrified because Leigh quickly shakes her head.

"No." She points to Leesa. "The drama llama."

"Oh, shut up," Leesa sobs.

They're really killing my post-sex buzz, but I can't tell them that. I cross to the bedroom and knock softly. No answer, so I chance it and peek inside.

Mel has earbuds in and is dancing her butt off.

I close the door behind me. "Hey," I say.

She doesn't notice.

I snap my fingers, and then when that doesn't work, I jump in front of her.

She shrieks and loses her step. "Are they still fighting?"

"I think it's a grumpy peace. Are you okay?"

"Mm-hmm. I'm marrying Javi tonight. Nothing can ruin today, not even my silly decision to do the cliched roommates-as-bridesmaids thing." She throws her arms around me. "Oh, Rosie. You would never put yourself before me this weekend. I'm so grateful for you."

Well, this is awkward. I hug her back because there's nothing else to be done. "Two hours until the photographer arrives," I say, my poker voice even better than my newly acquired poker face. "Let's feed you one last time—just a little nibble, all right? And then it's time to get this beauty show underway."

Food helps everyone move past hurt feelings. By the time Daniel returns—in a perfectly tailored black suit that stretches over his shoulders and shows off the length of his muscled legs—my hair and makeup are done, and I'm about to get into my dress.

I duck into Mel's room to change, my heart beating wildly.

———

Five hours and probably three thousand pictures later, it's time to go to the chapel.

Leesa walks down the aisle first. Then Leigh. For a moment, it's just Mel, Daniel, and myself waiting outside, and then I'm cued.

With one final glance at them, I step into the cozy space.

Step, pause, step, pause. All eyes are on me until I reach the officiant, and then I turn, and the music changes.

Mel walks down the aisle to a piano version of "Canon in D Major." She grips Daniel's arm, but her glittering gaze is all for Javi, who's waiting just across from me, his chest puffed with pride.

I'm so glad I have a handkerchief wrapped around the base of my bouquet. I'm totally going to cry as soon as they're holding hands.

But right now, all I can see is Daniel. The square set of his shoulders, the tense flex of muscles in his cheeks. He's staring straight ahead, a rock for his daughter, and I love him so much it hurts.

Why now? How did this happen?

And then, after he passes Mel to Javi, he slides his glance to me, pausing for a moment before taking his seat, and I don't need the answers to those questions.

It can remain a mystery as to why and how. All that matters is that this is happening. It's wild and unbelievable and perfect, so perfect.

As the ceremony begins, and all the way through the vows and exchange of rings, I can feel Daniel's gaze burning up my skin.

Have I gotten myself in over my head? Nobody knows about us. We've only had. . .whatever this is. . .for a few days. Is it crazy to think that this could be us at some point? Exchanging forever kinds of vows?

And why does it hurt *so much* to even consider that it might be impossible?

I try to picture telling my parents I fell in love with Mr.

Burke while we were in Vegas, and a horrible panic swells inside me.

I love him.

Dragging in a deep breath, I focus on that.

One thing at a time.

16
daniel

AS ROSIE STANDS after dinner to give her maid of honor speech, I'm still thinking about the play of emotions I watched her go through during the ceremony.

Another man would feel bad for watching the maid of honor more than the exchange of vows at his daughter's own wedding.

I am not that man.

Mel and Javi are married now, blissfully in love. What I do next is my own damn business.

The private dining hall is set up with two long tables, each seating twenty people. Rosie's standing at the center of one of them. I'm across the room on the far side of the other one.

Too far away, but I have the perfect seat to watch her entertain everyone.

She shares three different anecdotes about exciting and far-too dangerous adventures she and Mel went on as teenagers, all in pursuit of boys. Each anecdote ends in a humorous lesson about how it wasn't the right boy and definitely not the right time to fall in love. "And then she flew across the country to go to school. I had big plans to visit her in New York City and have more of the same adventures. But within a year, she met a certain Mr. Ruiz at the bank where she did a summer internship, and the fun and games were over."

Four years I made my daughter wait to marry the man of her dreams. Listening to the way Rosie tells the story and realizing how I feel now about a certain, sexy maid of honor, it's a miracle they didn't elope sooner.

So when it's my turn to speak, as the father of the bride, I tuck the prepared notes I made back in my pocket and just speak from the heart, starting with a confession. "When my baby girl told me she'd gone to New York and fallen in love with a man—an older man, set in his career—I didn't know how to take it. And he was a *banker*, no less, so not even someone who works with his hands. . ." Javi leads the laughing, thank God. I mean it with love. "I'll even admit that I didn't take it very well at all."

From across the table, Mel dabs her eyes with a napkin.

"But what Rosie left out of her speech, and what Mel and Javi won't tell you because they love me despite myself, is that I did refuse to support this marriage when I first heard that he had proposed. Not forever. Just until she finished college and had a job. Four years, I begged them. Just wait until she's. . ." I grunt around my feelings. Goddamn it. "All grown up. But Rosie's right. Mel went to the city and grew up fast. She fell in love. And despite my objections, she has been steadfast in that love. Very grown-up and very patient. Javi, you too. So despite my earlier misgivings, it's an honor to see the two of you make this commitment today. Mel, I am so proud of you. And Javi. . .I'm proud to call you family."

"Dad. . ." Mel sighed and swiped away more tears. "You old goof."

Beside her, Rosie mouthed those three words back to me as I circled around to give my daughter and son-in-law the tightest hugs.

I might be an old goof, that's true. But I'm Rosie's old goof. And I will fuck her into the mattress like a twenty-five-year-old when she makes the delightful mistake of repeating it later.

They thank everyone for coming and cut a small three-tier wedding cake, officially opening the dessert buffet, which people will need after the ten courses of tiny food art.

Then it's time for their first dance. In the intimate space between the two long tables, Javi takes my daughter in his arms and slowly starts to spin her around in practiced circles. She melts into him, their foreheads pressed together.

The photographers circle the room, documenting everything.

Mel drags me out onto the floor for the next dance, and Javi dances with his mother. I see Rosie dancing with the best man, and it takes everything in me not to grind my teeth.

As soon as the song ends and Mel is back in her husband's arms, I intercept Rosie on her way back to her chair.

"Can I have this dance?" It's phrased in the form of a question to be polite. It's a demand.

Let me hold you. Be in my arms.

She slides her hand into mine. There aren't enough

guests for us to get lost on the dance floor. There will only be a few of these dances tonight, and while most eyes are on Mel and Javi, twirling in the center of the room, I can feel some attention on my back as I twirl Rosie and then tug her close.

My hand finds its home in the small of her back, my thumb grazing her spine and my little finger resting on the curve of her ass.

She's taller than usual in today's heels, and her breasts brush my chest. Her breath is warm as she puts her cheek against my jaw, and her fingers wrap over my shoulder.

The lyrics are about love that knows no bounds, a thousand years of yearning, and my whole body throbs for Rosie to know that I want this to mean something significant.

When we get back to Conception Ridge, I'm going to be her best customer at the coffee shop. I'll pick her up from school and make her cozy dinners, then spend all night with my mouth on her cunt and my cock buried deep in her body.

But before we go home, she has a birthday to celebrate.

17

rosie

Sunday

"HAPPY BIRTHDAY, BEAUTIFUL GIRL," a husky voice whispers in my ear.

"Mmm. . ." I stretch, arching against Daniel's big body behind me.

His hand skates up my side and cups my breast. Immediately my nipple tightens against his palm.

"I've ordered room service breakfast because the post-wedding brunch will be more of that foam nonsense. . ." He rocks against me. "And then after that, we have the whole day to ourselves."

Mel and Javi are taking a helicopter trip to the Grand Canyon, just the two of them, and everyone else is splitting off and doing their own thing.

Daniel's going to take me to get my tattoo mid-afternoon, and then he's booked dinner reservations somewhere special.

I can't wait.

There's a knock at the door, and he leaps out of bed. My tummy rumbles, so I roll after him. I go to put on the robe hanging on the back of his bedroom door but spy his dress shirt from the night before.

Even better.

I do up a few buttons so I don't traumatize the room service attendant and lean against the doorframe as I watch Daniel hunt for his wallet.

I'm giggling as he opens the door, shirtless, but the laugh dies in my mouth when instead of hotel staff, the person on the other side is Mel.

"Dad, I wanted to give you this—" She cuts herself off as she looks past him and sees me.

Time slows, and my legs start to shake.

"What are you doing here?" Her face twists in horror. "Rosie, what the fuck?"

Daniel growls at his daughter. "Melanie, watch your mouth."

She spins on him. "Dad, did you sleep with Rosie? Oh my God, do not answer that. Gross."

He winces. "What did you want?"

"It's not important now." She gestures her hands between us. "Whatever this is, it's not appropriate."

"You're right," Daniel grates. "But it's *you* that's being inappropriate."

She pushes past him, and the door closes behind her. "You're twice her age."

"I thought age didn't matter when it came to love?" He gets between her and me, not that it does any good. I can still feel her zinging nasty looks my way.

"This is *not* the same as me and Javi. Don't you dare—"

She stops. Sighs. Glares up at the ceiling then stomps her feet. "Fuck, fuck, fuck. And don't tell me to watch my language, Dad. You guys should have tried harder to keep this a secret. Ew."

"We are in the privacy of my suite. I was expecting *breakfast*."

"Are you saying this is *my* fault? And why are you ordering *breakfast* when I'm going to be hosting a *brunch* in two hours."

"Jesus, Mel, not everything is about you."

"Excuse me for thinking that on my wedding weekend, it just might be!"

I cannot witness any more of this conversation while only wearing Daniel's shirt. Neither of them notices that I zip across to my room, and I'm grateful to close the door for a minute and take a breath.

Then I pull on clothes. Real clothes, *my* clothes, not the Vegas-only outfits I've been wearing so far. Sweatpants and a vintage Nintendo T-shirt. I wash my face and swipe on some mascara in the bathroom, then quickly put my hair in two French braids, one down either side of my head.

Staring back at me in the mirror is Rosie Johnson, regular girl from Conception Ridge. And she's slightly horrified that she ruined her best friend's wedding weekend.

Was it worth it?

My stomach twists.

I can still hear them arguing, their words muffled through the wall.

Another deep breath.

But when I open the door, they aren't in the living room

anymore. Daniel has gone to his room, and Melanie is standing in the doorway.

"You can tell them I had to go back for work," I hear him say. "Nobody needs to know. I know I made a mistake, and I'm not going to ask you to pretend to be okay with it."

What?

My stomach drops, that messy, twisted feeling giving way to a freefall of panic.

"And what about Rosie?" she asks, her voice sharp.

I hold my breath.

"She'll agree it was a mistake," he finally says.

I wish I wasn't sure he'd just said that. I wish his stupid voice didn't carry so well across the suite.

Stepping back into my room, I ignore the hot tears sliding down my face and start shoving everything I have back into my suitcase.

18
daniel

I NEED my daughter out of my face. As much as I love her, she's ruining Rosie's birthday. All I can think about right now is getting packed up so I can take Rosie anywhere but here.

Mel is about to open her mouth to chastise me again —*enough already*—when we both hear a scuffle in the living room. She turns, and I see Rosie heading for the door with her suitcase over her shoulder.

Fucking hell.

"Rosie," I bark.

Mel raises her eyebrows at me.

My little lover doesn't stop moving. She opens the door, not looking back.

I swear under my breath and grab my room key. "We won't make it to brunch," I snap at Mel. "And this isn't over. I love you but get out of my suite. Now."

Then I take off after Rosie.

She's not at the elevator, and it doesn't look like one just left our floor. I spin around in a circle. We're thirty floors up.

Could she have taken the stairs? I run to the nearest stairwell and push the door open.

Sure enough, an angry, dark-haired girl is stomping down the concrete steps a floor below me.

She's carrying her suitcase. This is madness.

"Rosie, stop."

"Go away."

"Listen to me."

"I heard what you said."

"Obviously not the whole thing."

"You said we were a mistake," she yells up the stairwell. "So fuck off."

Oh, she's going to regret that language.

I don't bother to tell her to stop again. I pick up speed and meet her on the next landing, getting in front of her.

Her face is streaked with tears, and now I'm the one who wants to swear.

"*We* are not a mistake," I growl, catching her as she tries to push past me. "Listen to me, goddamn it. Mel knows I love you. You didn't hear that part, did you?"

She freezes in my arms. "What?"

"I told her it was a mistake that I kept my feelings from her. I should have told her as soon as she arrived. That would have given her two days to process the news before the wedding."

She huffs in protest. "What the fuck, Daniel? No, that's not—" She grunts and tries to push away from me.

I spin her around and press her against the wall. "Stop that. We will talk about this like grown-ups."

"You didn't try to talk to me about what the *better option was* before telling Melanie it would have been better if we'd ruined the days before her wedding. You didn't include me as a grown-up in that part of the conversation. So don't fucking lecture—"

I crash my mouth against hers, needing her to stop swearing at me. It's that or take her over my knee, and I'm not prepared to do that in a public stairwell.

When we get back to the room, maybe.

She gasps against my mouth, then kisses me back, desperate little sips like she can't quite believe it.

I grunt as I haul her up the wall, fitting my body against hers. Her legs wrap around my waist, her arms tight around my neck. "Say it again."

"We need to talk about this like grown-ups."

"Not that part." She's shaking. "The other part."

"The bit about the fact that I love you?"

She lets out a shuddering sob and nods. "I love you, too. I'm sorry I ran from you."

"You were scared. That's on me. I was so annoyed, and I wasn't thinking about what it was like for you to be on the outside of a Mel and Daniel snap fest."

"I don't like that I came between you."

"You didn't. Oh, baby, if you had just heard everything I was saying to her. She's mad at *me*, not you. And she'll get over it. You're fine. You're perfect and so sweet. Still in trouble for telling me to fuck off, though."

"I was mad." She says it indignantly, like that makes it okay.

I'd have been mad, too, in her shoes. "Is it too soon to ask you to trust me?"

"You said it was a mistake!" There's still a tremor of fear in her voice, and I get it now.

"You could never be a mistake. I know we've only had this special connection for a few days, but I've been waiting my whole life for you, and I didn't know it. You're my everything, Rosie. I never want to let you go." I set her down and step back. I take her suitcase and hold out my hand. "Come on."

Her eyes are big and wary, but she takes my hand and lets me lead her back to the suite. Mel is long gone. I'll sort that mess out another day.

Right now, all I care about is the tight grip she has on my fingers.

19

rosie

I'M SHAKING by the time we get back to the suite. A lump has lodged itself in my throat, and I feel like a fool.

Daniel doesn't say anything. He takes my suitcase to his room—*not mine*—and then returns and sprawls out on the couch. When I don't move, he sighs and pats his lap. "Come here."

I fly across the room, launching myself at him. "I'm sorry."

"For what?"

"Everything."

He grips me against him, like I might run away again. I won't, and I don't know how to tell him that. The lump grows.

"I don't know how to do this." He grinds out the words. "I want to take you over my knee. When you told me to fuck off..."

I cringe.

He smooths an errant hair back against my braids, then gathers the two plaits in one hand and tugs. "Is this what it's going to be like?" His gaze darkens, and beneath me, his cock pulses. "When you have a temper tantrum, am I going to be equal parts terrified of losing you and deeply aroused at the thought of punishing you for your bratty little mouth?"

He's turned on?

The lump in my throat softens. "I won't do it again." I grind against him. "Please don't be mad. I really am sorry."

"I know you are. And I'm not mad." He drops his other hand to my thigh, pinning me against his body. He's hard all over, his muscles tensed, his cock flexing between us. "No, this isn't anger, little girl. This is something else."

Oh.

Oh.

"Daddy?"

"Stand up." He says it coarsely, his gaze glittering with intent. "Take off your pants."

Legs shaking, I climb off him and peel off my sweatpants.

Daniel groans when he sees my underwear. "How many pairs of little white panties do you own?"

"It's pretty much all I wear." This pair has *Sunday Funday* printed on the butt.

Which he discovers as he hauls me back over his lap, this time with my ass in the air.

"It is Sunday," he says, chuckling as he smooths his palm over my upper thighs and cotton-covered butt. "And since it's your birthday, maybe we should combine your birthday swats with a reminder that Daddy loves you very much and never wants to let you go."

"That's a lot of swats," I pant, my legs already shaking in anticipation.

"I don't want to hurt you." But he says it silkily like it's half a threat. *I don't want to do this, but it's for your own good.*

My clit zings in anticipation. "I'm safe as long as I'm with you."

"You sure about that?"

"Yes." I realize I'm absolutely certain of it. The lump dissolves completely. "There's nothing you might want that I don't want, too. I trust you."

"With your body?"

"Yes."

"And what about your heart?" His voice is rougher now. More vulnerable.

I exhale in a rush of joy. "That is all yours, too."

"Good." His palm lands heavily on the fleshy bottom curve of my ass. "That's one. Happy birthday, baby."

I rock from the warm sting of it, then press my face into the couch cushion.

The second, third, and fourth swats are the same. Five through eight are light smacks to the tops of my thighs, and those feel so good I moan on the last one. Daniel grunts and adjusts his position beneath me.

Nine.

Ten.

And then his fingers drift between my legs. He doesn't say anything, just breathes heavily as he explores the damp spot growing on my panties.

Eleven, again on my butt cheek. Slow and heavy.

His fingers return to my pussy. More heavy breathing, and I arch my back, wanting more of his quiet molestation.

Without saying a word, he peels off my panties.

Twelve.

Thirteen.

Fourteen.

"Daddy, I need you. . ." I'm babbling now, begging for him to touch me again. Each spank unleashes a fresh wave of slick, and when his fingers return to my pussy, he pushes that arousal up to my clit, then returns to my entrance and circles it.

Teasing me now.

Fifteen.

"Don't tell me to fuck off," he growls. "Not when you really want me to hold you down and touch you like you're a dirty little girl."

I whimper. "I'm sorry."

"I don't care if you're sorry. All I want to hear from your sweet little mouth is that you need this."

"I need this."

"What do you need?"

"Daddy's touches."

"Where do you need them?"

"My. . ." I bury my face in the cushion again and sob as he spanks me again and again.

Eighteen.

Nineteen. "Rosie."

"My pussy," I gasp. "And my ass. My legs. Everywhere."

He drags me up onto his lap, tossing my panties away and then arranging me so I'm straddling him. With quick, rough movements, he frees his cock and sinks me onto it. He shoves his hands up my shirt and squeezes my tits. "Here, too? You need Daddy's hands on your sweet mounds? Look at you. Little braids, cute T-shirt. Wet cunt taking all of Daddy's bare cock. Aren't you the dirtiest little girl?"

I bounce, trying to use his erection to get myself off.

He stops me with a heavy hand on my hip. "Don't you fucking dare come on me."

"What?"

He grins. "This is your punishment."

"Nooo. . ." I gasp and try to control my body, but my clit is throbbing. One touch, and I'm going to dissolve into blissful goo. "I'm sorry, I'm sorry, I'm so. . ."

He guides me down on top of him, curving my ass in the air. "Shhh. . . It's okay. Two more spanks."

But now, my clit is rubbing against his body. His cock is hitting me at a new angle inside, and my brain goes absolutely blank.

He reaches around my body and claps his hand against my butt. "Twenty," he whispers in my ear. "Good girl. Hold it in. Feel that? Feel how much you need me? Remember this feeling if you ever overhear something that sounds like I might not want you. Know that I will always give you this cock. Whenever you need it, it's yours. My mouth is yours; my body is yours. Because I love you."

I sob.

His hand comes down again. Twenty-one. Without lifting his hand again, he squeezes his fingers into my flesh and moves our bodies as if one. My orgasm explodes from the center of my body.

"Happy birthday, baby. I love you so much."

I cling to him and grind through the aftershocks. My whole body is shaking and twitching as he thrusts into me, faster and faster, taking his own pleasure from the remnants of my messy, beautiful punishment.

20
daniel

HAVING Rosie dissolve into sobs over my lap as I spanked her and stroked her slippery little cunt to the peak of arousal has changed me in a fundamental way.

I came to this city as I have many times before—a man searching for something. I will leave having found it, feeling truly whole for the first time in my life. I will leave with Rosie by my side and do everything in my power to keep her next to me every day for the rest of my life.

Today, on her twenty-first birthday, I mean that in the most literal sense of the expression.

We shower together, then get dressed for a day of fun. I leave my suits in the closet and put on jeans and a T-shirt to match her dressed-down look. She gives me a wicked smile and says, "There's the Mr. Burke I know and love to perv on."

I press her against the wall and make her ride my cock again.

When we finally leave the suite, it's for her tattoo

appointment. She grips my hand for almost an hour as the artist decorates the top of her foot with an intricate design.

Then we have to go shoe shopping because she wants to dress up again tonight, but the heels she brought have a strap in the wrong place.

The clerk at the shoe store calls me Rosie's dad, and she giggles and goes along with it.

I fuck her against the wall again as soon as we're back in the suite. Mating with her is a full-body workout every time, and I think it'll be weeks or months of this multiple times a day to calm my frenzy to claim her.

It's still a bit hard to believe that she wants me—needs me—as much as I do her.

"We should have a nap," I tell her as I carry her to the shower for the second time that day.

She nuzzles my neck. "Okay, Daddy."

I groan in pained delight.

Instead of sleeping right away, we talk for an hour about poker and the rules of playing in person. To my delighted surprise, Rosie has played before, at college and online. "Never for a lot of money," she hastens to add. "I've never needed a poker face tutorial before this trip. But I know how to play the game."

"Good girl. I'm looking forward to taking you to the poker room tonight."

Our conversation meanders after that, and we land on her school schedule and how often she can sleep at my house. I want her there every night. I want a ring on her finger by the end of this trip, but she wants to take things slower.

"A few weeks, then."

She smiles lazily. "Maybe we could get engaged in the summer?"

"What if you're pregnant by the summer?" I cup her breasts and imagine them full of milk.

"I'll stay on the pill until we're married."

I groan.

"Really?"

"What if I throw them out?"

She laughs and circles my cock with her little fingers. "Don't you want some time with me all to yourself, Daddy?"

The only thing that could distract me. "Keep talking."

Her fingers stroke lower, cupping my balls. "You wanted more babies after Mel?"

Once upon a time, that question would have sliced into my chest. Now I know the answer. "I did. I still do. And it turns out, the gap will be a bit bigger than I thought."

She snuggles closer. "And what about after we have one baby? Will you want more?"

I stroke her hair. My heart thumps hard against my ribs. "I would. If you could have them."

"I liked growing up with siblings."

There are four kids in her family. I close my eyes and picture Rosie a decade from now, herding dark-haired angels who look just like her out the door.

"Then we'll have as many kids as is right when the time comes." My cock flexes against her touch, but I don't roll her onto her back and take her again.

There will be time for that again soon. Tonight, tomorrow. When we return home and I can chase her naked through my house. We'll fuck in every room. I'll make her dinner and give her bubble baths, and then bury my face between her legs on my—our—bed.

But right now, in this moment, all I want is this tender connection. I grin.

She must be watching my face because she asks me, "What is it?"

"This is nice."

"Yeah."

"Rosie. . ." I blink my eyes open again and catch her chin in my fingers. "I love you. I will always love you. No matter what, I will put you first. And one day soon, I'm going to make some eternal vows to you in front of our families."

"Oh, Daniel." Her eyes shimmer, but she's smiling. "I love you, too."

———

"Okay, I'm going to practice on you."

I lean back in my chair, amused, as Rosie squares her shoulders, then points at the breadbasket. "Would you like more bread?"

"No," I say smoothly. "Thanks for asking."

She gives me a pleased smile. "Would you like my panties?"

"What?" My voice rises, just enough, and she claps her hands—and *now* her smile is actually *genuinely* pleased.

"I heard the difference." She grabs a piece of bread and slathers it with butter. "So when you're making small talk before the game begins, you're listening for that genuine tone."

"Exactly."

"Got it. So when I tell you that I'm not actually wearing any panties. . ."

I'm more prepared this time, and my response is smooth and controlled. "I put them on you myself."

She winks. "But did I take them off at some point? I heard the tremor. Just a little. Mr. Burke, maybe *you're* the one who needs to work on his poker face for the game tonight."

"I'll be fine."

But my confidence in my ability to command the game doesn't take into account the intense jealousy I feel as soon as we walk into the casino's poker room.

Every horny male gaze in the room locks onto her bouncy tits and curvy legs.

Biting down the instinct to hustle her somewhere, anywhere, else, I guide her to the main counter and let them know we've arrived for our reserved game time.

"Welcome back, Mr. Burke. And can I see some ID, young lady?"

Rosie gleefully hands over her driver's license. "It's my birthday."

I'm half-expecting another 'your father brought to a casino' comment, but I suppose in this environment, a young, hot girlfriend is more likely.

"Happy birthday. The same number of chips for the birthday girl as you usually get, Mr. Burke?"

"Yes, please."

Rosie's eyes go wide as the tray is lifted to the counter. "Daniel, this is too much."

"Nothing is too much for you." I run my hand up and down her back. Her dress dips low tonight, revealing her spine, and I love the access I have to her bare flesh. Nothing would ever be too much for the woman who woke up this hungry beast inside me. "It will make me happy to see you play."

Two other players interested in no-limit hold 'em, a man in his thirties and a woman closer to Rosie's age, arrive at the table at the same time as us.

We introduce ourselves, then I lead with my standard "get to know their unguarded voice" question. "How long are you in town?"

"I live here," the young woman says. "Lacey."

"I'm Greg. Arrived yesterday." The man gives Rosie a friendly smile. "How 'bout you, sweetheart?"

She tugs on my elbow before I can growl. "I'm Rosie, and this is Daniel. We're here for Daniel's daughter's wedding." She's definitely broadcasted to them that we are a couple. My inner caveman appreciates the public claim as she pats my chest, and I remember the same gesture at the florist. Her voice is different now, though. "We fly home tomorrow."

Little Rosie Johnson isn't letting these people hear *her* unguarded voice. She's carefully performing even before we sit down.

I'm impressed, and I let her see that in my expression.

She winks at me as the others sit. *Game on.*

During the first hand, everyone is a bit cautious. Rosie folds after the flop, which was a good call when Lacey wins with a full house. Nice for her, but she didn't make very much on it because of the early nerves. I file that observation away.

The next few hands are duds for me, so I'm the one to fold early. As I expected, it is a lot of fun to watch Rosie play.

She's more expressive than most, but I can't tell which of her faces are genuine and which are put on.

If I can't, there's no way the others can.

My little girl found her own way to bring a poker face to the table. I'll reward her for that later.

Two more players join us, filling up the table, and the next hour and a half fly by. In between hands, I stroke her back. She drops her hand to my thigh often, and the erotic touches don't distract me from the game.

They're foreplay.

The pile of chips she has in front of her is pretty arousing, too. Her natural enthusiasm plus a good dose of beginner's luck—and careful betting—means she's definitely leaving here with more money than she came in with.

Happy birthday indeed.

She yawns just before the next hand, and I kiss her softly. "Last one? Ready for bed?"

"Mmm," she says happily against my mouth. "Maybe."

I'm confident about my cards at the turn, looking at a flush. There's a pair of kings on the table, so there's a chance someone might have a full house or also have two hearts in their hand like I do, but I'm willing to risk a bit.

To my surprise, it's Rosie who challenges me for it. She has an earnest gleam in her eye. "Raise it up."

And she pushes a third of her chips over the line.

Well. That's hot. I adjust my stance and meet her bid. "Call."

Two other players call as well.

I lay my cards down first.

Then it's Rosie's turn.

"Pocket kings."

The others groan. Nobody can beat her four of a kind.

She flashes a wicked smile at me as the dealer slides her winnings across the felt. "Thank you. And I think that's it for me. Good night, everyone."

By the time we get to the counter to cash out, she's vibrating. She plays it cool, though, not saying anything until we're well away from the poker room.

"Oh my *god*." She grabs my hand and tugs me into a dark corner in the first slots room we pass. "That was so much fun."

"You don't look tired anymore," I growl against her neck as I kiss her. "You didn't want to stay and keep playing?"

"Can't get carried away. Need to control myself." She pushes my hands down her hips to the hem of her short skirt. "Oh, Daniel."

I grin. "Whatever you want."

"I want you. But first. . ." She tosses her head back and laughs. "Whew, I'm high off that adrenaline. Okay, what were you drinking the night before the wedding?"

"Scotch."

She peels a few bills from her purse. "How about a nightcap, Mr. Burke?"

Right. I should have expected that. Another chance to legally use her ID. "In a minute."

"Daniel!"

I rock my erection against her core. "I. Need. A. Minute."

"Oh." Her eyes sparkle at me. "I guess I deserve that."

"Come here, you vixen." I kiss her mouth, soft and sweet, and it doesn't help my painfully hard cock problem, but it does something magical for my soul.

It's well past midnight when we return to the suite. Rosie's birthday is technically over, and she's glowing.

"Thank you for today," she says, swaying in front of me. "I can't imagine anything that would make it better."

I slowly turn her around and point to the kitchenette part of the suite. "Not even a birthday cake?"

She gasps. "Oh, Daniel!"

The cake is decorated like a video game background. I took a photo of her T-shirt and asked the concierge to arrange for a special delivery tonight.

It was a gamble. On a day where she's so focused on celebrating being all the way grown-up, would she want something so playful? But the look on her face says I made the right gamble.

I light the sparklers on top and take a video as I sing her, "Happy birthday." She swipes a bit of icing on her finger and feeds it to me when I put the phone down.

"Delicious," I murmur. I catch her wrist and lick her finger clean, then bite her fingertips one at a time until she's giggling for me.

That sound is better than the fountain of youth.

I cut us a big piece of cake to share, and we curl up on the couch together. She gets the first bite and the last. In between, we again return to the conversation about what life will be like when we go home.

"No matter what, we'll be together," she promises.

I'm going to hold her to that. "I'll be patient as you finish school. And I know your parents may have some objections.

That would only be fair, given the things I admitted to at the wedding dinner last night."

She grins at me.

"But I won't water down how I feel about you." I pull her final birthday present from my pocket. "I've been carrying this around all day."

It's a gold chain, a diamond solitaire dangling from it.

"One day soon, Rosie Johnson, I want to get down on one knee and ask you to be my wife. I would do it this weekend if there was a way for you to wear my ring home and not bring on a massive storm. I don't mind Mel yelling at me, but I want you to have a softer landing with your family."

"Oh, Daniel." Her eyes are as wide as can be. "That's. . ."

I wait for her to say it's too much.

She surprises me. She presses her lips together, then smiles and sighs. "That's beautiful. And perfect."

"Good." I kiss her roughly. She tangles her tongue against mine, giving as good as she gets.

God, this *woman*.

Breaking away, I lay the delicate chain around her neck. "I do want the world to know that I want to marry you. I won't be patient forever."

"I know." She presses her fingers to the diamond. "Soon."

I crush her to me. "God, that feels good to get off my chest. I want you to be my good luck charm and travel partner for the rest of my life. I want to cook dinner with you and sleep in with you and steal away from the rest of the world for secret moments of pure filth with you."

She laughs lightly, her eyes dancing. "Filth?"

"The most depraved sort."

"Show me."

I pick her up in my arms and stalk to the window. One hand hooks under her hips, the other going tight to the back of her neck. I squeeze, my fingers pressing into her flesh, and I make her gasp.

"Like this, little one." I press her against the glass and thrust my hips between her thighs. "Feel that? Feel how hard you make me with your sweet little promise?"

"Mmm," she moans. "Because I love you?"

"Yes." I growl and snap my teeth as she wriggles in my arms. She's not getting away. Not now, not ever. "Tell me more."

"I like you a lot, too," she whispers. "You're fun to spend time with."

I'll show her fun. I drag my mouth down her neck to where her collarbone dips, and I lick her there, tasting the shadows on her skin.

"You're kind—"

I hike up her skirt and palm her ass, gathering the fabric of her panties in my fist as she clings to my shoulders.

"You're funny."

I rip away her panties.

She gasps and tightens her legs around my hips. I let her be a strong little monkey for a moment while I free my cock from my dress pants, then I find her slick entrance and thrust again, this time with nothing between us.

"You're so good to me." Her voice hitches. "Doting, even."

I silence her sweet words with my mouth, savage against her lips. But I can still feel her pure goodness, her delight in everything I do, as she kisses me back. Her tongue strokes against mine, eager and nimble. Her fingers sink into my hair.

And when I bottom out in her pussy, her whole body shakes with pure, sweet pleasure.

There are too many clothes between us. I need to feel her body against mine.

I rock my hips, driving my cock against her favorite secret spots, then ease her off me. I cut off her protest with another kiss.

"I need you naked," I whisper as I unzip her dress.

She spins for me, letting me plaster her soft tits against the window. My suit falls on the floor, too, and then I'm lifting her up and finding my way unerringly back inside her, this time from behind.

The press of her luscious ass against my hips and the wet contact my balls make with her clit as I fuck her against the window is amazing.

The way she cries out for me is even better.

But the best part of it is how she comes for me, a shuddering, full-body climax that milks my seed deep into her body. I drop my face to her neck and hunch over her, picturing it painting the walls of her womb.

Mine.

Forever.

21
rosie

Monday

I WAKE up to a text message from Mel.

Happy belated birthday. I'm sorry about yesterday morning.

I steal a look at Daniel. He's still fast asleep.

Thank you.

We're going to the airport in an hour. Can we get coffee first?

I let out a rushed breath. After telling her I'll be ready in ten minutes, I roll over and gently kiss Daniel. "Hey, sleepyhead. Don't wake up, okay? I'm going to get coffee."

"Room service," he mumbles.

I rub my lips against his stumbled jaw. "Takes too long. You want me to bring something back for you?"

"I'll come with you." His eyes are still closed, though.

I take a deep breath and fess up. "I'm going to see Mel before she goes to the airport."

His eyes snap open, and he frowns at me. "Just you?"

I show him the texts. "I think. . .yeah. Just me."

He props himself up on one arm. The sheet falls away, and I take a second to appreciate just how much I love his body. The visceral *oomph* I feel when he's bared for me like this is something more than I ever would have imagined for myself.

But now is not the time to be distracted by his thick, brawny perfection.

I have a peacemaking mission to go on.

"All right," he says slowly. "If you think this is best."

"I do. Thank you for trusting me."

He catches me, his hand warm on the back of my neck. "I love you."

"God, *same.*"

That makes him laugh. "Bring me back a fancy latte of some kind. Nothing too weird, but something good."

I roll my eyes. We have so much work to do on his coffee knowledge.

Downstairs, my friend—hopefully not former friend—is waiting at the coffee kiosk. She looks beautiful but a little sad, and I feel that right in my chest.

I don't want Melanie to be my former friend. I just want her to understand that we can't help where our feelings go.

"Hey," I say as soon as I'm in getting her attention range.

She starts, like she was lost in thought, and then opens her arms for a hug.

It's a better start than I was expecting. I squeeze her back.

"Coffee?"

"Definitely."

We order, and I decide not to get Daniel's just yet. I'll wait until we're done talking. She doesn't need to keep staring at two cups on my side of the table.

Once we're sitting, she goes straight to the point. "About yesterday."

"Yes."

"I handled that badly."

"So did we."

"My dad thinks he should have said something sooner, but—"

"No," I interject. "That would have been worse."

"Right?" She nods. "Yeah. I mean, I wish I hadn't seen that yesterday, either, but definitely wouldn't have wanted to know about it before the wedding."

"I told him as much."

"What did he say?"

He was too busy spanking me for us to get back to that particular point. *Poker face.* "It was a complicated conversation."

"I bet." She wrinkles her nose.

"Neither of us planned this," I say softly. "It just happened. And we really didn't plan for you to find out this weekend. All we wanted was for you to have the most wonderful wedding ever."

"You say that like you're a real couple." She gives me a beseeching look. "Rosie, he's so much older than you."

"You *just* married a man who is closer to your dad's age than yours!"

"That's different."

"How?"

"Because this is *weird*."

It's a rehash of everything she said to Daniel yesterday, but it's less hostile now.

And I can see how, for her, it is weird.

"Well. . ." I shrug. "Everyone's personal life is weird if you think about it too long."

"Yeah, I still think this is kind of ew." She's processing the news, and now she's working her way around to being mollified. She sighs. "It's really serious, isn't it? This wasn't just a vacation fling."

I shake my head. "No. It wasn't. And that took us both by surprise, I promise you."

"That's actually. . .I guess I knew that. I have something for you." She takes a deep breath. "The photographer sent me a preview pack of some of the highlights from Saturday."

She pulls out her phone and shows me three photographs.

The first one is from before the ceremony. Daniel is in the middle, with Mel on one side of him and me on the other. Leesa and Leigh bracket us. The other three women are all looking at the photographer.

Daniel and I are gazing at each other, sharing a private laugh.

"I don't remember this. . ." My breath catches in my throat.

"I don't know how I didn't see it," she says thickly. "Look at how he looks at you."

The second photo is exactly that. It's from the ceremony. I'm looking at Mel. Daniel, in the front row, is looking right at me.

And the third picture is from after dinner, when we're dancing. His hand is dangerously low on my back, and his head is dipped close to mine. His eyes are closed, and he looks like he's breathing in the scent of my hair.

Well, fuck me.

I love this man so much, and we didn't hide it at all. "I'm sorry," I whisper. "We thought—"

"You dork," she snaps. "Don't be sorry. I mean, don't be too gross about it, either, but look at how happy you make my dad."

"Oh." I bite my lip and try not to grin. "Well, yeah, I try. And I know it's startling and unexpected from the outside. But I promise we're just two dorks sharing some laughs."

"He is a big dork."

I laugh. "Right? I think what your dad would say is that our relationship is private. We're both grown-ups, and we make each other happy."

"My dad. . .happy. That's a novel concept."

"He's waited a long time to trust someone with his heart."

She makes a face. "I'm glad it's you, then. Two dorks who are perfect for each other."

"Listen. . .if you're feeling forgiving. . .do you want to come up and see him before you go? It would make his day."

We go upstairs together, and when Daniel opens the suite door and sees his daughter there, the look on his face is everything I need.

She shows him the pictures and makes us promise to keep the PDA to a minimum as she adjusts to this new normal.

And then she tells me again that she thinks he's a big dork, and he protests that he's right there, and he raised her better than to call people names.

It's as good an ending as I could hope for on the weirdest, wildest adventure.

Next up: going home. And explaining to my parents what happened when I went to Vegas. . .

epilogue

Rosie

Three months later

"HALF-CAFF MOCHA FOR LILY, iced chocolate for Summer," I call out, sliding the drinks across the counter to two students I recognize from Ridge College. Lily carries a little boy on her hip and gives me a happy smile before taking her coffee.

Over her shoulder, I see the door to Brewed Awakening open, and a familiar stern Daddy strolls in. It's the middle of the day, but instead of his usual T-shirt and jeans, he's wearing a preppy polo shirt and khakis.

The outfit doesn't succeed in hiding his muscles, but it tries. The haircut I gave him last night in his kitchen helps, too. He looks very. . .nice.

He stops in front of the counter and gives me a slow, sexy grin. "Hello, beautiful."

"Welcome to Brewed Awakenings. What can I get for you?" There's an eagerness in my voice I don't bother to try and hide.

"When's your break?"

"It's overdue by almost an hour, but we were slammed." I glance at my co-worker, who waves me on. "I can take it now."

Daniel glances at the display cabinet. "Can I have a brownie, too?"

You can have whatever you want.

I ring him up and then pour us a glass of iced coffee to share.

People are used to seeing us being all lovely-dovey. Daniel either drops me off at work, comes in for a visit midshift, or picks me up.

Sometimes all three.

We kept our relationship secret for four weeks. It was so hard to sleep apart from him that, in the end, I told my parents in an unexpected blurt over breakfast.

And then I went to school and to Daniel's that night. I got a terse, one-word reply when I sent a text letting my mom know I'd be gone for the weekend.

Understood.

We haven't talked much about it since. I spend most nights at Daniel's house, and they expect me home for Sunday dinner at the very least.

But the closer I get to graduation, the less it matters what they think.

What really matters is how right it feels to be open about my relationship with Daniel.

He leads me outside to the courtyard beside the coffee shop. We have it to ourselves. He holds out a chair for me, then scoots his own chair closer to mine so he can play with my ponytail as we share the brownie.

This. This is what matters.

"How's your day going?" I give an appreciative once-over of his nice outfit. "Business meeting?"

"Not exactly." Now his fingers drift to the back of my neck and the gold chain. "I was going to wait and tell you at home tonight, but I've waited long enough."

"What are you—" And then I realize.

The nice clothes.

The hair cut.

The fact he's taking off my necklace. . . .

My breath catches in my throat. I search his face. "Daniel?"

"I went to see your parents this morning. I took flowers for your mom and a bottle of scotch for your dad. I told them that I want to marry you and spend the rest of my life making you happy."

"Oh. . ." The diamond solitaire lifts off my chest and glints in the sun before he captures it in his hand, and then it's out of sight. "How did they take it?"

He strokes my cheek with his thumb. "They knew I wasn't asking their permission."

I'm trembling, my chest full of butterflies. "No," I breathe. "I'm yours no matter what."

"That's right." His expression is serious and unwavering. "But if you're wearing my ring by Sunday, I'm invited to dinner."

A surprised gasp escapes my chest. "Oh. *Oh.*"

"So I needed to steal your necklace as soon as possible, you see."

"Right."

"I know this isn't how it's done, exactly. I should surprise you—"

I cut him off with a kiss. This is perfect. This is exactly how it should be done. With honest, earnest communication. Non-stop touches. And sharing a brownie in the afternoon sun.

———

He still manages to surprise me, though. I don't work on Friday, and I don't have class until the afternoon, so when he wakes up and leaves for work, I lounge in bed a bit, reading.

Then I go downstairs, thinking I have the whole house to myself.

And by whole house, I mean. . .Daniel's place is massive. There are four generous bedrooms upstairs, but that's only part of the second floor. Downstairs is a combination big kitchen and family room, with a large great room behind that. Above the great room is another set of rooms. Melanie's room is up there, and now that she's moved out, Daniel's home office is up there, too.

As I'm making coffee, I hear a faint noise coming from up there, so I go to investigate.

His office is empty. I take a different set of stairs down then I took up—again, the house is massive—and wind up at the front of the house, in the foyer.

There's a glittering chandelier above me, and it's not on right now, but the sunlight coming in the window catches the crystals, making them look like they're on fire.

The first time I came here as a teenager, I thought Melanie was the luckiest girl in the world.

The first time I came back after Vegas, it really hit me that Daniel wanted to share this space with me, too. That I was that lucky girl as well.

I do a little pirouette under the chandelier, giggling to myself.

And when I stop, facing the kitchen again, I realize the family room is filled with pink balloons.

Shiny ones, like we picked out for Mel's bridal suite.

"Where did. . ." I trail off as I move fully into the space and realize Daniel is down on one knee in the center of the room. "You didn't leave!"

"I had something important to do this morning."

I glide over to him, feeling like I'm floating on air. "Oh?"

"Rosie Johnson, you're the prettiest girl I've ever seen. The kindest, sweetest woman I'll ever know. And the sexiest, most perfect friend. Will you marry me?"

I'm already nodding. No poker face power moves here. Not right now. I'm nodding, and I'm crying.

He's got a ring that I can see through the blinking blur. I hold out my hand, but he doesn't put it on yet.

"Rosie. . ."

"Yes," I finally burst out. "Yes. A hundred times yes."

"This summer. No waiting." He stands up and slides the ring on my finger before spinning me around. "You said yes."

"I said yes."

He pushes a balloon out of the way and hauls me onto the couch. He sprawls on his back, and I crawl on top of him, eager to get my mouth on his.

His kiss is hungry, and his hands are extra possessive.

I'm going to be his wife.

Soon.

My clothes peel off as if by magic. Or talented Mr. Burke hands. Then his mouth is on me. On my breasts, and then between my legs. I arch my back as he licks my pussy in slow, hungry swipes. He doesn't let up until my thighs clamp around his head and my clit pulses in his mouth.

Then he covers me with his body and fills me with his hard, throbbing Daddy cock. "You know what this means," he growls.

I do.

I definitely do.

"I'll stop taking my pills tomorrow."

"Good girl." He's breathing hard, shuddering now. "You said *yes*."

"I'm going to be your wife," I whisper as he thrusts into me.

"We're going to do this every day. Twice most days."

"Until I'm knocked up?"

"Until the end of time." He captures my mouth in another kiss, and we roll, tumbling to the other end of the couch. Now I'm on top of him, and he fucks me from below, his hands digging into my hips.

His cock swells inside me, and my whole body flexes from the pleasure of being filled so perfectly. His shaft strokes me in all the right places, and he holds each thrust deep inside me, knowing what that pressure does to me.

I'm so close now. Already. "Daddy," I plead. "Please."

"Please, what?"

"Make me come."

"Oh, I will." His grip shifts, and now he's driving into me from a different angle. "You're such a good girl. Holding still for Daddy. Letting go for me, too. You'll make such a good wife." His gaze burns up at me, making me gasp. "I dream of our wedding night, Rosie. Of filling you with my seed."

"Soon," I breathe. "I'm yours to breed."

His expression shatters, his head thrown back, and as my whole sex convulses around him, I feel his heavy spurt deep inside me.

Yes.

I'm going to marry this man and have so many of his babies.

———

If you want another delicious slice of Rosie and Daniel's life, five years later, turn the page for a bonus story, *Daddy's Birthday!*

daddy's birthday

a Father of the Bride bonus story

daddy's birthday

Five years later

daniel

"HAPPY BIRTHDAY TO YOU, happy birthday to you…"

Rosie's eyes twinkle as she carefully supervises our son carrying a cupcake.

The candle in it isn't lit, but it's still a precarious task for a three-year-old.

The one-year-old on her hip has evidence of icing on his fingers, too.

A group effort, and my heart is full for it.

"Happy birthday to *Daddy*, happy birthday to you."

I hoist Benji onto my lap and thank him for the cupcake. He's halfway through explaining the sprinkle selection when my phone, sitting on the hutch in our dining room, rings.

Rosie glances at the screen and her face lights up. "That's Mel," she coos to Mikey in her arms. "Your big sister is calling."

Benji abandons the cupcake, a more important task now at hand. "I do it," he says solemnly as he grabs the phone. "I know how."

"You sure do," I say sternly.

Rosie bites her lip.

Now we need to be careful about what naughty texts we send each other, because Benji loves anything with a screen and seems to memorize our passwords just from brief observation.

We have a nice call with Mel and Javi, and promise to visit soon, and then it's time for the boys to have their bath, which spirals into tooth brushing and stories, and finally bedtime.

I get them settled in their room, Mikey in his crib and Benji in his toddler bed, then turn on the monitor and go in search of Rosie, who excused herself to have a shower once she'd nursed Mikey.

I find her in our bed, wearing panties and a Star Trek t-shirt. She's braiding her damp hair, and pauses when she sees me in the doorway. "Happy birthday, Daddy."

My cock flexes as I strip down to my boxer briefs. "Perfect day just got even better."

I take the elastic from her fingers and finish her braid myself, then secure the end of it before tugging it gently, tipping her face up.

She smiles as I kiss her.

"Next year is the big five-oh," she whispers against my lips. "What do you want to do to celebrate?"

Easiest answer ever. "Take you back to Vegas. Put another baby in your belly."

"You want to wait a year to knock me up again?"

I growl and push her onto her belly. Laughing, she lifts her hips so I can peel off her panties.

"An excellent point, little girl. Maybe I should breed you tonight."

She moans into her pillow and spreads her legs wider.

It is my birthday, after all. Whatever Daddy wants, Daddy gets.

I graze my fingers up her inner thigh, groaning as I find her slick and open for me. She went to the spa yesterday and got waxed, so she's freshly bare. Baby soft and vulnerable in the best way. Nothing stopping her arousal from slicking all over her pink skin, her plump pussy lips, and onto the tops of her thighs.

A messy little girl whose body is primed for attention.

"What were you thinking about as you sat in Daddy's bed and braided your hair?"

"Uh…" She rocks back against me as I free my cock. I rub the head against her puffy pussy. "This. You."

"Waiting for me to find you?"

"Mm-hmm."

"Knowing I would want to fuck you tonight? My favourite birthday treat."

"Yes…" She sighs as I find her slit wet already, enough to fit the flared crown just inside her entrance.

Wet enough to take just the tip inside her, but her body is still tight. It might feel like she's too small for Daddy.

Wicked, wicked games.

In five years, neither of us have tired of the filthy talk when it comes to being Daddy and his little girl. It only got worse when she was pregnant. Watching her bloom with my future child inside her made me ratchet up the caregiver kink. I picked out her clothes before she woke up in the morning, made her lunch when she went to work, and gave her baths at the end of the day.

And then Benji arrived, and the fun stopped for two months. Survival mode kicked in, and we were just Daniel and Rosie, adjusting to being parents of a newborn. For her, the first time ever. And I was almost twenty-five years out of practice.

But loving a wee baby is easy. And loving the woman who carried that baby safely for nine months is even easier.

If Rosie had wanted me to put the Daddy kink away in a box for the rest of our lives, I would have. I could happily just fuck my wife in the most vanilla of ways—three times a day some days, of course—and be the happiest man on earth.

But it was her need that brought it roaring back when Benji started sleeping longer stretches. She crawled into lap, dragged my hand to her soft belly, just inside her shirt, and asked if I was still *her* Daddy, too.

My cock roared to life. I made her a promise that afternoon that I would always be, in every meaning of the word.

After Mikey arrived, it was a little longer before she got her sex drive back. And that first time, sinking into her soft warmth—so damn snug, like she was a virgin all over again—she'd whimpered that I was too big.

A whine she had promised me she would make. Wanted to make, because it got her all hot and bothered.

Whatever my wife wants, my wife gets. Even on my birthday. It's just convenient that we like the same things.

Like Daddy's cock being wedged in a little cunt, too small to take him.

"I can't…"

But she can. I smooth my hand down her back, then squeeze her hip, my fingers sinking into her luscious flesh. "You're doing so well, baby."

"Oh god…"

"Just a little more. Relax for Daddy. You feel so good." I brush my thumb against her asshole, which makes her whole body tremble. "Good girl."

"Fuck you," she mutters.

I grin and smack my hand on the side of her hip. "I'm starting to think you're never going to learn your lesson about swearing at Daddy."

She's smiling. "What lesson was that? I couldn't hear it over the loud pounding of my pulse because *you're too big*."

My lippy little brat. My gorgeous wife.

"Whose birthday is it?"

"Yours."

"And what do I like?"

"Torturing your little girl."

"Giving you your hottest fantasies, that's right."

She groans and arches her back, pressing her hips against mine. "Please…"

She wants me to pin her down and force her to take my fat cock. But we've skipped an important step. "No."

"Why not?"

"Because this is more fun." I spank her again. "That's two."

"Wait, what?" She cranes her neck. "Daniel…"

"It's my birthday," I say sternly. "Forty-nine birthday swats."

"For *you*. Not for me! That's not how this works!" But

she's gone slick around the thick tip of my cock, her pussy pulsing in delight.

She'll be even wetter when I'm done.

I pull out and turn around, sitting with my back against the headboard. My cock head glistens from being inside her, and she dives for it, her mouth gobbling up the throbbing shaft.

"Good girl," I praise her again. "Feel that? Feel how hard you made me? With your cute little t-shirt and your barely there panties. Waiting in Daddy's bed for him to braid your hair and fuck your brains out. Hoping to skip the birthday swats."

She protests around the big, fat cock she's happily choking on.

"What's that?"

She groans.

"I know, it's not fair. Nothing about this is fair. I get this soft, pretty body to touch and spank and violate, and you just have this big old cock to choke on."

She slurps off. "Emphasis on old."

"Watch it."

She gives me a saucy smile and returns her wet mouth to where it belongs.

I sigh happily and drop my hand on her jiggly bottom. "Three."

The next ten swats are lazy. They're all lazy, really, although by the time I get to forty, she's gasping with each strike. None of them hurt her. I would never *hurt* my wife. I'd only threaten to because it makes her whine in delight, that edge of promised danger making her wet and ready for me to lose myself in her body.

I love how her bum turns pink. How it stays warm when I gather her in my arms, how her cheeks are damp with near-tears as she sinks onto my cock again, and we cling to each other at the end of a fuck that is more intense for the ritual, more erotic and private and wonderful for the secret role-play.

Every birthday is like this now. Hers and mine. Birthday spanks and a pink ass. Her riding me until we come together, my cock twitching heavily inside her, her cunt squeezing all the milk from my balls.

My beautiful young bride. My lifelong love.

rosie

As the aftershocks of my orgasm fades, I sink into the wonderful feeling of Daniel still inside me, plugging up the mess he's made.

His cock is still half-hard, and I wonder if he'll want to go again. We don't usually, but there's something about baby-making talk that is better than Viagra for him. Give the man a chance to flood my bare pussy with live shooters, and he'll maximize the opportunity.

"You didn't even take my shirt off," I murmur into his neck.

"I love your fucking t-shirts."

"Mmm." I lick the taut skin where his neck meets his shoulders. "I know."

Inside me, his shaft flexes. "God, your pussy feels good tonight."

He eases me back, so I'm still straddling him, but there's space between our torsos. His eyes are hooded and lusty as he slides his hands under my shirt, his warm, strong fingers seeking out my tender tits.

His breath hitches when he cups my flesh, my nipples hard against his palms. "I want you to come again."

"Like this?" I push up on my knees, riding him slowly.

His gaze drops to where we're connected, to the visible evidence that he's already spilled inside me once—now sliding out around his cock. "Touch yourself."

I reach down and gasp at the wetness. My clit jumps against my fingertips, and Daniel groans.

"Like this?" I circle my fingers. "Oh, Daddy."

"You're so fucking hot, Rosie. Taking my cock. Letting me breed you all night long."

"I'm going to have your baby," I whisper. "Again."

His hands tighten on my breasts. I quiver all over, already on the cusp.

"Shh…" His gaze goes dark.

And then he's flipping me onto my back. I yelp as he peels off my shirt, then sigh as he covers me with his body. His big hands trace all of me. My hips, my belly, my breasts. Up my arms, to my wrists, and then he pins me to the mattress.

"You are the love of my life," he grinds out. "So good to me. So fucking hot, Rosie. How did I get this lucky?"

I arch into his touch, our bodies finding their way together. His thighs brace against mine, and then he's inside me again.

"So lucky."

But I'm the lucky one. I'm adored and supported and fucked to within an inch of my life as often as I want.

"Happy birthday," I whisper.

He groans in delight and steadies himself above me, his hips moving just enough to drag his thick girth against all the right spots inside me. Then he catches my mouth with his as he thrusts deeper again. His tongue does wicked things, amping up my arousal and carrying me right to the edge.

Five years in Mr. Burke's bed. His hot little secret, even after we made it official.

I can't wait to see what the next five years bring.

————

Thank you so much for reading Father of the Bride and wanting a little more! If you want to stay in touch while I write it and all the other future books set in Conception Ridge, please join my Secret Chloe Maine Book Daddy Appreciation Club on Facebook: facebook.com/groups/chloemainebooks

cabin mates

a Virgin Peak why choose story

cabin mates

My plans for a solitary weekend of hiking and hot-tubbing at my family's cabin in the mountains take a turn when I arrive at dusk, only to discover it's been rented out.

The unexpected guests aren't actually strangers, though. They're construction workers who renovated my college dorm. Who growled at any boy who dared to look in my direction while I was trying to study.

But I don't need protection this weekend. I'm looking for a sweet kind of oblivion that it turns out only four strong arms can provide. Little do I realize they want a lot more than forty-eight hours of uninhibited bliss. These possessive men want double the happily ever after.

1
emily

ONE OF MY favorite things about going to college in Conception Ridge is the proximity to my family's cabin in Virgin Peak.

When I need a break, all I have to do is check the online calendar, and if it isn't rented out, I can make the hour and a half drive in my trusty little hatchback. Which is exactly what I do Friday afternoon when the annoying guy in my lab gets on my final nerve. We both live on campus, and the thought of bumping into him in the cafeteria over the weekend is not appealing. I'm taking an accelerated program with extra credits, and the end is almost in sight. A bit of rest and relaxation is exactly what I need to allow me to throw myself back into my all-consuming studies for the summer term.

Lucky for me, the cabin is available this weekend. My dad and his siblings all own the cabin together, after inheriting it from my grandparents, but none of them live close by. My parents are in Seattle, my aunt is in Los Angeles, and my uncle is in Houston. They use a rental agency to manage the property, but I don't need to go through them. I just text my dad to let him know I'll be at the cabin, and I hit the road.

Two hours later, after a quick stop for groceries, I arrive. It's not quite dusk yet, but in the dense forest on the narrow mountain roads, it's pretty dark.

I can't wait to get a fire going in the woodstove.

I unlock the cabin using the combination code—technology is great—then immediately go through to the back deck and peep at the hot tub. It's on, and it looks like the caretakers who check in on the cabin did a chemical treatment within the last day or two. My lucky night. I check the pH, set it to my preferred temperature, and skip back inside to put away my groceries.

Dinner tonight will be a frozen pizza, so I stick that in the oven, then crawl under a warm blanket to read while my food heats up.

I'm lost in a delicious story about a Navy SEAL when there's a knock at the door, then the unmistakable whirring sound of the lock being opened.

"Hello?" a deep voice calls out.

I shriek—not my smartest move—and scramble off the couch, clutching the blanket around me.

The blanket will protect me, right? From the intruders who are politely calling out a greeting?

"Excuse me, is someone here?"

"Me!" My voice catches. "I'm here. Hello?"

Two big men step into view. They're both wearing jeans and work boots. The younger one is wearing a hoodie, the older one a plaid shirt over a T-shirt. They're handsome and muscular in a "we work outside" kind of way, and if they wanted to, they could snap me like a twig.

I hold my breath as they crowd into the space in front of me. A confusing energy charges the air around us as they look me up and down.

At the same time, they frown.

"It's you," the younger one says. He turns to the other man, a surprised—but not unhappy?—look on his face. "Heath, it's—"

The man called Heath nudges him. "Shut up, Wyatt."

Well, now I know their names. My eyes dart back and forth between them. They're both older than me. Wyatt might be in his late twenties, and Heath looks like he's my dad's age. But like, in a hot way. A very hot way.

Don't crush on the potential murderers.

I pull the blanket all the way up to my chin, nerves rioting through me. "Do I know you?"

"Probably not." The one named Heath frowns again, his eyebrows pulling together and the corners of his mouth turning down. Is that frown familiar to me? "Did you rent this cabin for the weekend?"

Oh shit. "No. Wait, did *you* rent it?" I peel the blanket off my body and frantically fold it. "I have a pizza in the oven, but you can have that. Consider it a welcome gift from the, uh, owners, and I'll just be on my way."

"No, wait—"

"It's fine." I drop my book. So klutzy. Laughing nervously, I lean over and pick it up. Goose bumps skitter over my skin, and I'm rambling now, I know it, but I can't stop. "This is very unprofessional of me. Please don't rate the cabin less than five stars on my account. I thought it would be empty this weekend because nobody had rented it earlier today."

"You just hoped this cabin would be empty?" Wyatt looks genuinely confused. "You're a squatter?"

Wyatt might not be the smartest tool in the shed, so maybe I'll get out of this alive. Dumb, handsome potential murderer. "Actually, this is my family's cabin. We rent it out through a service, but when it's not booked, I sometimes come up for the weekend. And well...oops." Okay, I think I have all my stuff now. I spin in a slow circle. "Do you want my groceries?"

"Emily, *wait*." That's Heath again. He's bossy. And unlike Wyatt, he doesn't give off sweet, sexy himbo vibes.

I skid to a stop.

He's effectively bossy. Sexy, dominant vibes. But...

Now it's my turn to frown. "How do you know my name?"

"You go to Ridge College," Wyatt says helpfully. Then he grins, full of boyish charm. "I painted the hall outside your dorm room."

All spring, we had renovations at school. I think my floor was painted like three times. I try to picture this guy, but his face doesn't ring a bell. Although now that I think about it, there's something about that grin... But I would remember a guy this hot being outside my room a lot, right? Have I had my nose buried *that* far in the books?

My eyes go wide. "You know where my dorm room is?"

2
heath

IF EMILY WOULD STOP LOOKING like she thinks we're serial killers, it would make this easier.

It would also go more smoothly if she didn't keep flashing us her little white panties by bending over and whirling around. That fucking sundress will be the death of me. It barely covers anything at all.

My brain is scrambled with thoughts of *Emily is here, too* and *What are the chances* and *Fuck Wyatt, take her for yourself.*

None of which helps, because we've definitely gotten off on the wrong foot here. And I used her fucking name.

Time to introduce ourselves. "I'm Heath Taylor. This is Wyatt Dane. We happen to recognize you from the college. It's a coincidence that we're in your family's cabin, I promise."

"He knows where I live," she repeats, her bright eyes flashing.

I can practically hear Wyatt swallowing around the protest he wants to spit out.

His damn crush on Emily is one of the reasons I

suggested we get away to Virgin Peak this weekend. Hoping that escaping Conception Ridge and all the rules there—where I'm his boss, and she's an off-limits fantasy, and we're both tangled up wanting things we cannot have—would fade away. Because one thing Wyatt already does better than me is talk about his feelings. The man is an open book about what he wants. Me? I've locked down my real desires for a very long time. Since I was younger than Emily.

And I'm tired of living a half-life. All work and no play has made me…well, wildly successful in business.

And miserably alone in my personal life.

"We renovated your dorm. No reason for you to remember us, but, uh…" Fuck, I can't lie to her. "You made an impression on us." I cock my head at Wyatt. "Him, in particular."

That's a bit of a lie. We were both taken with her. I recognized Wyatt's crush, the way he lingered outside her room and timed his trips to the truck to get more supplies with her class schedule.

And I knew what he was doing, because I was fucking doing it too.

I clear my throat. "You don't need to leave."

"She doesn't?" Wyatt sounds surprised.

Emily looks confused. "I don't?"

"No." I shove my hands in my pockets to keep from grabbing her and hauling her up my body. Rubbing those panties against my thick erection as she squirms to get free. "It really wouldn't be safe for you to drive down the mountain in the dark."

And fate delivered her to us. After all the resistance we exhibited over the spring… I flick a glance to Wyatt. His gaze is locked on her bare shoulders. Exactly as he used to look at her when we were replacing the windows in her dorm room, and she was studying at her desk, her noise-cancelling headphones making her oblivious to his hopeless lust.

Hopeless, because I forbade him from acting on it.

That wasn't just professional interest as his boss, though. A darker thread of jealousy was woven through my order. Secretly, I felt it too. There was something about this girl from the moment we laid eyes on her. We were both drawn to her so much we kept returning to her wing to make the most minor of touch-ups.

Wyatt must have painted the walls outside her dorm room three times.

"I couldn't stay," she says nervously.

"How many bedrooms does this place have?"

"Four. And the loft."

"So there's more than enough space for all of us." I hear a ding from the kitchen. "And your pizza is ready. At least stay and eat it first? We brought our own dinner. Let us give you a chance to get to know us and make up for the weird introduction."

"I don't know." She laughs slightly. "This is so weird, I'm sorry."

"God, no, don't be sorry. What are the chances, right?" I step back, giving her lots of room, and gesture to the kitchen. "Your pizza, miss."

"Miss!" She laughs again, harder this time. "Oh no. Don't do that."

"That'll be hard. We've been calling you little miss for months," Wyatt says.

She blinks at him. "Months?"

"I shouldn't have said that." He cringes.

There's a long, agonizing pause, then she shakes her head and laughs. "Are you going to kill me?"

"What?" His eyes go comically wide. "Gosh, no."

Gosh. This fucking kid. Except he's not a kid, he's a grown man, but he's closer in age to Emily than to me, and it shows.

She shrugs. "Then I guess I want to hear the story about how you know all about me, and I have no clue who you are. As long as it's not creepy."

I clear my throat. "Wyatt's a puppy dog." The least I can do is vouch for my employee. "The best young man you'll ever meet."

The horniest too, but that's just because he's never gotten laid.

She gives us a careful, measured look, then nods and heads into the kitchen.

Wyatt turns on me, his gaze full of fire. "What are you doing?"

I honestly don't know. But holy fuck. The tight little body, the bright eyes just as wild as Wyatt's, and the stubborn lift of her chin...it all works for me. Too well.

She's Wyatt's, by all rights. He saw her first. He's waited for her, listened to me when I told him he had to stand down, even though he's never been with a woman, and deep down, he knew he'd been saving himself for Emily.

He told me that, straight up. As if it made any sense in the world. I told him to shut it down, because he couldn't hit on her when she was a student and we were working on her dorm.

I cockblocked him.

Now, I want to haul her into my arms. And given the way he's tensed up beside me, he wants to do the same.

Fuck, fuck, fuck.

Maybe I can't have her. But I can spend some time with her and facilitate the big dope beside me finally having his chance.

"I'm just being friendly," I tell him. "Grab the food. It's time to eat."

3
wyatt

I WANT to follow Heath's lead here, but... I look to the kitchen, where Emily is taking her pizza out of the oven.

Her yellow sundress crawls up her thighs when she bends over, her bare legs begging to be licked.

Goddammit, she's pretty. And nervous, holy shit. I should wrap her back up in that blanket and haul Heath out of this cabin. I don't care if it's a perilous drive back to Conception Ridge in the dark; we should leave her be.

No licking her legs. No devouring of her tiny, perfect titties.

What is Heath playing at, suggesting that we stay for dinner? He knows how I feel about her. And even though he tried to hide it before, I know he has some of the same instincts.

He once put protecting her at the top of his priority list.

As soon as he realized how I felt about this stranger, this little slip of a girl who had no idea who I am, he took me under his wing and tried his best to help me manage those feelings—and learn to channel them more appropriately.

You'd never know to look at me, but I'm a shy guy. Always have been. Girls make me tongue-tied. I didn't have any interest in dating in high school, and then by the time I was in my twenties and started thinking about what a forever kind of life situation might look like, everyone had passed me by.

Luckily, I had work and the gym to bury myself in. It didn't matter that I hadn't found the right girl yet. I had faith she would one day appear in front of me.

And then she did. Dark curls spilling all the way down her back, relaxed jeans that hid the perfection of her little body, and an oversized hoodie that loudly identified her as a Ridge College student.

In an instant, I knew she was the one for me.

And in the next moment, Heath cuffed my shoulder and dragged me around our truck. "You can't look at the students like that," he'd growled.

I didn't. Not any other student.

Just her. A dark-haired angel who was gone by the time I tore myself away from my boss.

And now, that same man wants to insinuate us into her evening?

"Wait," I say, raising my voice.

Emily turns back, that sundress swirling around the tops of her thighs, and as soon as her gaze meets mine, everything changes. My chest expands, my muscles all flex and relax, and I…fuck, I just *know*.

"Emily, is it all right with you if we stay?"

Her eyes widen. "Of course it's all right. You booked the cabin. *I'm* the interloper here."

"We don't want to make you uncomfortable."

"You aren't." She laughs lightly. "I was reading this heart-pounding book about two people on the run because their lives were in danger. I think I overreacted when you arrived." She gives us both the prettiest smile, and I know it's real because I've watched her for months. This girl doesn't smile often. "I'd love to share dinner with you both."

"Then we'll just grab our food and be right back," Heath drawls. Then he gives me a significant look as he stalks past me to the door.

Once we're outside, he gives me that same look again.

"What?"

"What was that, *wait*?" His eyebrows arch up. "I've never heard you bark like that."

"I didn't bark at her."

He shakes his head. "No, you didn't. You barked at *me*. About her."

My mouth drops open. Then snaps shut. "So maybe I did. Maybe you were presuming too much."

"I saw an opportunity and I took it. You're the dumbass who practically told her that you've jerked off outside her window."

"Fuck you, I've never done that." Thought about it. Recreated it at home, growling my way through my horny shame. Repeatedly. But never for real. "I wouldn't."

"I know. Hey, lighten up, man. That's the whole point of this weekend. To unwind and consider all your options in life."

Instead of my previously held pipe dream of holding out hope that one day Emily might realize I exist and fall deeply, madly in love with me too. "That was before she was *here*, inside the cabin we're going to spend two nights at. What are the fucking odds?"

"A million to one." He grabs the cooler from the back seat and shoves it at my chest. "So don't blink. Take the chance in front of you." A new expression skitters over his face, and his jaw tightens up. "There aren't any rules up here, kid. You're a young man. She's a young woman. See how the night goes, and don't trip if you're given a chance to show her how good you could make her feel. I'll get out of your way, too."

"But we drove up together."

Now his expression is completely readable. He thinks I'm a fucking idiot. "I'll go to bed early. Let you get to know her one-on-one. I'll head out for a hike by myself tomorrow. Not abandon you here."

"Oh. Right." In the fading twilight, I know he can see me blushing.

He claps a hand on my shoulder, the warmth of his touch grounding me. "Hey, this is all normal. It's normal to be rocked when the girl you like is unexpectedly in front of you. Don't panic."

I take a deep breath when he squeezes my arm. "I'm not panicking."

"Good."

I turn toward the house then stop. "I'm not *not* panicking. But it's a good kind of panic."

We're both chuckling as we step back inside, and the way Emily lifts her head immediately, smiling when her gaze lands on us, does something intense to my chest.

Is this what hope feels like? Wild horses galloping against my ribs?

"What did you bring?" She gestures to the pizza she's set on the table. Beside it is a bowl of salad. "I'm happy to share."

Her dinner would be an appetizer for one of us, but I still grin like a goof as I thank her.

Heath puts away our groceries as I add our steak sandwiches to the dinner table.

"So, you guys really just decided to rent a random cabin?"

I nod. "And we found you waiting inside it."

"What are the chances?"

Heath joins us. "That's what Wyatt said."

As if it was meant to be. As if maybe we were meant to have a second chance at a proper introduction. Except I've spent three months thinking about how good her tiny pussy must look and taste and feel. "We should eat," I say sharply.

Emily laughs, a pure giggle, and I wonder how much of my desire she can sniff out. For a little bit of a thing, she's not scared of us anymore.

She's having a great time being the guest of honor, suddenly. "So, if you know everything about me, tell me something about yourselves."

"First of all, we don't know everything," Heath says.

Just where she sleeps, what she studies, and how fucking cute she looks first thing in the morning.

"And you know that we're in construction," I offer. "Heath owns the company with his business partner, Daniel. I've worked for them for three years."

"And what did you do before that?"

"I spent a few summers planting trees." I shrug. "It was a good way to stay fit for the winter."

"Why?" Her eyes are wide as she nibbles on a slice of pizza. "What was in the winter?"

"I worked as a ski instructor here in Virgin Peak."

"What?" She shakes her head. "I took so many lessons here as a teenager. How many times have our paths crossed and we had no idea?"

"Almost like it's meant to be," Heath grunts. But then he shakes it off. "Emily, I think that's a sign you should stay for the whole weekend."

"I don't know… I don't want to intrude."

He looks at me, and I know we're thinking the same thing. It would be no intrusion at all.

"She should stay. She wants to stay, right?" There's something electric the way he says it. Hypnotizing, and it turns my pulse into a drumbeat of need.

I follow his gaze to Emily's sweet face. Her gaze slides back and forth between us. "I do want to stay," she says, barely above a whisper, then she grins. "Is that okay?"

Fucking hell, it's more than okay. It's a bloody miracle. And a gift.

"We'd love to see the mountain through your eyes," I admit. "Since you're local."

"You worked here, too."

"But only in the winter. And only at the ski hill."

"Then it's settled." As we eat our dinner, she tells us all about her favorite trails and the little market that pops up on Saturdays, if we want fresh salad fixings for dinner tomorrow night.

I want her for dinner, but that's probably not on the menu. Maybe not.

Who knows. With every passing second, I'm pulled

deeper into a weird place of hope where all my fantasies feel like they might just actually be possible.

Except Heath is here. And Emily is still a relative stranger.

But on the other hand, Heath already knows about all my horny dreams when it comes to Emily; I can't stop running my mouth to him about how perfect she is.

And Emily…

As we're tidying up, she does this exaggerated stretch that draws both of our attention to her swirling sundress and the tight swells peeking out the top of it.

"I was going to have a soak in the hot tub." She glances at Heath, then me, dragging her gaze down my body. "Did you bring a swimsuit?"

Even though I'm fully clothed, her gaze is baldly assessing. My cock rises swiftly, eager for her attention. I don't miss the moment when she realizes my jeans are being tested to the limit, my erection straining at the fly. Her eyes go wide, and her cheeks turn pink.

But I don't feel any kind of horror. To my shock, I like the way her attention locks on to my jutting bulge. It's hers, after all. She's the only woman who has ever made me feel this way. Who has ever stripped away my nerves and left me nothing but wild, rampant need.

"We did," I hear Heath say. "Right, Wyatt?"

I can't speak. I nod in agreement. Yes, we knew there would be a hot tub. I shoved a pair of board shorts into my duffel bag.

Yes, I want to see her in a bathing suit.

And out of it.

The longer her gaze stays latched on my straining cock,

temporarily trapped in a prison of denim, the more I think that I might just get a chance with Emily.

It's not until Heath clears his throat and says he's going to hit the hay early that I realize there's just one problem with this whole plan—Emily doesn't know we've talked about her and made a choice.

She doesn't know that she's mine.

And her face just fell at the idea of Heath getting out of my way.

4
emily

"HEATH, YOU SHOULD JOIN US," Wyatt says, his voice strained.

His friend turns and frowns. "No, it's—"

"Emily wants you to." Then Wyatt turns to me. "Right?"

An odd, powerful calm slides over me. I nod. That is what I want. "I'd like to get to know both of you better," I admit. Then I smile at Wyatt, so thankful that he noticed. "You read me well. Not that I would have minded it just being the two of us."

He ducks his head, and I swear he blushes.

That's really cute.

But just as attractive is the stern way Heath almost glares at both of us, then mutters something under his breath.

"That's a yes," Wyatt says to me once we're alone. "He's gonna get changed and join us."

I grin conspiratorially at him. "Excellent. Good job."

"Oh, that was all you." He smiles down at me for a moment, then his expression shifts, his gaze getting...more serious. "You need a swimsuit, too."

I glance down. "I'll be right back."

"We'll be waiting for you."

I feel his gaze on my back until I'm out of view, and then I shiver.

What are you doing, Emily? When they first arrived, I was confused and worried I'd done something wrong. But then over dinner, Heath's quiet air of command kept drawing my attention.

And just now, the way Wyatt looked at me?

For a bookworm who has never kissed anyone, this is a lot to process all at once.

And as a bookworm who has read a *lot* of kissing books, it would be easy to get carried away with a fantasy. Because my body was definitely giving me mixed messages about what to do with these two men this weekend.

How could I be attracted to both of them? That doesn't make any sense. In real life, I mean. On the page, I know exactly what would happen next.

A game of truth and dare in the hot tub would lead to swimsuits being tossed aside and…passions to flare wildly? I flop on my bed and curse myself for devouring horny books instead of carefully studying them like instruction manuals.

There's no time to obsess over something that isn't likely to happen.

I scramble off the bed and open my bag. I only have one swimsuit, and it's nothing fancy. Just a turquoise one-piece I've had for a couple of years. I tug it on, then grab a few towels from the closet in the hallway—wrapping one around my body securely—and meet them back in the living room.

I'd thought they were good-looking when they arrived at the cabin. Now?

I nearly stumble when I catch sight of them waiting for me.

They're both massive. Broad-shouldered, thickly muscled all the way down their bare torsos. And their swimsuits are riding low enough on their hips that I can see…things.

A line of hair down Wyatt's belly, starting just below his navel and disappearing into his shorts in a way that promises there's more of it there. I think about the neat little triangle of hair between my own legs and try to picture what his must look like.

Heath, on the other hand, has no hair on his lower abdomen that I can see, but he does have ridges of muscles curving over his hips that point in the same direction.

Both of them have bodies designed to draw my attention to the private space behind their swim trunks.

They're built for sin, and I'm a curious little coed ready to find out how to be bad. *Stop it, Emily.* I can't, though. My imagination is a dangerous thing. *It's just like a naughty book.*

Oh, if only.

But the way they look at me definitely helps my vivid imagination. Heath does a slow up and down, then tells me to lead the way to the hot tub. Wyatt's gaze is less controlled, pinging back and forth from my face to where my boobs are hiding under the towel and then back again.

When I scoot in front of them to open the back door, I imagine he's looking at my butt too.

My imagination is very brave.

I, on the other hand, stand next to the hot tub, refusing to take the towel off my body. *I'm getting in a hot tub with two strange men.*

Heath picks up on my hesitancy right away. "Do you want us to get in first?" He grabs Wyatt's shoulder and turns him around. "Or you can."

I drop my towel and scamper into the water, lowering myself into the bubbling tub until everything is submerged from the neck down. "I'm in."

Wyatt snaps back around, eager like a golden retriever puppy, and gives me a happy grin as he climbs in. Heath is more careful, taking his time, his gaze never leaving my face. What is he thinking?

"I just want to make sure you're comfortable with us."

My eyes go wide.

He smiles. "You have a very expressive face, little miss."

"There's that nickname again," I whisper.

Wyatt frowns. "Does it bother you?"

I'm surprised, but no, it doesn't. "I just don't understand it."

His expression slides from concerned to…chagrined?

"Wyatt," I say, affecting my best "stern teacher" voice, which isn't that bossy, but I'm trying. "What does it mean?"

"Emily." Heath says my name, like a command or a caution.

I twist in the water, giving him my full attention. "Yes?"

"It's a term of endearment. We will stop using it if you don't like it, but we don't know one another well enough to fully explain it with the right context. Can you trust us to share the story in time?"

I nod, surprised again. And even more shocking to me is

how warm I feel inside when Heath smiles, genuinely pleased at my answer.

"Good," he murmurs, and I feel that deep inside me.

What else can I do to get that kind of satisfied purr from this man?

It makes me feel bold. I hold his gaze for a long beat, until I sense that Wyatt needs my attention too. When I turn to the younger man, he's watching me as intently as I was looking at Heath.

"What?"

He shakes his head. "Nothing."

"So, what should we talk about, then, if not your curious nickname for me and not the reason you are staring at me?" I don't need to look back at Heath to know he wants to caution me again. "And before your boss says *Emily* again, I'm genuinely not sure how to entertain two strange men in a hot tub. This is a first for me."

Heath laughs out loud at that. "Well, that's fair, isn't it, Wyatt? She's never done this before."

Wyatt grins boyishly. "How do you entertain one strange man in a hot tub?"

"I wouldn't know, haven't done that either." I lift my chin. "I'm just a little miss, after all."

Something wild flashes in Wyatt's gaze.

Heath glances between us. "That's interesting."

I cross my arms over my chest. "Why is that interesting? Lots of people choose to focus on school or work instead of dating."

"Oh, I'm aware," he says. "Wyatt—"

His friend slaps Heath in the chest. "Shut up."

"What is it?" I push across the hot tub, getting between

them so Wyatt doesn't slap Heath again, and I give him an earnest, *you can trust me* look. "Are you not interested in dating either?"

"I wasn't in the past. But that changed this spring."

My heart flips upside down. Why does that distress me so much? *Who did you find?* "Oh."

He searches my face. "I haven't acted on it yet. I've never been with a woman before."

"Really?" I squeak out the word in absolute shock, which makes Heath laugh out loud, good-naturedly.

I sputter and shake my head. "I don't mean that to be a criticism. That would be hypocritical of me. Wow. But you must be curious?"

I have a wild idea to seduce him, so he doesn't pursue whomever he fell in love with in the spring. If he's never been with anyone else, then my own inexperience won't matter.

"Of course he's curious," Heath says.

Heath.

Guilt floods my chest. I can't seduce Wyatt while Heath is here. And how am I so sure Wyatt would be the right person to take my virginity anyway, when Heath's praise makes me feel like I'm walking on air?

I nod nervously. "Well, it's kind of nice to find someone who has also decided to wait—and it's not like I'm waiting for marriage or anything."

Wyatt shakes his head. "No, of course not. Not me either. But it's just, it has to be…"

And then we say it at the same time, "Right."

Heath grunts and heaves himself out of the water. "I'm going to find some drinks. Anyone want a beer? Pop?"

Before either of us can answer, he's grabbed a towel and gone inside.

I feel awful. "Wyatt, I—"

"You're fine," he says quickly. His eyes are wide as his gaze darts down to where my body is mostly hidden under the bubbling surface, then back up to my face. He takes a deep breath. "Emily, I don't know how to tell you this, but in all that time that Heath and I were aware of you, both of us thought you were real pretty."

"Oh!"

"The thing is, you caught our eye at the same time. Our first day on campus, I saw you coming back from class and…" He looks a little embarrassed. "My feelings were obvious to him. He reamed me out. But later that day, I found him growling at some kid from your lab who was coming around your dorm room."

I gasp. I remember that. Not the growling, exactly, but my nemesis used to come to my room to irritate me and then that stopped.

Wyatt has no idea he and Heath are my heroes. He keeps going. "And one of the reasons you didn't know about us until today was neither of us wanted to get in front of the other guy. I could never compete with a man like him, and he is too much of a good guy to stop me from my first crush."

"Your first crush was…*me*?"

"You're the smartest, prettiest girl I've ever laid eyes on."

"So…I'm the girl you noticed in the spring?"

"The only girl I've ever set my most impure thoughts to, that's right."

I can't breathe. Wyatt actually has feelings for me? But

that wasn't all he said. "What are the other reasons? You said that was one of the reasons. What else? Why didn't you approach me?"

"Heath owns the construction company. He signed a code of conduct agreement with the college. None of his employees could act inappropriately toward the students. And neither could he."

"Asking me out would be inappropriate?"

Wyatt's eyes blaze. "Don't mistake us for boys, Emily. We weren't interested in taking you to the movies."

"So, you…and Heath…had…impure thoughts about me, and that was against the rules?"

"That's right."

I lick my lips. "But we're not at the college right now."

His eyes flare as he follows my meaning.

"Right, Wyatt?"

"That's right."

"And are you going to be doing any more construction in my dorm?"

He shakes his head. "We finished a week ago."

"And if I had impure thoughts about you…"

"You should trust your instincts and do whatever feels right."

"So, the only question is, how much trouble are we going to get into with Heath if I kiss you?"

5
heath

I PALM MY COCK, willing it to go down, but that's a lost cause. This was a mistake. Bringing Wyatt up here, telling Emily she should stay, humoring her innocent questions in the hot tub. All of it was a fucking terrible idea, because those two have a real shot at something special, and I'm a dirty old man who will ruin everything.

I see the way she looks at me. Laughing and giggling with Wyatt, but all the while tracking how I'm leering at her tits. Her little fingers playing up and down the strap of her bathing suit, her tiny nipples getting harder and harder with each pass of her hand under my hot, bruising gaze… She's a temptress, and she has no fucking idea.

But instead of pointing all that seductive innocence at Wyatt, a young man who deserves a girl like Emily, she's playing that game with me.

A man old enough to be her father.

And it turns me on more than I want to admit. My cock is pulsing for her, my little miss, my good girl with the clever questions. I want her to ask me anything and everything while she perches naked on top of me. Innocent inquiry and then beautiful patience when I tell her she can't know something yet.

Can you trust us to share the story in time?

Us.

Fuck.

I shove my swimsuit low on my hips, needing to fist my cock properly.

She's not mine; she's Wyatt's, and I'm supposed to be helping him get the girl. Not thinking about whispering all his filthy secrets in her ear for my own pleasure. Not because I get off on the pink of her cheeks and the wide, uncertain gaze that turns bold when she realizes she's safe.

In a perfect fantasy world, Emily would be my little slut, and I'd teach her how to blow Wyatt's mind, and then she'd crawl into my bed and tell me about it between giggles. I'd stroke her between her legs and discover the mess he'd left, mixed with her slick, and use that to slide inside her.

My naughty little girl.

Daddy's secret seductress.

The way she lit up when I told her she was good. Fucking hell, why does Wyatt have to want her all to himself? The first woman I've ever felt this fucking protective over, this unique mix of caring and depravity...

I groan her name and pick up speed, my hand slick now from the seed pulsing at the tip of my cock.

"Heath?" My bedroom door swings open, Emily silhouetted in the doorway, all bare arms and legs and that tiny fucking swimsuit hugging her torso so tight it leaves nothing to the imagination. "I heard my name."

Wyatt stumbles into the space behind Emily. "What the hell? Heath, put that thing away!"

"No, don't." Emily's eyes are wide and glued to my hand. "Can I see it?"

"What?" That's Wyatt's bellow, but I could have said the same thing.

"I'm sorry," she squeaks. Then she shoves past Wyatt and disappears down the hall.

6
emily

I RACE DOWN the hall and into my room.

I slam the door behind me and lean against it, trembling.

This has been my room at the cabin since I was a little girl. It has two twin beds and a pullout couch. When all my cousins are here at Christmastime, we bunk in together. This weekend, it was just supposed to be mine, and my stuff is spread out on the second twin bed.

I can hear them down the hall, arguing. Oh God, if my parents ever hear about this—if anyone ever hears about this—I...

I don't know. I've completely stepped over a line, though. They are guests in this house, and I got carried away with the flirting. I'm totally going to get in trouble for taking advantage of the fact that I am the closest family member to this cabin.

There's *no way* this ends well. The thought repeats on panic mode in my head, and I pace away from the door, peeling off my bathing suit. Clean, dry clothes might help. I pull on a T-shirt and a pair of sweatpants.

They don't really help, but at least they're dry. I grab a hair elastic and push my hair up into a bun, then crawl under the blankets to warm up.

There's a knock at the door. "Emily, can we come in? Can we talk?"

That's Heath.

Then Wyatt's voice. "Emily, you didn't do anything wrong. You have nothing to apologize for."

But if I weren't here, if I hadn't said that... *Can I see it?* Who says something like that?

A shiver races through me. Again, they knock.

"Go away," I say, my voice unsteady.

"Oh, we can't do that." That's Heath again, and there's something about his voice. The confidence, that bossy calm. It reaches through the door and wraps around me. "I'm going to open the door now."

He says it as a statement, like he's not asking anymore. Maybe like he knows this is what I need. How can he know what I need? When I don't even know myself?

The doorknob turns, and despite my worry, my attention is locked on the gap revealed as the door swings open.

They have matching looks of concern on their faces as they glance into the room, first looking at me, then taking in the dated 1970s decor.

"Most people don't use this room, so it's— This is just my room. And my cousins', I guess." I'm stammering, embarrassed for no good reason. But compared to the renovated rooms they are staying in, this one has a very retro, throwback feel to it. I usually love it, but now I'm seeing the fake wood paneling and orange quilts through their eyes.

Maybe also because it reminds me of my childhood, and right now, I feel very small and childish.

Heath eases in past Wyatt, who takes up the entire doorway, and takes a seat on the couch. "How long has this cabin been in your family?"

He's making himself small and nonthreatening, I realize, by sitting across the room from me. I read about that in a book. Maybe he's the good cop. Wyatt's still glowering in the doorway.

"My grandparents lived here when they first got married. When they had kids, they moved to Conception Ridge."

"So, you're local," Heath says. "But you live in the dorms?"

We're not going to talk about how I asked to see his erection? Which he's now covered up, I realize. With real clothes. Like me, he pulled on a pair of sweatpants and a T-shirt. Wyatt's still shirtless, but he changed into a pair of workout shorts.

"I..." I swallow hard. "Yeah. I mean, no. My grandparents are gone, and their kids all moved to big cities. I picked Ridge College because I love this area. We come here for the holidays, but that's it. I grew up in Seattle, and that's where my family lives."

"Will you be going back there when you graduate?"

I blink in surprise. "To Seattle? No, I don't think so. I love Conception Ridge. There are a couple of biotech firms I've done co-op placements with, and when I finish my summer lab, my plan is to apply for a job with them."

Wyatt's scowl lifts. "Really? That's awesome."

Heath's reaction is harder to read.

I want to crawl into his lap and smooth out the furrow

between his eyebrows with my fingertips. Kiss his frowning mouth until he tells me why it matters where I go after graduation.

"So, you'll be around," Wyatt says, rubbing his hand up and down his washboard abs. Drawing my attention to how his shorts hang low on his hips, and below his waistband, that impressive bulge is back. He can't be the bad cop with a hard-on, right? That's gotta be a rule.

Which means they really aren't mad at me for being weirdly slutty.

My embarrassment shifts, crystallizes, and narrows to a laser-beam focus. I feel all hot and uncomfortable, not about wanting to see Heath's cock—he said my name while jerking off, after all, and Wyatt's got a hard-on right now, so the horny feelings are all mutual—but about my reaction immediately after.

I freaked out, and *that's* embarrassing.

I just don't know how to talk about any of this, because this has never happened to me before.

"I'll be around," I repeat, nodding, looking back and forth between them. "Staying in Conception Ridge."

"That's great news," Heath grinds out. He glances over at Wyatt, then stands up. "I'll get out of your way so you can discuss that further."

Again? He abandoned us in the hot tub, and now in my bedroom?

Oh, heck no. I jump off my bed and join Wyatt at the doorway, blocking Heath's exit.

heath

"JUST WAIT A SECOND," Emily says, her gaze darting back and forth between us. She licks her lips. "I shouldn't have run off like that. That was…childish. And immature. I think we can talk about this like mature grown-ups."

I swallow a strangled groan. She was a teenager a hot second ago. And the mature grown-up conversation I want to have about that is how much her innocence turns me on. *Not* appropriate for someone so tender and young.

"Here's what I want to say." She props her hands on her hips and nods. "I'm tired of being a never-been-kissed bookworm."

Wyatt hauls her into his arms, one hand palming that sweet little bottom I was just devouring with my eyes, the other hand sinking into her bouncy bun of dark curls, holding her head still. "If you want me to kiss you, just say the word."

"Word," she breathes.

He pulls her tight against him, her whole body lifting up

and into his arms. He turns them both to the side, so I can see them as his mouth covers hers. As her tongue—*I can see her eager little tongue*—licks against his.

My cock throbs, loose in the sweatpants I pulled on in a hurry. I adjust myself, feeling every inch the pervert in the shadows watching his little girl being mauled by the boy next door.

The light spilling in from the hallway illuminates every inch of their bodies. Wyatt's erection strains at the front of his shorts. Emily's lithe little body shakes in need.

And the sounds they're making... I've never heard anything sexier. Wyatt is moaning like he's just discovered heaven. Emily is panting every time they break apart.

The best fucking part is the little smiles they give each other before they crash together again. Because they've just discovered how fucking good it feels to share a kiss with a lover.

I know how long Wyatt has waited for this.

Ever since I saw him fall in love with Emily right in front of my eyes, we've shared each other's secrets. I know he's never been with a woman. And he knows I have kinky fantasies I've never fully been able to explore—and that Emily is my dream girl come to life, the perfect embodiment of my little one I want to share.

A confession I regretted immediately, but he's never betrayed my confidence.

Maybe because I've made it clear that I won't get in his way. Fuck, he probably knows I'll get off on watching what I can.

But it never occurred to me that he might like *being*

watched. That he might get off on having Emily in front of me.

And if he does, then I might just get a slice of heaven myself this weekend before I let them both go.

"Wyatt, wait…" Emily presses her hands against his bare chest, then moans.

"What is it, baby?"

She turns in his arms to face me again. Wyatt doesn't let her go, but he doesn't stop her from turning her full attention to me, and after a beat of holding my gaze, she drops her eyes, looking at my straining dick tenting my sweatpants.

Whatever Emily wants, Emily will get. We've tumbled into something here; I can feel it. A weekend of whatever this little girl desires, even if it is me as well as him.

A myriad of complicated feelings spirals through me at once.

I shouldn't taint their new connection.

But God fucking damn it, I want her too. I want this, whatever it turns into, for however long I can hold on to it. I may never get it again.

I say her name, low and urgent. "Emily…"

I need to make a promise here, but words are coming slow. All I can see is Wyatt's big mitt moving up and down her side, pushing at the bottom of her T-shirt, his fingers sliding under the cotton to stroke her bare skin. The way he plays with her flesh, as if he can't get enough of the softness. As if just touching her makes him happy.

Touching Emily would never be enough for me. I want to bend her in half and plunge into her, make those tiny mounds bounce and jiggle as I work my way into her strong little body.

"I can't help it." Her eyes are pleading with me. "I need to kiss him, I can't explain it."

"You don't need to explain it to me." The words rasp out, honest and rough. "I know you need to explore this connection with Wyatt. I won't get in your way."

"But what about you?"

I shake my head. "I'm not really the guy for you, Emily. Not like Wyatt is."

"But—" Emily cuts herself off as Wyatt pushes his hand higher up her shirt. "Ah…"

He murmurs something I can't hear, and she nods.

I know he can feel her nipple in the palm of his hand, and that's enough to twist my brain inside out.

Which is why I'm not sure I hear Wyatt correctly when he fixes his gaze on me—that wild look I've seen before, when he told me he was going to marry this girl—and says something impossible to Emily. "We could share you. Would you like that? Heath's fingers between your legs and my mouth on your pretty little tits?"

She nods, her gaze locked on my face. "I want you both."

Is this a dream?

Of course I want nothing more than to sink into her tight little body. It's been too long since I've been with a woman, and never like this. I shake my head.

This little girl has bewitched me.

Not a girl. A woman on the brink of adulthood. Innocent but ready. No wonder Wyatt was drawn to her. She's perfect for him. The two of them have found each other in the universe, and now I'm in the way.

But I'm not dreaming, because Emily reaches out her hand to me. "Don't go."

Wyatt lifts his heavy gaze, and when his eyes meet mine, they're unexpectedly challenging.

"Stay," he says. And his voice is firm. "She wants you too."

8
wyatt

I SPENT a long time thinking that because I didn't want the type of casual sexual relationships I saw other people have around me, I was less of a sexual being than the average guy. That maybe I just didn't care that much about sex.

I couldn't have been more wrong. It isn't that I want less than what others have. I actually want more.

I'm not jealous at the thought of Heath taking Emily beneath him. I'm turned on. I can share her with him—if he feels the same way. I *will* share her if she wants us both. After months of the most possessive thoughts, I surprise myself.

She's mine. Yes.

But she might be his too.

Heath's glittering gaze meets mine. I see a matching possessive claim there, as I have many times before. But I see something different this time. Now the pulse of desire doesn't make me growl in competition with this man.

I hold his gaze. *She's ours.*

Can he even fathom it? Is there something I can teach the older man?

His eyebrow arches. *You'd share her?*

Only with him. Because there's something special about Heath too. We have a deep bond, a friendship that I've always labelled as a brotherhood connection. Except, I have three brothers, and I don't want to watch any of them thrust home inside Emily.

He's my mentor, my friend, and when it comes to how I feel about this woman, my confessor, too.

He knows how fucking horny I am for her. How I want to fuck her into the ground. My brain can't handle all the dirty things I want to do to this girl. Heath, though—current situation excluded—is always in control. He'll be able to teach her things I don't even know.

"Go to him," I murmur to her, and she breaks free of my possessive hold, crossing the room.

Heath catches her and lifts her up, urging her to put her legs around him as he kisses her.

I feel her mouth all over again as I watch. I don't know what the fuck I'm doing, but kissing her felt damn right. Her tongue slid against mine, and everything clicked into place.

I move farther into her childhood room. I'm not sure where to sit, because they're in front of the little couch against one wall, and there are only two beds. One is clearly hers, where she was curled up in the blanket, and the other is covered in little scraps of clothes and piles of books.

Fuck it.

I sprawl out on her tiny twin bed.

That confidence lasts ten seconds, then I hop back up,

neatly fix the blankets, and sit on the edge so as not to disturb too much.

I think it's the last bit that Heath sees, because he's laughing suddenly and whispering something to Emily.

"What?" She gasps. "Why not?"

"Because you're special, and we have all weekend." Heath kisses her temple and guides her onto the bed next to me. "Tell Wyatt what I just told you."

She wraps her arms around my neck and curls one thigh over mine.

"What did the boss man tell you?" I rub my hand up and down her leg.

"He says we can't have sex tonight."

"Get the fuck out, Heath," I bark.

"It's not your room to order me out of, and we've just established that I'm wanted here." He sounds so fucking smug.

I don't think he knows how hard my dick is.

"And I only said Wyatt can't fuck you tonight, little miss. Not that we can't get you off. There's a lot more to sex than fucking."

9
emily

"I MAY HAVE MISREPRESENTED what he meant," I whisper to Wyatt.

He gives me an incredulous look. And then he grins.

If I'd known talking about sex was this much fun, I'd probably have spent less time with my nose in a book for the last three years.

"There's more to sex than fucking," Wyatt repeats slowly. "Let's call that lesson one. I want to know everything about that."

"It's probably lessons one through fifteen," Heath drawls as he joins us on the bed.

Wyatt slides a possessive hand over my hip from behind as I twist and wrap my arms around Heath's neck. "So, what's lesson two?"

Heath brushes his lips against the corner of my mouth. "You've already had a taste of it. Kissing."

I shiver. "Tell me more."

"We could spend all night just kissing you, Emily. Make you burn so good."

My pulse pounds as he takes my mouth again. This time, it's a slow, lazy exploration. His tongue licks along my bottom lip then glides deeper, showing me how to thrust and parry at a we've-got-all-night kind of pace.

A little less desperate, a lot more promise. This kiss stokes a fire I didn't know could burn this hot inside me.

And the way his fingers press into my upper arms, holding me ever so still, I know I shouldn't rush him. He's trying to show me something here.

So I give in to the searing gentleness of his tongue in my mouth, this heady invasion that makes me think of bodies moving together in the middle of the night, of slow, drawn-out sensations. It's all-consuming, hot, and possessive, just like Wyatt's grip on my hip.

And everything else fades away.

The only three heartbeats in the entire world are in this room.

When Heath finally slides just an inch away from me, his lips hovering above mine, he smiles lazily. Proud, because he must be able to tell from the glassy, unfocused look in my eyes that I'm punch-drunk now.

Lost from his intoxicating kisses and bruisingly slow pace.

"How was that?" he murmurs with an arousing confidence.

He knows.

My heart wants to burst with the goodness of it all. "That was perfect."

He turns me around, lifts my whole body up like I'm a little rag doll, and sets me on his lap. He curls one of his hands over the top of my thigh, brushing his fingers just an inch from my aching core. "Now, kiss Wyatt, just like that. Take your time. Explore his mouth and find out what he likes."

I want to lunge at our other lover—*I have two lovers*, I think drunkenly—but Heath's grip strongly advises I take my time. He's literally holding me back, even as Wyatt licks his lips, his eyes wild and needy.

"Come here," I whisper, and Wyatt surges into me, sandwiching me between him and Heath's broad chest. I catch his face in my hands, slowing his approach.

His chest heaves against mine, his hands landing on my torso, just below my breasts.

"Kiss me slow," I tell him, breathless in my newfound knowledge. "Almost lazy-like. Like we have all night."

Heath groans at my description, then murmurs his agreement. "That's exactly right. All weekend, in fact."

Wyatt's lips hit mine, soft and teasing. His version of lazy is even slower than Heath's, and I'm the one who caves first, thrusting my tongue into his mouth.

He catches it and sucks, a leisurely pulse of his lips around my tongue, then a release. I gasp and suck his tongue into my mouth, trying that out. He surges against me at the first pull, and Heath holds us upright.

A rock behind me.

"You two cannot be restrained," he growls, but even through my needy haze, I know it's a form of praise.

Wyatt mutters something that sounds like *damn straight* and moves his mouth down my neck, to the collar of my shirt, and then peels that back, licking my newly exposed flesh.

Heath catches my jaw in his hand, his fingers warm and

just a little rough against my skin. "Do you want to give Wyatt a taste of those tits he wants so much?"

I whimper and nod.

"Pull up your shirt," he whispers, his breath hot against my temple. "Show us your sweetness."

I don't have a lot going on, little almost-B cups, which isn't much when you're petite to begin with.

But the way Wyatt's mouth drops open when I tug my T-shirt up, baring my breasts, makes me feel like a porn star. He makes a feral grunt, his hands immediately squeezing my sides, stroking the bottom of my breasts with his thumbs.

"Look at you," he breathes, then he full-on gropes the left one while he presses his face against the right. He takes a long, shuddering inhale, then begins to brush the gentlest kisses over my slight swells.

Heath pulls my shirt over my head, then presses his face next to mine, watching. He curves his fingers over my thigh again, higher this time. Very close to my aching core.

The combination of two burly men—*these* two men, in particular—caressing me all over is enough to make me spontaneously combust.

A powerful need coils inside me, a restless ache that makes me feel empty. I know it won't be answered tonight; Mr. Boss Man has said I need to sleep on it to be sure, but I already know what I want.

They belong inside my body.

I'm not sure how that will work, the two of them at the same time, but I'm wild with that need. I twist my head, catching Heath's mouth with mine. Kissing him, nipping at his lips. Showing him I'm ready for more, anything to soothe the ache.

And then Wyatt's mouth opens against my nipple, his tongue wet as he laps at me for the first time, and it's *my* turn to go feral. I writhe against his mouth so fiercely I slide off Heath's lap. He catches me, hauling me back up. Wyatt follows, and then Heath's sitting back against the headboard, and I'm safely between his legs. Wyatt's on top of me, caging me between their bodies, and it feels so good I can't even stand it.

Heath strokes his fingers up and down my neck. "Can we strip you down, sweetheart?"

I nod mutely, and he murmurs for me to lift up. I'm trembling as Wyatt tugs my sweatpants down my legs.

He covers me with his body, his mouth soft as he kisses me. "You're so pretty," he says quietly, his gaze locked on mine. A moment of pause, before he rears back and takes his first, long look at me naked and sprawled on top of Heath.

And for all that this is his first time too, Wyatt's not like me. He's not *innocent*. He's full-blooded and clear-eyed in his wicked intent for me.

He grins at Heath over my shoulder. "She's our pretty little plaything for the weekend, isn't she?"

Heath growls appreciatively in my ear. "Ours to do whatever we want with."

"I like the sound of that."

They're talking about me like I'm not perched on Heath's lap, panting in anticipation. Just having a casual conversation as he gropes me. His hand is hot on my hip, his fingertips brushing just shy of my mound. *Little closer.*

But instead, he sweeps his touch north, pinching at the nipple Wyatt sucked on. I moan, a bit desperate now.

"I love that you're just a little slip of a thing," Heath says reverently, and it sears into my brain. *That's important,* I think dimly. He likes the size difference between us. Likes that he can manhandle me. I like it too.

"Yours to do...whatever you want." I lick my lips, trying to find the words for what I want next.

It's so hard to spell it out when I'm turned on. And I'm not the only one fighting the effects of arousal.

Heath cradles me against his chest, his touch gentle even as his body flexes beneath me. His thighs are rigid, his cock a hard brand against my ass.

And in front of me, Wyatt is blatantly stroking himself through his shorts as he stares between my legs.

Yes. That.

"Lesson three," Wyatt growls. "More kissing, yes?"

Oh. My. God.

"Look at how he's watching you," Heath murmurs in my ear. "Our hungry boy. He wants to eat you up. Nobody has ever licked your perfect pussy, have they?"

I shudder in anticipation. "Ahh, no."

"He's never buried his face between someone's legs either. This will be new for both of you. You have to tell him what feels good."

Everything will.

"Spread your legs, little miss."

I'm shaking as I do as he instructs, hooking my thighs all the way over the outsides of Heath's, and I feel my pussy bloom open, revealing that I'm already soaked in arousal.

Wyatt drops down, making an unholy sound that I feel deep in my core, and he presses his face to the inside of my thigh for a moment, kissing me there before bringing his fingers forward to stroke my slick pussy.

I buck my hips at his touch.

But when I reach for his head, to tangle my fingers in his hair and bring him to where I need his mouth, I realize he's shaking too.

"It's okay," I whisper, my breath catching.

His gaze locks on mine, and he smiles, wolfish instinct overruling whatever momentary nerves just rocketed through him. "Can I lick you?"

All the air whooshes out of me. "Please," I beg.

He groans and gives me a slow, pointed lick, right on the seam, and I practically climb up Heath from how good that feels.

It's followed immediately by a grunt, a pause. Then his tongue goes flat, covering every inch of my inner sex from lip to lip, and then up to my clit, and both of us make a sound when he circles that throbbing bud.

Then it's only me crying out, because he's caught my clit in his mouth and he's sucking.

I had no clue *this* is what it felt like. "Oh. Oh, yes."

Wyatt pulls off, looking up at me for approval.

Heath laughs. "When she says, 'oh, oh, yes,' whatever you're doing then, just keep doing it."

Wyatt latches back on, and I wrap one leg around his shoulder, pinning him in place.

I never want him to leave his post between my legs.

"Is it always this good?"

Heath kisses my temple, his hands on my tits now, my nipples his willing captives. "It will be with him. Every time. And he'll get better as he learns your body."

"Every night," Wyatt promises, then licks a slow,

promising circle through my folds. My eager fellow pupil. We're in this together.

Every night?

Could I be so lucky?

Wyatt curls his hands under my ass, lifting my hips as he realigns himself to lick lower, teasing my entrance with his tongue now. He's watching my face as he tells me, "I want to put my tongue inside you."

I push my hips up in a wordless offer. But he's not done yet.

He's using his words to set a scene, to play with me. Turn me on before he devours me again. "Can I taste where Heath's gonna put his cock tomorrow?" Lick. Swirl. "Where you'll take us both by the end of the weekend?" The barest of thrusts, and a groan when he tastes more of me. His eyelids hood as he glances up at me one more time. "Perfect little untouched hole gonna taste so good."

I cry out, and he gives me what I need. His tongue, thrust into me. Someone else, *inside* my body. Wyatt's tongue is the first intrusion. Their fingers might be next. And by the end of the weekend, their cocks.

That's what Wyatt's dirty talk promises. *Take us both.* The picture that conjures lights me up inside, makes me burn.

But it's the quiet that follows that pushes me over the edge. The groan, and then nothing, because his mouth is *very busy*, so it's just the sounds of sex that swirl around me and sink into my skin. Wet and quiet and irreverent at the same time. Unholy and perfect.

And in my ear, Heath's ragged breathing as he watches me writhe on Wyatt's face. I start panting as my climax approaches, and Heath squeezes my breasts harder, holding me firm, giving me something to push against as Wyatt licks another path up to my clit and then latches on.

I shoot into the atmosphere like a lone, overpowered firework. Higher than anything else, shockingly bright. A star, burst into a million pieces.

When all those pieces of me come tumbling back down to earth, I find myself sagging back against Heath, my thighs wrapped around Wyatt's head.

"Did I almost strangle you?" I ask, out of breath.

He grins at me. "Would have been worth it if you did." He licks his lips. "Wanted this for so long, Emily. Your pussy on my face. Your slick taste on my tongue. Wanted it forever and still didn't know it would be this good."

"You say the nicest things." I reach for him, but I'm too weak. Turning into a magical, sky-high firework is exhausting.

Heath sweeps his hand down my belly, making me shudder again at the grazing touch. "Mark her. Come on her."

Wyatt shoves his shorts down, his fist a blur, and then he's groaning so low and deep I feel it in my chest. Warm, thick lines paint my skin. I gasp at the shock of it. Heath said it, but I didn't know...

That really just happened.

A man knelt between my thighs and jerked off furiously, painting me with his come.

We're *both* panting hard now, staring at the mess he just made.

"Get a washcloth," Heath murmurs to Wyatt. An instruction.

The other man crawls off the bed and disappears, and

Heath wraps his arms around me. "Good girl," he whispers. "You're so beautiful when you come. I knew you would be."

I can feel how hard he is behind me, but my head is spinning, and then Wyatt is back before I can ask Heath if he wants a release too.

I yawn as Wyatt cleans me up. Heath dresses me, extracting himself from behind me, saying it's bedtime for me, and I protest.

He bends over and kisses me, his mouth both demanding and soft at the same time. Like he wants so much more but knows we have time for that tomorrow. Everything he said already. I clutch at him, not wanting the kiss to end.

But then, when he stands up, another yawn takes over my entire body.

Heath doesn't take no for an answer this time. "Bed. Sleep. Think. And tomorrow, if you still want this, then we are all yours."

10
heath

I WAKE up at the crack of dawn, my arms empty and my whole body restless. I check on Emily. She's fast asleep, her covers thrown off and her legs akimbo.

The urge to kiss her awake, my head between those thighs, is almost overwhelming. But she needs to make the next move. Last night was a free pass for all of us. There was no way Wyatt wasn't going to get a taste of her, and wild horses couldn't have kept me away from sharing that first step with them.

But going any further? It needs to be her choice, made after enough time to have second thoughts and give them fair weight.

Instead of crawling into her bed, I force myself through a punishing workout and a cold shower, then set about making breakfast.

I have pancake batter prepared and sausages on the griddle when Emily wanders into the kitchen, rubbing sleep from her eyes, her hair twisted up into two buns on either side of her head.

She's pulled on socks, but otherwise is wearing what I tucked her into bed in. Those little shorts and that super soft T-shirt.

And a shy but determined look on her face. "I still want this," she whispers, her voice shaking.

That hits me square in the chest, and I pull her in close. "Good girl," I say, my voice rasping. "I'm so fucking glad."

I haul her up and set her on the counter. She wraps her arms around my neck and her thighs around my waist, clinging to me as I wedge myself against her.

And then I give her a proper good-morning kiss.

A teasing hello, a lingering play of lips and tongues, then a deeper, serious exploration of how fucking good she tastes. And finally, smiles and laughter. Her breath hitches at the end, and I chase her mouth once more, needing another sweet hit.

Holding her in my arms like this unlocks something inside me, something dangerously close to what I've always craved and known was impossible. A sweet girl of my own, a little miss to take care of.

I'm not sure I can even name it as a real thing—or if I want to even try. Not yet. Because she's not *mine*; that's not possible. Not exclusively.

Ours.

Is that even possible? And what would Wyatt do if I wanted her to call me Daddy?

What would Emily say?

Questions best punted down the line.

"Good morning," I murmur as I try to regain my equilibrium. "How'd you sleep?"

"So well." She bites her lip, her gaze dropping to my mouth.

Fuck it. Equilibrium is overrated.

I dive in again, just as hungry as she is for more. I bite at her lower lip, a nip that she returns then soothes with a gentle lick. Our little miss is a natural.

That's how Wyatt finds us. When we finally notice him, he's got a matching hunger in his own eyes, so I step out of the way, pulling him in. Showing him that she's his first, and I'll never stand in his way.

He gives me a look that's hard to read, then Emily grabs the front of his shirt and hauls him in close. "Good morning, my sex buddy."

He laughs and groans at the same time, then dives into her mouth.

When they're finished—for now—I urge them to eat something while we debate the merits of going hiking.

"If we stayed here," Emily says boldly, her eyes twinkling, "we could fool around. Work our way through some of those lessons on the way to bang town."

Wyatt points his fork at me. "She makes an excellent point."

"Lesson number…" I've forgotten how many we covered last night. "Let's call this lesson number six. Anticipation is foreplay. So is getting to know one another better. And fresh air builds up a good appetite."

"That sounds like three lessons. Six, seven, eight. We're getting closer, Wyatt." Emily winks at him. "Eat up. You're going to need your energy."

"That sounds like a threat." And not one he minds in the slightest.

After breakfast, Emily scampers off to her room to put on hiking-appropriate clothes. When she comes back, she's got on the right footwear, solid hiking boots, as well as a light-weight but long-sleeved shirt and a pair of khaki shorts that are perfectly suitable.

All I see is the easy-to-access zip fly and the short leg holes that flare around the tops of her thighs. So many possibilities for touching and teasing her. Lessons nine and ten, maybe, if the path is private enough.

An hour later, and the long stretch of bare leg between the hem of her short shorts and the top of her hiking boots is driving me to distraction.

Emily took my instruction to heart and led us up a path right out the back of the cabin, promising it as a popular hike and a vigorous challenge.

Keeping my hands off her is proving to be a vigorous challenge, too.

Those *legs*.

Tanned thighs I ordered her to spread for us last night. Strong, lithe legs that flexed and pushed, then went soft and boneless after she came on Wyatt's face.

Legs she wrapped around me this morning. Thighs I want to spend the rest of the weekend between.

After we stop at a wild flower meadow and start climbing again, she spins around and catches me looking at her ass. She winks and tugs her shirt up, flashing me her bare tits.

I trip and just barely catch myself before I face-plant in the dirt.

"What the…?" Wyatt turns from his spot in the lead, and

Emily giggles, turning back to face him—shirt still rucked up. He growls and comes charging back down the path, catching her around the waist.

I collide with them both as she winds her arms around his neck, and she twists, giving me her mouth as he covers her tits with his hands.

"No bra, Emily?"

"Oops, I forgot." She bats her eyes at me.

"What if you ran across some dangerous men while hiking?"

"Horny men," Wyatt adds. "Who will take one look at you and do anything to be inside you."

She shrugs. "Haven't met any of those men yet. Only you two."

Wyatt growls and drops his mouth on her neck, kissing or biting or both, maybe. She shrieks and pulls him closer, giggling as he roughly shows her just how much he wants her.

I brush my lips against her ear. "Is your patience running low, little miss?"

She rubs her ass against my erection. "I thought I could wait…"

I reach around her and deftly unbutton her shorts. "But you need to come?"

"Please," she pants as I slide my fingers into her panties, finding her slick. Her clit is hard, throbbing against my fingertips.

Wyatt lifts his head long enough to shoot me a warning look. *Not on the trail.*

But we haven't passed a single soul, and I can't stop

touching her, not until she's found her release. "Wyatt's going to keep an eye out," I murmur to her. "Make sure nobody sees you riding my hand. Such a dirty girl, letting me touch you in the middle of the trail. A good girl, too, because you know I've wanted your scent on my skin. When you flood my fingers, I'm going to lick them off."

She squeals and writhes in my arms as I keep stroking her, my dirty words and capable fingers working in tandem.

"Should I give Wyatt a taste too? Or should we make him wait until we get back to the cabin?"

"No waiting," she pants. "For anyone. I want you to come too."

"Do you?" Fuck, she's so perfect. "If you come for me, then you could help us out."

"Ah!"

"That's it. Fuck my hand, little miss. Show me how much you want to suck Wyatt off as I feed him your sticky juices."

Wyatt groans, grabbing her hips. My hand is pressed between them now, his cock a heavy brand against her belly I can also feel against my forearm.

My erection is just as hard behind her.

"Lift her up," I bark at Wyatt. "Grind your cock against her untouched hole."

She cries out as he pulls her up his body. I keep circling her clit with my fingers, and then she's there, her clit throbbing in long, pulsing beats against my hand.

"You're such a good girl," Wyatt croons in her ear as he hugs her tight.

I slip my hand out of her shorts. Her scent is devastatingly perfect, and my mouth is watering, but Wyatt's gaze is locked on my fingers.

Fuck. I feed him the first taste, as promised in the swirl of lust. His tongue shoves against my hand, hungry and uncaring if this is unusual.

It's fucking hot. That's all that matters.

After he pulls away to kiss her, I lick my other fingers, letting the scent of her imprint on my brain. Her scent and his hot, branding lick. If I get my hand on my cock, it won't take more than a stroke or two to get off.

But I don't want to do it myself. I glance around, then hook my hand around Wyatt's upper arm and drag him—carrying her—off the trail and behind a fallen tree.

"Our turn, baby girl," Wyatt says, setting her down.

Emily drops to a bouncing squat in front of us, her attention laser-focused on getting our cocks out. Biting her lower lip, she furrows her brow in concentration as she pulls at Wyatt's zipper with one hand, the other grabbing at my belt.

We help her, and then both of our cocks are free. She has her hands on them immediately, then her mouth. Glancing licks at first, then more confident bobs deeper into the warm, wet pull of her lips. Back and forth she goes, never letting go of us, and with each slurp, she pulls us closer together.

Wyatt clamps his hand on my shoulder, and I wrap my arm around his waist, bracing against each other as her sweet little uncoordinated pulls do their magic.

The only thing hotter than seeing her little fingers wrapped around my surging dick is the competing sounds they both make every time her mouth pops off his cock.

He groans in desperation and she moans happily, and my balls pull a little tighter each time.

Topping that is the gasp of delight she makes when the final sliver of air between our bodies disappears. Wyatt twists toward me, and our cocks slide against each other, bumping into her lips, trying to force their way into her mouth together.

"Take us both," I growl, an impossible ask.

"Lick your tongue between us," Wyatt pants. "Can we come like this, Emily? Will you let us?"

Like there's any stopping the churn of my seed. "You can pull back," I tell her, stroking her cheek.

She shakes her head, her eyes wide as she licks her lips and pulls our crowns together again, rubbing them against her tongue.

Wyatt groans and pumps his hips, his dick thrusting past mine to pulse the first spurt of his come down her throat, then he rocks back. The sight of his seed on her tongue makes every cell in my body tingle, and the corners of my vision go black. With a shout, I follow him, my balls contracting, the base of my cock pulsing too. My release paints her mouth, the head of his cock, and then overflows, dripping onto her chin and the ground below us.

Emily beams up at me before swiping her tongue and swallowing as much as she can.

"Look at you," I say as I catch her face in my hands, not caring that my cock is still out, still throbbing. "Such a fucking good girl for us. Taking everything we had."

Wyatt smooths his thumb over her chin, and I help on the other side. Cleaning up our little miss.

Then she rises on shaking legs, and Wyatt helps her do up her shorts. I tuck my cock away and drag her up against the front of my body. Wyatt, too, in for a group hug.

My heart pounds in my chest.

Holy fuck.

What was that?

And how soon until we can do it again?

11
wyatt

WE DON'T HIKE MUCH FARTHER after that unplanned addition to our day's itinerary. Emily suggests we climb a few more minutes to the crater lake that was our original destination, but instead of hiking all the way around it, we simply sprawl out on a wide viewing dock.

Emily puts her head on my abs, and Heath pulls her legs over his lap. From above, we'd make a letter H, and I wish I had a drone with me to capture the image. It'll have to be enough to snap a point-of-view shot on my phone, a photo where my hand is holding one of Emily's and her other hand is tangled up in Heath's fingers.

The same fingers he fed me her taste with.

Fuck, my cock throbs at the brand-new spank-bank memory. Right up there with shooting down her throat together. I went first, then Heath. His jizz had spilled all over me, too.

And now I just have a raging erection. Good thing Emily is looking toward my face and not the other way.

Or what? She'd figure out that you're an absolute horndog?

That cat might be out of the bag.

I replay the blow job in my head, a lazy smile pulling at the corners of my mouth as I remember my big hands pawing helplessly at her head as my whole body throbbed for her, ready from the first swipe of her tongue. I wanted to press her down and pull her off at the same time. I needed to come so hard, but there was something else blaring in my head. *Not like this*, I'd thought for a second. Some misguided idea that the first time I came in her, it should be in her pussy. Inside her body, but not like that. Except yes, like that, because flooding her hungry little mouth?

Fucking perfect.

"Wyatt, bud, are you having an erotic daydream over there?"

I blink my eyes open and find Heath having a good laugh at my expense. At my erection straining the limits of my fly.

Emily rolls over and covers it with her hand. "Do you need another blow job?"

I drop my hand on top of hers and squeeze. "I'm not going to say no, but—"

"No." Heath shakes his head forcefully. "Not here. There's a cabin just over there."

"Who made you the boss of us?" Emily teases. She gives my cock a squeeze, then flips around so she can crawl on top of Heath. "We need to behave in public? That's the rule?"

"Jesus, Emily." He gives her a tortured look.

Because he would very much like to be the boss of her.

And in that moment, I see it. I've never had a problem with what turns Heath on, but until right now, I didn't really understand his particular kink. In the same way he never really understood me wanting to wait until I fell in love with someone to bang them endlessly.

We all want what we want, and as long as we don't cross any lines in the pursuit of it, it's all good.

But now, with our little miss biting her lip and pretending not to grind her hips, and him being absolutely tangled up in his feelings about wanting to either punish her or make her scream or both, I can *see it*.

Heath as Emily's informal teacher, her patient caregiver, her secret Daddy.

It makes my cock throb in a new way. "You should listen to him," I say, my words thick with lust. "Or maybe he'll take you over his knee."

"Ooh," Emily says, giggling. "Am I being that naughty?"

Heath squeezes her ass in his hands, getting in a good grope before he lifts her off. Then he stands up. "You're not naughty," he says tenderly, helping her to stand. "But I will spank you if it makes you feel good. It might make you feel…secure."

Her eyes light up as she glances back to me. "How about you, Wyatt? You want to paddle my bottom?"

I clamber to my feet and join them. "Not me, little miss. But if you need something to make you feel better after, my tongue is always available."

She grins at me. "Speaking of tongues…We should discuss a few things before we go any further, right? Like, I know this is casual fun, no biggie, but it's also my first time."

"It's not casual—" I start to protest, but Heath shoots me a look to shut up.

He wraps his thick arm around her shoulders. "Talking is always good. What do you want to know?"

"Well, I take the birth control pill every morning," she says with a little smile. "Started it a few months ago, just in case. Felt like it was time. So that's covered, but have you both recently been tested?"

"That's a non-issue for Wyatt, since it'll be his first time, too. But I got tested twice last year. And since then, it's just been me, my hand, and fantasies of you learning all the ways to make my cock hard."

"Fantasies of me?"

"Bent over your desk, showing me your pink slit. Climbing up my body to sit on my face. With your wet little tongue—"

"Okay," she breathes. "I've got the picture."

Something shifts after that teasing conversation. On the walk back to the cabin, Emily has a new, curious adoration thing going on with Heath. She's hanging on his every word, giving him her rapt attention as he lays out a plan for the afternoon. A soak in the hot tub, then a trip to the farmers market. He gives her a detailed rundown of all the food options we have for dinner, which is frankly not nearly as interesting as skipping dinner and eating her instead, but I'm just a twenty-nine-year-old virgin who has finally gotten the green light to fuck his secret obsession, so I'm biased.

Then he says she might need a nap after shopping. "You can nap with Wyatt while I make dinner."

That's not subtle at all, but I'm not going to argue with him.

I'd love some alone time with her, but I'm pretty sure that, for Emily, we're a package deal. She likes me a lot, but she likes Heath just as much.

And every time he tries to push her in my direction, she

gets a hurt little look on her face.

Maybe because she's meant to be a Daddy's girl, through and through. It's an intoxicating idea.

And there's my cock again, so hard and ready it's dripping against my leg. Because there's no jealousy, only arousal, only an aching pulse to dig deeper into what this could be.

Our girl.

I don't want to scare her off, but I'm all in. I fell for Emily months ago, and I've lived with the knowledge that Heath loves her too. I've had time to sit with that—and his secret fantasies, as well.

They don't turn me off.

Nothing about Emily turns me off. If she's into it, I'm into it. Watching her climb all over him and be precocious? I want to see that naked. I want to see that at the end of the evening, when she's teased him all day and he's pushed to a limit and flips her over and pins her down.

But only if she wants it too. I feel like we have a window of opportunity here, while we're in Virgin Peak, that might close if we don't put all our cards on the table.

Heath is more relaxed up here. Like he thinks that what happens in Virgin Peak, stays in Virgin Peak. It won't, though. I'm not letting her go, and she isn't going to let *him* go, and so we're going to have to figure out a way to keep this going back in Conception Ridge.

Which means being honest with her now, rather than later. I have everything I've ever wanted. I think Emily does too. We'll make sure she does.

So that leaves Heath.

Can we trust Emily with his secret too?

12
emily

WYATT HAS something on his mind. I was wrong yesterday, when my first impression was that he isn't that smart. He's very clever, and quite observant, but also very much an open book.

And something happened on our hike back down to the cabin that has him thinking hard.

On the way to the farmers market, he tries to get me to sit in the front seat of Heath's truck, but I insist on sitting in the back row so I can observe them together. There's something they aren't telling me. A stark reminder that I've only known them for a day, even if they've been watching me for months.

Months.

The annoying guy in my lab has been less present in my dorm since the renovations began. Come to think of it, no guys have knocked on my door since the workers have been around.

I chew on that thought, shocked at the secret thrill I get. I should be offended, but I'm not.

They were being overprotective from the very start. Both of them, probably, but in very different ways. Wyatt would be like a jealous, possessive boyfriend. And Heath… Boyfriend isn't the right word for Heath.

And it's interesting to me that Wyatt isn't jealous of his boss, when he would be jealous of anyone else sniffing around me; I know that in my bones.

I grin to myself.

"Having fun back there?"

I glance up and meet Heath's gaze in the rearview mirror. "Yep."

His mouth tugs up in a lazy, pleased grin. "Good."

No, Heath doesn't give off jealous boyfriend vibes.

———

Back at the cabin, Heath puts away the groceries as Wyatt and I start a fire in the woodstove. I didn't get to that last night, and it was a bit chilly overnight.

Wouldn't have been that cold if we'd all slept together. That's my big plan for tonight. Heath doesn't get to put me to bed and put off the big sex finale.

Not that I think he will. He held my hand through most of the farmers market, even when I was also holding Wyatt's hand. I liked being in the middle of the two of them.

I want that again, tonight, but we're all going to be naked.

Once the fire is going, Wyatt tackles me onto the couch. I stretch out beneath him, savoring his eager kisses. He doesn't make a move to take off my clothes, seeming content to make out hungrily, and I get lost in how good he tastes.

When he finally releases me, it's only to roll up onto his knees so he can strip off his own shirt because the fire has gotten quite warm.

And that's when I realize Heath is sitting in the chair across from us.

"Hi," I say breathlessly. I scamper off the couch and cross to him, crawling into his lap. "How long were you watching us?"

"Long enough to get hard." He thrusts his hips against me. "Ready for another lesson?"

I squeak in delight. "Yes."

"Yes, what?"

"Yes, please?"

"Mmm, good girl." He kisses me, his tongue where Wyatt's just was, his hands hard on my hips. "I think it's time to talk about fucking."

From behind me, Wyatt groans, a deep, appreciative sound.

"Hear that? He wants to be inside you."

I shiver. "I want that too."

"There are many ways to fuck someone," Heath continues. "But for your first time, I think it's important that you be very turned on. Achingly so."

I nod, in full agreement. I'm already halfway there.

"And you should be in charge."

I blink in surprise. "Me? I don't know what I'm doing."

"But you will know what feels good—and what doesn't." Heath nips at the soft spot at the base of my neck. "And once you've done it a few times, then you can endlessly pretend play that it's your first time, and that big, horny beast behind you can pin you down and take you as much as you want."

"I want," I breathe, and he chuckles.

"I know, little miss." His mouth latches on to my skin, sucking hungrily.

Making me hot.

My shirt comes off next, leaving me topless on Heath's lap. He sucks at my nipples, back and forth, my breasts plumped up in his hands, until I'm writhing against him.

"Ready, little one?" He looks up at me, his gaze hot and hooded.

I nod.

He pats my ass. "Stand up and take these off."

I climb off, my legs and arms shaking, my heart racing, and when I turn around, I see Wyatt sprawled on the couch, naked. His cock is thick, rising up against his belly like a staff, and between his legs, his balls rest full and heavy, on display like it's nothing at all.

My eyes go wide, and he crooks his finger. "Come here."

I cross to him, an eager fawn, stripped bare.

He takes my hand and pulls me onto his knee, ignoring the fact that we're both naked. His gaze is locked on my face, and his arms hold me tight. "We'll only do what feels right," he whispers, the ragged edge of his words the lone betrayal of any nerves. "Can I touch you?"

I nod, burying my face in his neck as he strokes his fingers between my thighs. My legs fall open, and I picture Heath sitting across from us, watching Wyatt slowly pet my glistening folds.

That turns me on even more, heat swirling to my core, my limbs going liquid.

Wyatt croons to me, "You're our beautiful girl. Look at

your pretty pussy. I can't believe it. Can't believe how lucky I am."

Next, I feel his fingers circling my entrance. I whimper, my legs tensing up, and Wyatt eases his touch back to safe ground, to my clit, where it only feels good, and I've got nothing to fear.

Then from across the room, Heath says, "Who's in charge, Emily?"

I peek over at him. "Me?"

"Is that a question?" God, his stern, no-nonsense face does something wild to my heart.

"No." I take a deep breath. "It's just that I like it when he plays with me. Both of you. I like being your..." I like my lips. "What did you call me yesterday? A little slip of a thing?"

Heath's eyes darken and his jaw flexes. "You are just a little slip of a thing. A little girl playing grown-up games, is that it?"

Wyatt hooks my legs over his lap, turning me so I'm braced against him. In very much the same position Heath held me yesterday. Now it's Wyatt's turn to present me to the other man. "Is that right, Emily?" he murmurs in my ear. "You like Daddy watching you get fingered?"

Shock ripples over Heath's face, his whole body tensing as he surges out of his chair. "Wyatt—"

"Yes," I gasp, the wild need that has consumed me since last night crystallizing now. "Watch me..."

Wyatt groans in my ear. "Say it, little miss." He strokes between my legs again, and this time, I don't tense up. This time, I go languid and soft for him, because Heath's gaze is locked there, where his friend's fingers are circling my untouched entrance.

"Watch him touch me, Daddy. I like it." I lick my lips and mewl, caught in a silent firestorm between the two men. Heath glaring at Wyatt, and Wyatt—my sweet, happy himbo—taking control of the situation in a way I did not see coming.

Heath sinks back in his chair, his expression tortured and his erection clear. "Are you going to fuck him, Emily?"

I nod slowly. "I need to."

"We could go upstairs," Wyatt drawls, clearly enjoying this. "If you don't want to watch."

"No," I gasp. My nipples tighten, my little breasts feeling suddenly heavy. "I want to do it here."

"Dirty girl." Wyatt chuckles and shifts me forward, so I can brace myself on his thighs. And then I feel his cock, nudging between my thighs. "Rub against that, sweetheart. Show Daddy how much your pussy likes my cock."

"Like this?" I keep my gaze locked on Heath as I shift my weight again and wrap my fingers around Wyatt's erection.

I really do like it against my slick core. Just like earlier, I marvel at how hard it is, rigid in my grasp, but soft on the surface. Velvet-wrapped steel is a cliched euphemism that would have made me laugh a week ago, but right now? That's what I'm frantically grinding my clit against.

And it feels so good.

But I can't figure out how to get it inside me, not from this angle. And I can't look away from Heath.

"Turn around, little one," he says, his voice rough and raw. "I'm watching. I'm right here."

"I..."

"Turn around," he repeats. "And once you and Wyatt have this together, then it'll be Daddy's turn."

Oh, it's so much hotter when he says it.

I cry out, my need rabid now, and I twist around. Wyatt catches me, and I brace myself on his shoulders, aching with how much I need him inside me.

His gaze hitches on my face for a moment, then drags down to the juncture of my legs, where I'm fumbling with his cock—it's so big—rubbing it against my swollen, hungry pussy—still so small, despite how much I want this. And he watches as I find the spot, the place where just the tip of him notches into the entrance of me, and we both stop breathing.

He feels huge. Throbbing, solid, and unyielding. I try to sink onto him, and nothing happens. He slides his hands up my thighs, his breath dragging in and out of his massive chest as he tries to hold still.

"Does it feel good?" I whisper.

He groans. "You're perfect. Gonna make a mess in you, I swear."

"You aren't even inside me yet."

"I am, baby. Just a little. But you're taking me in. Oh fuck, Emily, that's the hottest thing I've ever seen. Your little pussy is stretched so wide around me."

My eyes feel like they're saucers. "It doesn't hurt yet."

"Maybe it won't." He grins at me. "Does it feel good?"

I roll my hips, trying to find the words to describe it. "It's…a lot." Another roll, and this time, it's his eyes that go wide.

"Oh fuck."

"Am I going to make you come?" I'm so pleased at the thought, but he looks horrified.

"Not before you."

"I might not. I read that, in a book."

"Fuck that book. You come first." He glances over my shoulder. "Right, Heath?"

Losing my virginity by committee is a very surreal experience. And I'm too stuffed full of dick to turn around and look at Heath's expression. I imagine it's a glower of some kind, and that gives me another burst of slickness. I roll my hips, trying to take more of Wyatt's thick length, and—oh.

He freezes. "Em?"

I bite my lip, trying not to cry, because that hurt. It was sharp and stinging and definitely on the ouch-y side of what I expected.

Wyatt's chest heaves. "Say something, beautiful. It's okay. God, you're so pretty. I just want to make you feel good. What would..." He shifts his hips, moving inside me, and I cry out.

"No!"

"Hang on. Oh fuck, that feels good."

"For you, maybe."

"And you too, if you just—" He snarls and pulls my hips closer to him, his body curving so he can suck one of my nipples into his mouth.

It's too much. It's so good, but he's all the way inside me now, and I can't breathe. I wrap my arms around his head, holding him to me as he starts to move inside me.

All I can do is hold on. Heath's plan for me to be in charge lasted as long as it took to bust my cherry, and now Wyatt is pinning me against him, rutting into me from below.

And his mouth...

I close my eyes, giving in to the swirling pressure. The burning has subsided, and now I feel a new sensation deep inside. Like there's a line between my nipple and somewhere else, and Wyatt's erection has found that somewhere else.

Don't move, I want to command him, but I can't speak. I can only hold on, grip him as tight as I can, and focus on that spot.

Behind me, Heath is watching.

Daddy.

Watch him fuck me, Daddy.

Can Heath see Wyatt's cock, buried in my pussy? Is he touching himself or gripping the sides of the chair, waiting for his turn?

"Goddammit, Emily," Wyatt grunts. "I can't hold back."

"It's okay," I whisper. "Come in me."

"You need— I'll get you off. I'll lick your sweet little pussy. Such a good girl, she's been. Fuck, fuck—" And then he's coming, all of him throbbing against me, and deep inside, a heavy pulse.

He pants against my chest for a few long beats, then swears again, and pulls me off, rolling me onto my back on the couch.

He crouches in front of me and softly licks me, his hands squeezing and kneading my thighs and ass.

"Did I hurt you?" His tongue slowly circles my swollen clit. "Don't answer that. Can you come like this?" He groans. "Fuck, you're all swollen. I'm so sorry, baby. But God, your pussy is pretty like this."

I whimper and reach for his head, needing to show him that I'm okay, and yes, this feels good, and oh God, he's licking me where he just came, and that's so fucking hot.

He glances up, catching my gaze.

I bite my lip and nod.

He groans in relief and goes to town, lapping at me with a slow rhythm I liked yesterday and love today. It doesn't take long to make my coiled arousal yank tight, then send me flying. Again, I wrap my thighs around his head as I come, and again, he seems to like it. He bites the inside of my thigh when I finally let him go, then licks that spot softly.

Then, together, we turn our attention to Heath.

He's standing, unbuckling his jeans.

"Look at how hard he is," Wyatt says, his voice steeling up. I recognize it now. His dirty-talking voice. His *get Emily ready* voice.

I shiver.

"You know why he's that hard, Em? Because it's his turn next in this tight little cunt."

13
heath

I DIDN'T HAVE a plan for this, but Wyatt jacking the dirty talk up to level ten wouldn't have been a part of it if I did.

I grunt in appreciation.

Then I lose my clothes and take his place between her thighs.

She's so little beneath me, and her face is pure innocence. She gives me a shy smile. "I'm a little messy. From Wyatt…"

My cock flexes, straining to get inside her. His seed and all. "That's not a problem. I'm gonna take you messy, and it's going to be—as he would say—so fucking hot."

She giggles, her cheeks turning pink. I stroke my thumb there, just beneath the blush, then trail my hand down her neck to her flushed torso. Jesus, her tits are soft. I stroke her as gently as I can, and she whines.

"You're not too sore?"

She shakes her head. "I don't think so."

"I'll be gentle." A proud warmth fills my chest. "Do you trust Daddy?"

Her breath hitches and she nods. Then she spreads her legs wide for me. My balls pull tight at the perfect vision in front of me. Her pussy looks soft, so puffy and slick and hungry for more. Pink lips framed with a light dusting of dark curls. I nudge my cock against her, holding it firmly in my hand as I rock it up to her clit, then down again. Up, then down. On the third rock, she lifts her hips, and the crown sinks inside her.

Her eyes go wide, her lips part. Two cocks in one afternoon. A big day for a little slip of a thing.

"Good girl," I murmur, leaning forward to cage her in my arms. "You feel incredible."

"You're so big," she whispers.

Wyatt's hung too, but where he's longer than me, I take the girth award.

My fat cock is going to stretch her wide open; there's no way around that. Her little-girl pussy is no match for Daddy, but she wants me inside her and I've fantasized about this for months.

I'm not stopping.

I curve one of her legs high on my side, changing the angle, and draw my hips back before sinking into her again. Using the slick from Wyatt fucking her to ease my entrance.

She's so hot and tight, I can see how he couldn't hold back, but I'm not an eager young buck. As much as I want to paint her insides white, I'm in no rush.

Fucking Emily is a dream come true. I want to savor her tight, sweet heat as long as I can.

Beneath me, she's still staring up in breathless wonder. "I'm inside you, pretty girl," I murmur before I kiss her.

Her eager tongue chases mine, wanting to play. I let her mouth set the rhythm. When she licks me, I rock my hips back. When she retreats, wanting my tongue in her mouth, I give it to her in tandem with my cock in her pussy.

A Daddy and his little who got carried away on the couch, and now we're fucking in the quiet cabin, nobody knowing our dirty little secret.

Nobody except Wyatt, who's stroking himself slowly.

Show Daddy…

Would I have told her if he hadn't brought it up?

I don't know. But now that it's out in the open, I'm rejoicing in it.

"Shh," I growl in her ear, her nipples grazing my chest with each thrust. "You have to be quiet for Daddy."

She's a perfect little church mouse, but she nods and presses her lips together.

"Good girl." I groan as I work my hips faster, fucking her into the couch. "I'll give you back to Wyatt, full of my come. We'll trade you back and forth all weekend. Fill you up. I want you in my bed tonight. Be my little girl all night. Let Daddy fuck you, while we're all alone at the cabin."

"Wyatt, too?"

"You want to sleep between us?" I roar at the thought, fucking her right next to Wyatt in the big king-sized bed in my room. Trading her back and forth until she's shaking and exhausted, and then maybe one more turn.

"Both of you," she whimpers. "Need you."

I kiss her hard, then rear up, hauling her legs around my waist. I'm half kneeling on the couch, one foot planted on the floor, and I'm using her body like a cocksleeve now.

Gentle was a lie.

Gentle was the promise to get her to take me. Gentle isn't what she needs.

I squeeze her hips, her waist, holding her tight as I pound into her. She looks so pretty like this. Stretched open, full of cock. Little tits jiggling, thighs shaking.

Eyes still wide, gaze locked on where I'm sinking into her body over and over again.

Right below her hard little clit, standing at attention.

I curve one of my hands over her belly, bringing my thumb to her clit, and I add a rolling stroke there.

Her eyes roll back, and her mouth falls open.

There.

That's my girl. *Our girl.* Sexy little thing just needed Daddy's cock in her belly, his thumb on her clit, and the right—*thrust*—fucking—*deeper thrust*—pace.

With a cry, she seizes around me, inside and out. She locks her thighs around my waist, pulling me deeper into her, and her cunt convulses, milking my release out of me with a matching shout.

When she sags, her body sated, I hitch her hips up, tilting her pelvis so I can watch my cock slowly pulse in her opening. I don't want to pull out, but there's another instinct warring with my desire to stay inside her forever.

I need to see it. Proof we both filled her up. Our seed, mixed together.

Of course, it'll all look the same. I've probably fucked Wyatt's come deep into the walls of her pussy by now.

But symbolically, I know we're both there.

This morning, she was our hot little virgin. And now… Now, we've both claimed her.

My heart hammers in my chest. We get to do it again tonight. And tomorrow morning.

I will get to be her Daddy for at least one more day before I need to give her to Wyatt and return to real life.

14
wyatt

I CAN'T STOP TOUCHING Emily, all afternoon. Heath is extra handsy with her too—he carries her to the nearest shower big enough for three people right after we have sex —but there's something urgent in my pull toward her that seems missing with him.

Because he's fully satisfied in how he fucked her, and I'm... Well, I have work to do.

Good thing I have the rest of my life to fuck her like a sex god. Starting tonight, after dinner.

First, she teaches me how to play backgammon, and I teach her how to find a stud in any wall by knocking along it. Heath watches all of it with a detachment that worries me, but just when I think I should pull him aside and say something, he'll kiss Emily deeply or wrap her in a bear hug, and all seems right with the world.

He gets dinner started ahead of us, but once it comes together, we work as a team to finish a salad and warm up dinner rolls.

Emily wiggles a bottle of wine at Heath. "Am I allowed,

Daddy?" He hoists her onto the counter and kisses her so long and deep, we're all aroused by the time she slips past him and winks at me. "I'll take that as a yes."

Three wineglasses it is.

Two for the grown men, and one for the jailbait co-ed who has stolen our hearts.

Over dinner, it's my turn to sit back and observe as Heath digs into what companies Emily might want to work for when she graduates. I swear he did some research since she mentioned staying in Conception Ridge last night, and I feel dumb for not thinking of doing the same.

Another point in the *we make a good team* column.

And then after dinner, when she stands up, pulls off her shirt, and announces, "Last one in the hot tub is a rotten egg," we manage to get in at exactly the same time.

Excellent fucking teamwork.

No rotten eggs. Just two lucky guys who get to pass the girl back and forth until she's breathless.

Emily insists we cannot fuck in the hot tub, because her family also uses the hot tub, so after we make out for a while and gaze up at the stars, Heath climbs out first and gets a towel for our girl.

Then he carries her upstairs and puts her in the shower while I lock up the cabin and turn out the lights.

When I find them, he's deep inside her, steam swirling around their entwined bodies.

"Daddy," she whines, pulling my balls tight. Like I'm watching something I shouldn't, and it's the illicit and hot and perfect. "You're all the way inside me."

"Gonna fill you up, make you messy for Wyatt," he grunts. "Share my little girl."

"Yes, please." She kisses his shoulder, then lifts her head, catching sight of me. She smiles as she tells Heath I'm watching.

"Good." His thrusts get harder.

I miss what he says to her next, his words lost in the spray of the shower, but she nods, her gaze locked on my hand as I stroke myself.

Then her eyes go wide, her lips parting, and Heath's hips jerk as they find their release together.

She clings to him, and he holds her in his arms as he turns the shower off. It's my turn to take her in my arms as soon as he steps out. I wrap her in a towel, but only to carry her as far as the sturdy-looking counter.

Maybe we'll make it to the bed for round two. Right now, I need to be inside her. She leans back against the mirror as I fit my mouth against hers, tasting her again.

Never gonna tire of her sweetness. Her tongue thrusts eagerly against mine, and her legs twine around my body.

As if we've always been doing this, my cock finds her entrance.

She gasps at the blunt intrusion.

I groan at the sweet, swollen embrace of her cunt. So hot, so tight, and so slick there's no stopping my heavy erection.

That first thrust takes me all the way in. It makes her shake, and God damn it, I could lose my nut again, she's that fucking sexy, but I'm not going to.

This time, she really is coming first. I count backwards from ten, and on three, I drag my length out of her.

Then I break our endless kisses and look down between our bodies. Her pussy is stretched wide around my throbbing shaft, and her clit is standing proud. I watch in awe as that sweet nub visibly throbs, then I rock my hips and sink back into her lush slit. Her body clings to my shaft, pulling her clit taut.

"Oh, oh…yes," she breathes as I bottom out.

Keep doing that, don't stop doing that, my brain remembers.

Every muscle in my body fights for control as I repeat exactly the same stroke. Drag out, pause, fight that desperate urge to claw my way back into her, then a slow, deliberate thrust.

Again, she cries out once I'm in her to the hilt, my heavy balls pressed against her bottom.

I fucking love this counter. It's the perfect height for me to fuck her nice and slow, make her make that sound over and over again.

One of my hands finds her tit, squeezing her flesh and then pinching her hard little nipple. The other cradles her body, making sure my hard thrusts don't bash her into the mirror.

My precious little miss. My sweet Emily. My horny, hot lover, full of another man's come, and shaking around me as I prepare to give her even more.

"I want you on the bed next," I growl. "Ass in the air, face buried in Heath's lap. Lick his cock, get it ready. I'll lick you first, get you right on the edge, and then take you so hard. Just power fuck you from behind, Emily. Because you can take it, can't you?"

"Anything you give me," she babbles. "Always."

Always.

I don't know if she means it yet, but I do. That one word sends me to a whole new place. It's hotter than any dirty talk.

"Come on my dick, Emily. Let me feel it." Drag out. Pause. Long, slow thrust inside, pulling her clit taut, raking over that spot inside her that makes her eyes go wide and her mouth pull into a perfect O. "Make me come too. Your pretty little pussy gets me so hot, you know that? I'm ready to spill, pretty girl. Fill you all up, swell that belly."

She shudders and slaps at my chest, which I can only take as a compliment, then she throws her head back. I drop my mouth to that gorgeous stretch of skin and suck, leaving a mark on her body to match the one she's stamped on my soul.

Her cunt clutches around me, and I roar. The rippling contractions of her orgasm suck my climax from me as well.

Goddamn. God. Fucking. Damn. I mutter some shit that is perilously close to *I love you*, but I think I turn it into *love your tits*, which is also true, and then everything dims, the corners of my vision going back, and I yank her hard onto my dick.

Finesse, all gone. I need to be deep, need to pulse the final spurts all the way inside her.

She kisses my temple and strokes my hair, soothing me like a wild beast.

Yes.

Fucking yes.

15
emily

WHEN HEATH TUCKS me in at bedtime, it's in his bed. And instead of letting him go, I hold him tight. All night long.

On Sunday morning, I wake up between them. Wyatt is in front of me, soft and sprawling. My comfortable teddy bear.

Behind me is Heath, and even asleep, the man is tense.

Doesn't stop me from clinging to him, though. My hand is wrapped tight around his forearm, as if he's a brand-new security blanket I'm trying to break in.

We need to leave the cabin by noon. The caretakers come between noon and three, every Sunday, and then a few times during the week, depending on the booking schedule.

The countdown is on. We need to return to Conception Ridge and our real lives.

How do you ask weekend fuck buddies when you can do it again? Would tonight be too soon?

Hey, Heath, just how big is your bed?

As if my thoughts were loud enough to wake him up, he stirs behind me, his arm tightening around my waist.

"You're awake."

"You can tell?"

"All night long, you were a soft little handful of perfection. Now, you're a tense stress ball of perfection."

Takes one to know one, I guess. "How long have you been up?"

"A while."

Ah. So it wasn't my filthy thought that woke him up, a poke through the ether. Maybe he was worrying too.

I turn around, and he scoops me into his arms, hitching me right close to his body. His cock rises to attention between us, tripping a spill of arousal through my own core. *Hello, Daddy.*

Lifting my leg high on his hip, I rub against him. "So, another lesson? What do you say we do next, when we have to head back to reality soon?"

He flips me onto my back, shoving the light blanket we all slept under down to the foot of the bed. "Quickies. How to get turned on, fast, and work together as a team to achieve a common aim."

Wyatt rolls over, giving us a sleepy grin as he discovers Heath wedging himself between my thighs. "Good fucking morning."

"School's in session," I pant.

"I'm an A+ student," Wyatt drawls, sliding his hand between our bodies to cup my pussy. He drags his fingers through a pool of slick at my entrance, making me moan. He pulls the moisture up to my clit, easing the path of his touch. "What were you saying about turning her on?"

"Put him in me," I breathe. I glance sideways, then back up to Heath above me. I lick my lips as I hold his gaze. "Let's pretend Daddy isn't sure if he should fuck me, but you're his friend from work who fucks me all the time, and you know I'm hot for him. You know I want him to hold me down and take me."

Heath tightens his fingers around mine, and his nose flares wide, his eyes bright.

It's a mash-up of the fantasy he told me yesterday. Wyatt's not the only horny beast who can pin me down and take me for the first time, over and over again.

Daddy stealing my innocence as I pant an uncertain protest? Top of the quickie inspiration stack, I think.

"Maybe I don't want this." I wink so we're all clear I do. "Maybe Daddy's under some sort of spell, and—"

Heath groans out loud, deep and long, as Wyatt turns his hand, fisting Heath's erection now. Roughly dragging it through my folds he's slicked up.

"Feel how wet she is for you, man." We're all breathing hard now as Wyatt jerks his friend off against my pussy. "Nobody will know if Daddy takes what he wants. She slept curled up in your arms for a reason. She needs you inside her. She feels empty without your cock buried deep."

"No...." I faux-plead.

Heath grunts.

"She has to say that, she's a good girl," Wyatt whispers, his eyes wicked and hot. "But she'll be saying yes soon enough. She'll be crying out for Daddy to come deep inside her."

"Stop talking," Heath growls, and I squeak, worried we've gone too far.

Wyatt shuts up. But he doesn't stop jerking Heath off, so he can't be that worried.

And then Heath's hips move, just a scant little shift. Enough to push the tip inside me and hold it there as he breathes heavily above me.

My whole body feels alive, and I know it won't take much for me to go over that glorious edge. Dirty-talk-driven quickies is my favorite kind of sex yet.

Heath drags my wrists together above my head and pins them with one hand. He wraps his other hand around the side of my neck, his thumb trailing a firm line down the front of my throat. "Shh," he rasps.

I say nothing.

"Hold still for Daddy," he growls. "Be a good girl."

My breaths jerk in and out of me, tight little sucks of air. Wyatt rolls away, and it's just the two of us. Heath's thighs shove my legs wider, and then that hand coasts down my body. A rough, gasp-inducing squeeze of my breast. A ghost of his palm over my belly, where his hand spreads from hip bone to hip bone.

He's so much bigger than me, he could overpower me in a heartbeat.

I am entirely at his mercy. My pleasure is his to give, or to deny. And he wants me to be a silent little thing for him, so Daddy can secretly fuck me in this big bed on an early Sunday morning.

He finally settles his hand on my hip, lifting me up, tilting me to take him better.

And then he plunges into me, his whole body driving forward and down. He pins me beneath him, and the angle he's entered me at puts my clit right against the rigid lower plane of his belly.

On the next rocking thrust, his whole body works against mine in perfect tandem. The pressure on my clit scrambles my brain, and the heavy push of his erection, claiming space inside me, is a one-two strum against my arousal.

His grip tightens on my wrists. Another thrust. Oh God. Need coils tight.

"Don't fucking come on me," he snarls. "If you come, I'll follow. Daddy can't come inside you."

I cry out, a bad girl now who can't keep quiet, because I'm lost, that image tipping me over into ecstasy. He bites out a curse word then barrels into me, three times fast, before locking up his hips when his cock is deep in my belly.

His eyes are burning embers as he sucks in a breath, staring down at me. "Couldn't help myself," he says slowly. He rocks his hips, his cock slowly pulsing inside me. "You're too fucking sexy."

"Need your mouth, little miss." Wyatt climbs up the bed, and I turn my head, parting my lips as his cock thrusts forward, even as Heath is still inside my pussy. Three hard pulls against my tongue and I'm gulping down his release, hot spurts right to the back of my throat.

He holds himself in my mouth as his long length softens just a bit.

I'm filled to the brim now, and I suckle happily at Wyatt's tip to let him know that was everything I wanted.

Heath drags himself off me and nestles in behind me, sending Wyatt to find me a washcloth.

"This was incredible." His voice drags, a ragged edge to his tone underlining the middle word in a way that pings my brain, even through the sex fog. "The perfect end to a perfect weekend."

"We still have breakfast." I nuzzle into his neck. "Pancakes again?"

"A sweet treat for Wyatt's sweet girl?" He smooths his hand over my hair. "Absolutely."

Wyatt's girl?

I recoil.

And the slash of pain in his gaze confirms my reaction is on point.

This was *incredible.*

Wyatt's girl.

But, of course, it was only one weekend for him. We're too different. He has a whole life—respectable, responsible— that doesn't have room for a twenty-year-old girlfriend and her himbo boyfriend, who just happens to work for Mr. Respectable Businessman.

"Emily…" His voice cracks, and I shove the searing pain down as deep as I can hide it.

"I know…" I stroke his cheek. "Pancakes."

"Wait—"

I hop off the bed just as Wyatt returns, pushing past him. I keep going, quickly, to the bathroom first, where I scrub between my legs, then down to the kitchen.

I can hear them talking upstairs, sharp tones, words too quiet to make out. Words I don't really want to hear anyway.

Clattering some pots and pans together covers that nonsense up nicely.

But it's hard to escape them when we're sharing a cabin, and they arrive, pushing past each other, moments later.

Wyatt starts. "Emily, we need to talk."

I glare at him. "Did you know? That this was just a weekend?"

"It's not just a weekend."

"For you? Or for both of you?"

He hesitates long enough that I get my answer. Clatter clatter. Bang bang.

"Emily, stop for a second."

"It's my turn to make breakfast," I say brightly. "Thanks for all the sex lessons, Heath."

"Whoa." That's Heath now, finally finding his voice. "Wyatt said we need to talk. That requires you to actually listen to us."

I pause, properly chastened. My heart doesn't want to listen, though. He doesn't need to spell anything out. I'm a big girl. Everyone's supposed to get their heart broken, anyway. Rite of passage.

"Put down the wooden spoon."

I set it on the counter.

"Look at me."

That is harder to do, but I slowly lift my chin, and I find Heath waiting for me, his face tight. "Wyatt told you that we both caught feelings for you at the same time. We've shown you those feelings a lot this weekend. What just happened now…" He scrubs his hand over his face. "Fuck, Emily, you turn me inside out. Before you, all my secret cravings were just that—secrets, and only in my head. And then over the last couple of months, as Wyatt told me how much he felt for you, he somehow got me to fucking confess to being an absolute pervert where you're concerned. This guy? He's the fucking best. And all he's ever wanted is to find his other half. His mate. A pretty little wife. You could be his bride—"

"This is too fast," Wyatt growls.

But it doesn't feel fast. That part feels right and perfect. Wild and free.

Heath gives me a pained look. "I thought it would be better if I got out of your way."

And *that* part feels like absolute bullshit. I open my mouth to protest, but he holds up his hand.

He's not done. "I *thought* that. I don't think it now. Holding you last night, all night long...I could never let you go. And I tried to show you that with my body because I wasn't sure how to put it into words, when I also know that Wyatt has forever plans for you. And I cannot stand in the way of that."

I nod hesitantly, reeling at the unexpected turn of events.

"So—" Heath starts, then stops again. "We'll figure it out. But we all need to be a little patient."

"Mmm."

Wyatt frowns at me. "You don't look happy."

"I wouldn't say that." I frown too. Frowns aren't always about grumpiness. Sometimes it's a thinking face.

I cross to him, leaving Heath standing alone for a moment. "You told me to trust my instincts," I say softly, carefully. I need him on board here. I think he is, but I've never done this before.

"I did."

"I need more. I can't just be a bride. A wife?" I swallow around a lump as Wyatt ducks his head. "I need to be a little miss, too."

Wyatt's head jerks up.

My breath catches in my throat. Does he feel the same way?

16
heath

"THAT'S RIGHT. She needs you. You're her Daddy." Wyatt's eyes burn with an emotion I can't quite identify and don't expect because we've talked about this.

It's a punch to the gut, as is the way he wraps his arms around her. Protectively, the way I should be holding her. *Holding both of them.*

"It's more complicated than just saying that." They're both too pure to understand.

They don't know how hard it is to give people your heart after a lifetime of guarding it like a fierce dog.

"Tell us, then." Emily lifts her pretty little chin, jutting it at me. A challenge. "Unless you think we couldn't possibly understand."

Fuck.

She growls when I don't answer. "That's it, isn't it? You think *we* couldn't possibly get it. We're too young, too—"

"Damn it, Emily, I love that about you," I bark out. "I don't want you to understand. I want you and Wyatt to have a perfect life together. Do you know what a gift it is to find your mate the first time?"

"Yes, I do. I'm deeply aware of how wonderful it is—and how hard it is at the same time when one of them refuses to admit what is right in front of him." She elbows Wyatt. "Baby, tell him."

I grin despite myself. Bossy little girl.

He catches her arm and lifts her hand to his mouth. His gaze locks on my face as he kisses her clenched fist. "I don't think he's ready to hear it, sweetheart."

My throat goes dry. "Hear what?"

He shakes his head. "Nothing."

Emily growls at him.

He just keeps kissing her hand, his lips soft on each of her white knuckles.

My pulse jacks up. "You think you know me better than I know myself?"

His gaze doesn't waver. "Yeah, Heath. I know you."

Fucking punk. "You don't know shit."

"I know you want to have your mouth on her right now. You're fucking mad as hell that I get to kiss this little fireball right now and you can't, aren't you?"

Even though he's got a lock on my attention now, I can still see Emily's eyes go wide. "Wyatt," she breathes. "That's not—"

"Nice?" He shakes his head. "Heath doesn't need nice right now. He needs to be shown that we'll be just fine without him. That maybe you *don't* need him to be your Daddy."

I surge forward, stopping just a foot away from them.

Between us, Emily takes a shuddering breath. I can see

her little body straining toward me, but Wyatt is holding her tight. No more hesitation, no more big puppy energy. He's all man now, confident and strong for his little one.

Everything I knew he could be.

But it's wrong.

"You just said she needs me. Now you're saying she doesn't?"

He shrugs. "Isn't that what you said you wanted? And then, sure, you walked it back, but not enough. Not all the way, because you have to keep one foot in a safety zone."

I ball my hands into fists to stop myself from grabbing him and shoving him against the wall. Taking Emily from him and wrapping myself around her. "Maybe what I want is too fucking complicated."

"Is it, though?" His mouth is moving up her forearm now. He guides her hand to his neck, encouraging her to hold on to him—and to present her tight little body to me at the same time. She's stretched taut, her nipples pointing straight at me through the thin fabric of her T-shirt.

His other hand moves against her waist, tugging the hem of her shirt up, revealing a slice of her skin at her belly. "Nothing about this feels complicated to us."

My cock thickens despite my resolve to let them go.

"We need you," he rasps out. "We both need you. She needs you. I need you. We're not complete without you as our third. It's not about her being mine, and her also wanting you."

"Do you hear him?" Emily breaks free of him and leaps at me. I catch her easily, holding her close as she cups my face in her hands. "You told me I had to be in charge the first time."

"That was sex."

"I'm taking that lesson and applying it to our first fight too. If you think you know me so well, despite us never exchanging more than a few words before this weekend? That we have some special connection? Then accept that I can see you too. And I can see him."

"She has you there, man." Wyatt shrugs roughly. "What? It's true. And of course she's upset. She loves you."

"And you," she throws back over her shoulder. Then her eyes go wide. "I love you," she breathes. "Both of you. I can't believe in love at first sight, because I must have looked through you so many times over the last few months, and I hate that. I should have seen you both. I hate how one-sided it was. But on another level, I felt your presence. I felt safe and protected—"

I frown, cutting her off. "From what?"

"What?"

"Safe and protected… Did you not feel safe before we started working there?"

She waves her hand. "There's this guy—"

"He's as good as gone," Wyatt barks.

"I think you already scared him off, to be honest. He bugs me in labs now, but that's it."

"The little shit weasel. He won't be bugging you at all after we have words."

"You can't—"

I cut her off with a kiss. "Yes, he can. We can. We'll find a way."

"On one condition." She gives me the stern, baby-is-in-charge look again. "Listen to what Wyatt was saying. I don't want to gloss over that part. *He* needs you. *You're his too.*"

My arms shake as her words sink into my thick skull. I pin her to me, wanting her closer than is humanly possible. I lift my gaze to meet Wyatt's piercing eyes. There's no fear there. No hesitation.

But he's not going to come to me the way she did. I need to go to him.

Lifting her with ease, I cross the gap between us and pull Wyatt into my arms, too. There's room for them both, Emily snug between us.

"I love you," I say roughly, pressing my forehead against his. "I love you because you love her, and because you see me, and because you're so fucking pure."

"God, this is so hot," she whispers between us.

He grins. "Want to show her how much you love me on your knees?"

"Fuck you."

"Yeah, if you want." He licks his lips, his gaze bright. "I love you too. I told myself it was because you're a mentor and a friend and an older fucking brother, but it's deeper than any of those."

I grip the back of his neck. "We'll figure it out."

"Together," Emily whispers.

Wyatt nods. "Forever."

I squeeze them together. "All of us, no matter what."

"Wyatt?" Emily squirms between us, turning around, then climbing up him like a tree, until her ass is nestled against my cock and her tits are pressed against his chest. "I love you."

"I love you too." He kisses her, deeply, and I tangle my hand in his hair, my heart moving outside my body to exist in that embrace with them. *Mine.*

I nudge her hair out of the way, then drop my mouth to the back of her neck. *Mine.*

And then they turn, Emily kissing me, Wyatt's arms holding us firm. *Theirs.*

The rest will sort itself out. Our love is all that matters.

17
emily

FOR THE DRIVE back to Conception Ridge, Wyatt joins me in my car, while Heath drives his truck just ahead.

He's comically too big for the passenger seat of my hatchback, but they wouldn't take my gentle suggestion that he could just go home the way he came up—in the man-size vehicle.

"Is this what it's going to be like now?"

Wyatt gives me an innocent look. "Like what?"

"One of you being over-protective and ever-present."

He pretends to think about it for a long second. "Yeah."

I laugh out loud.

We spend that night at Heath's house, and when they go to work in the morning, I head to campus.

I have a meeting with a faculty advisor in the morning, then in the afternoon I spend a couple of hours in the lab.

The annoying guy isn't there, but when I push out the back doors of the science building, he's waiting against the wall.

"Emily!"

I keep walking.

"You were gone all weekend."

No comment.

"Whose bed did you sleep in last night?"

I whirl around. "I was out of town."

He leers at me. "Not last night. I saw your car—"

"Is this guy bothering you, miss?"

I gasp in relief at the sound of Wyatt's voice and turn toward him. He looks fierce and rugged. I want to nuzzle my face into the toolbelt slung around his waist. *My hero*.

But I don't want him to get arrested for smashing a student in the face.

Also, I'm not sure why he's on campus with his work gear, because I know for a fact he spent the morning putting a new roof on a house. Very much off-campus. He texted me a few shirtless selfies to brighten my day.

"He is," I say carefully. "I've asked him to leave me alone in the past, and he isn't getting the message. Could you escort me to my dorm?"

Wyatt steps between us. "With pleasure. But is there something I can do to reinforce that message? Drag this shit-for-brains to the Dean's office and report him for harassment, maybe?"

I swallow hard. I should do that, really. I just don't want to go through the long, drawn-out process only to be told that he always stayed *just* on the right side of the line.

And I only have two credits left to complete this summer, and then I'm graduating. The end is in sight.

I smooth my hand over Wyatt's bulging biceps. "Maybe you could stay with me in my dorm room tonight? Keep me safe, all night long?"

Annoying Guy narrows his eyes at me.

Fuck him.

"Just like you did last night," I purr.

Wyatt scoops me into his arms, hitching me up over his tool belt, so I can wrap my legs around his waist.

And he carries me all the way to my dorm room. "That guy—"

"I know." I kiss his face and wiggle out of his arms. "I'll be safe."

"Heath will want a copy of your class schedule."

I kiss him again. "Okay."

"Emily—"

"Wyatt." I press his cheeks with my hands, turning his head. "Look where we are. Do you want to channel Mr. Bossy Pants, or do you want to touch me inappropriately in my dorm room?"

He groans and nods. "You have no idea how long I've wanted to be in here with you."

"Tell me everything you want to do."

"This, to start." He kisses me deeply, inhaling as our mouths fuse together like he's just found a sense of inner calm.

Or maybe that's just me, because kissing Wyatt is my happy place. "I know, I love kissing you, too, but like…the dirty stuff." I waggle my eyebrows at him. "Blow job at my desk? Rail me from behind on my tiny bed? Stand in the doorway and pretend to paint something while I get changed?"

He's breathing hard as I unbutton my cardigan, revealing a little bralette underneath. Nothing but a lace band and delicate ribbon straps. The panties I'm wearing under my skirt match. I had big plans to play the innocent co-ed tonight at Heath's house, but in my dorm room is even hotter.

"Do you like what you see, mister?"

"You're the prettiest girl I've ever laid my eyes on," he whispers, his gaze locked on my breasts. "You make me thirsty, little miss."

"Thirsty for what?"

"You." He catches me around the waist and tumbles me onto the bed. My skirt sails up, settling around my hips, and his breathing stops as he catches sight of the lace scrap barely covering my mound.

My bare mound, because I shaved before lab today. Totally smooth and baby soft for my favorite sex buddy.

"Little miss," he breathes. "Your panties are indecent."

"Can I tell you a secret?" I crook my finger at him, and he tosses his tool belt across the room, then climbs on top of me, his legs bracketing mine. "I'm a very naughty girl. I've been watching you for weeks as you restore this building, and all I can think about is that big bulge behind your tool belt, and what it would feel like pushing into me."

"Show me what you imagined." He holds himself still above me. "Would I pin you down?"

I roll beneath him, getting on my belly. "Like this," I pant.

"Your tight little nipples grazing the mattress, fuck…" He palms my ass. "Do I lick you first? Or are you already slick for me, desperate to be filled?"

I cry out, *that one*, and he swears under his breath. His zipper rasps loud in my quiet dorm room, then he yanks my panties down my thighs and hitches my hips in the air.

"Fucking tight little coed cunt," he growls. "No way you can take me like this."

I mewl and arch my back, presenting for him. His cock thrusts thickly against my pussy, and it feels for a moment like he might be right, like I'm too small for him, but then he squeezes my ass cheeks in his fists, pulling everything between my legs taut—my pussy, and my asshole now feel like they're very much on display.

"You're wet for me," he breathes. "Aren't you, Emily? Saw me in my tool belt and your body ached for what I'm about to give you."

I groan and nod desperately.

He pushes against me again, and this time the hard crown slips inside.

Just the tip, pulsing inside my pussy.

We both exhale lustily, almost at the same time, then he squeezes my hips and thrusts all the way in.

Fuck, fuck, fuck. *Yes.* I shove my hand between my body and the mattress, blindly reaching for my clit. I'm already there, holy crap, and just—another—

I come on the third deep thrust, crying his name into the sheet, and he thunders to his own climax behind me, his whole body covering mine as he fucks me into the bed like a rutting animal.

My clit pulses and my whole pussy clenches around him as he spurts deep.

It's filthy, and raunchy, and perfect.

He kisses the back of my neck once he regains his breath. "We're going to be late for dinner. Heath is making spaghetti."

"It was worth it."

I'm still blushing as we get dressed again.

He carefully helps me into the nothing-but-lace under-wear, then buttons up my cardigan. "I dreamed of this for a long time. I'm glad we got to be together in this room."

I press up on my toes, kissing him softly on the mouth. "Me, too."

18
wyatt

WHEN WE ARRIVE at Heath's, another truck is in the driveway. I instantly recognize it as Daniel Burke's.

Heath's business partner.

And my other boss.

We talked a little about how to handle this conversation with Daniel, but I thought we'd have a few more days at least before we had to come clean that we are in a relationship with Emily. All three of us.

I'm prepared to stop working for them, because I can do any kind of manual labour. But Heath swears up and down it's fine.

I guess we're about to find out.

Before I can explain that run of thoughts to Emily, she jumps out of my truck. "Rosie?"

A pretty brunette about Emily's age appears from around Daniel's truck. Emily must have seen her from the passenger side.

"Emily?"

I get out and follow at a polite distance.

"What are you doing here?" Emily asks.

Her friend blushes and plays with a diamond pendant hanging on a strand around her neck. "Daniel wanted to introduce me to his business partner."

"Your boyfriend is…" Emily giggles. "This is a very small world. Come on." She links arms with the other woman and drags her inside.

Which leaves me standing on the driveway, looking at my other boss, who's just stepped out of his truck. "Wyatt?"

He glances to the house, where his very young girlfriend has just disappeared with my very young girlfriend, and then frowns back at me. "What are you doing here?"

"It's a long story. You're here to see Heath?"

"Yeah. It's been a busy spring, and…" He grins. "I've been keeping Rosie a secret, but she's told her parents we're together, so now it's time to share the news more broadly."

"Mmm." Well, that should take the sting out of what we have to tell *him*. "Let's go inside, then."

He gives me a strange look, like who am I to be so casual about inviting him into his business partner's house?

I don't have an etiquette guide for this. That's Heath's role in our dynamic.

Luckily, the man in question is waiting at the door. His gaze meets mine in a *are we doing this?* question, and I nod.

"So I've met Rosie, officially," he starts. "Emily introduced her as your girlfriend. But I'm pretty sure we've met before, right? Isn't she Mel's friend?"

Daniel's *daughter*? I grin. Fuck yeah, we're fine.

To his credit, Daniel doesn't look away. "We discovered a mutual attraction in Vegas."

"Mel's wedding." Heath looks like he's enjoying this. "The hot date you texted me about?"

Daniel grins. "Rosie."

"Fuck you."

"She's perfect, Heath. I can't help who I fall in love with." Another grin. "And if I could help it, I'd pick Rosie over and over again. She makes me so fucking happy."

Heath slings his arm around my shoulders. "So, about that. We have some news."

Daniel blinks. "You? And…*you?*"

"And me," Emily says, sliding into the conversation as Rosie joins Daniel.

Our little miss wraps her arms around Heath, giving him a tight squeeze, then holds her hand out firmly in Daniel's direction. "I'm Emily, by the way. We haven't met yet, but I know Rosie from school, and obviously I'm a big fan of your colleagues here."

I choke on a laugh. *Colleagues.*

But her brazen redirection of the conversation works.

Daniel nods a few times, visibly processing what he's just learned. "Are they taking good care of you?" he finally asks.

She beams. "The best."

Rosie kisses Daniel on his cheek. "Isn't this fun? We'll have to all get together to celebrate Emily's birthday."

At the same time, Heath and I turn to Emily and say, "When is your birthday?"

19
heath

two weeks later

EMILY BLOWS out the candles on her cake with gusto. Our little miss is twenty-one now, and we celebrate with chocolate cake and free-flowing champagne.

Everyone claps, then she carefully removes all twenty-one candles, setting them on a plate before cutting the cake into even slices.

"What did you wish for?" I ask her after she crawls into my lap to share a piece with me.

From across the room, I notice Daniel's raised eyebrow at the adoring way I hold my little one, but I don't care. He's just as besotted with Rosie.

Emily licks a bit of chocolate frosting off her thumb, her eyes twinkling. "It's a secret."

I lower my voice. "You can share your secret with Daddy, though."

She leans in, her chocolatey breath warm and intoxicating. "I wished…"

I squeeze her hip, encouraging her to tell me what she wants. Whatever it is, I'll make it happen.

She smiles nervously. "I wished that I could move in here when I finish school at the end of the summer."

My cock thickens. Time for Daniel and Rosie to take their cake and hit the road. "You can move in tonight if you want. You're sleeping here almost every night anyway. Let's make it official."

The only nights she's spent on campus have been at her demand, because she has studying she needs to do and two boyfriends eager to please her at all hours of the day competes with that.

But we can be better about that.

Maybe.

Definitely, if it means she's in my bed permanently.

Wyatt comes in from the kitchen and sprawls beside me. I tangle my fingers in his hair, tugging him close.

He chuckles. "What?"

"Tell him what you just told me," I urge Emily.

She climbs onto his lap and whispers that she's going to move in here.

I squeeze Wyatt's neck. We've already talked about this. When she's ready to move in, I want him to move in, too.

He gives us both one of his happy, goofy grins. "Sounds like a plan. I'm off tomorrow, I can do the bulk of the move out while she's in class."

"Excellent." I stand, leaving Emily in our lover's arms, and catch Daniel's eye.

He kisses Rosie, murmuring something about leaving shortly, then follows me down the hall to my den.

For a long time, this house was my bachelor pad. Now

I'm moving two people into it, and every space will change. Maybe I'll give Emily this room for her studies, since I also have an office at our headquarters.

"It's nice seeing you happy," he says when I close the door behind him.

"Thank you. And the same, of course. Rosie is a wonderful partner."

He nods. "She is."

"Speaking of that…" I lean back against my desk. "I'm not asking a question here, but I want to give you a heads up. I'm going to be getting my lawyer to draft a trust that provides Emily and Wyatt the same legal protections as they would have if they could both be my spouse."

"Okay."

"And I know that as my business partner this—"

He frowns. "I said okay. I mean it. Look at how happy you are. And honestly? Wyatt? I should have seen that months ago. He's been a bright light in your life since he joined our team, but something happened earlier this year, didn't it?"

My chest goes hot. "We saw Emily. At the same time. And she was off-limits, because she was a student and we had that big contract with the college. But I knew he fell for her, like…so hard, and she was everything I'd ever wanted, and he recognized that in me. It should have torn our friendship apart, but it only made us closer."

"You love her."

I do. I nod.

"And you love him."

"Yes."

"Then do what you need to protect your family. And our

business will be behind you one hundred percent." He holds out his hand, and when I take it, he yanks me into a tight hug. "You fucking jerk, keeping secrets from me."

"Same."

He laughs. "God, we're lucky, aren't we?"

So damn lucky.

20
emily

A GIRL COULDN'T ASK for a better birthday than a day spent with her men. But for the day to end with a night also spent with them…wrapped up in them both…that would be extra perfect.

I'm sitting in front of Wyatt on the couch, teaching him to braid my hair, when Heath returns from having seen Daniel and Rosie off.

Heath stops in front of me. "Have I told you today how pretty you are in that little sundress?"

Will I ever tire of that rough burr in his voice, the way he gives me a compliment like it's foreplay?

I smile. "I think at least twice."

"Did I tell you that it would look even better hiked up around your waist?"

Mother of… my whole body melts for him as he drops to his knees in front of me and spreads my legs.

As I hoped, he growls as soon as he sees that I'm not wearing any underwear. "Emily!"

"Yes, Daddy?" I ask innocently.

Two can play the teasing foreplay game.

"When did you take your panties off?"

Wyatt dangles them over my shoulder. "That was me. We thought it would be a fun surprise for you."

Heath growls and dives in, licking my bare slit.

Wyatt had already stroked me a little, getting me worked up before we did the hair-braiding thing—because we wanted to wait for Heath.

Tonight should be about all three of us, each step of the way. Panty removal aside.

As Heath nuzzles my clit and sucks on my pussy lips, Wyatt pushes my sundress down, baring my breasts. His hands cup me from behind, tugging on my nipples and squeezing my flesh.

"Our little miss is all grown up," he grunts in my ear. "Think you're big enough to take us both tonight?"

I shiver.

They've been playing with my bum for a few days now, hinting at a birthday treat.

From between my legs, Heath glances up. "Only if you're ready for us," he warns Wyatt.

My boyfriend really wants in my ass. I know it, we all know it. That's the plan. Heath buried in my pussy, Wyatt pumping into me nice and slow from behind.

My sex clenches at the image. It's hot as heck…in theory. In reality, I'm not sure I'll ever be *ready*. But I want it anyway.

I stroke Heath's hair as Wyatt pets my tits. "Yes," I finally breathe. "I want you both tonight."

Heath gives me one more, very enthusiastic lick, then stands up and scoops me into his arms. "Then let's take this to the bedroom."

Heath's bedroom overlooks the back yard and a forested park beyond that. It's private and luxurious, and I have to pinch myself to think this is really my life—and he wants us to move in here. Share this room with him forever.

Yes, tonight is definitely the night to take this next step. All three of us, together at the same time.

But when he sets me on the bed, and Wyatt peels my dress off me, neither of them reach for the lube. Not yet.

Heath strips down first and stretches out next to me in the middle of the bed. He pats my thigh. "Sit on Daddy's face. Show me that you love me."

I laugh and climb onto his torso, wiggling my hips until I'm within licking range, then he clamps his hands on my ass and drag me the rest of the way. I gaze down at him as he leisurely circles my clit with his tongue, a pussy-drunk look on his face already.

Wyatt joins us on the bed, now naked as well, and kneels beside us, his cock a heavy brand against my hip as I turn my head to kiss him.

"We're going to lick you all over," he murmurs against my mouth. "Make you squirm before we fuck you between us like the little rag doll you want to be."

God, I love it when they're bigger than me, all over me, making me feel helpless and small. And utterly adored.

Heath kisses the inside of my thigh. "All over," he repeats. "Lie down."

"What?" I shriek as he lifts my hips. Wyatt catches me and stretches me out, so my back is on Heath's torso, my head resting against his lower belly.

Almost close enough I could twist my head and kiss his erection, but not quite.

"Our little Emily," Wyatt croons, squeezing my tits. "Relax."

Relax? "Why—"

Oh.

Heath's tongue traces the edge of one of my butt cheeks, then slides into the crease.

Oh!

I tremble as he explores my most private flesh, where they've been touching me more and more.

And when his tongue circles my back entrance, lighting up the nerves there, I cry out. Everything tightens up, but he just keeps licking and the tension quickly morphs to a wonderful, arousing heat.

Around and around he goes, groaning as his tongue preps me for what will come next.

My pussy pulses at the unexpected sensations.

Wyatt looms over me, his attention darting from my face to between my legs and back again. "She fucking likes it, Heath. Her little pussy is fluttering." Then, as if to himself, "Gotta taste that."

He bends over, and then there are two heads between my legs, Heath licking my ass and Wyatt eating my pussy with an enthusiasm that takes my breath away. I writhe between them, aching for release, but needing them inside me first, too.

As if they know that, they don't intensify their licks. They're not going to make me come like this, just drive me almost out of my mind and get me so strung out, I'll be begging for both of their cocks anywhere and everywhere.

I have truly genius boyfriends.

Did they plan this? The thought of them talking casually on a work site about how they want to lick every inch of me at the same time makes me flush even hotter. My nipples are tight, my breasts swollen, and I need…

"Hear that?" Wyatt asks, lifting his mouth for a second. "She's begging for it."

Was I?

"I need you, I need you…" Oh, yes, I was.

I'm shaking as they rearrange me, turning me so I'm facing Heath. His cock breaches my pussy in a demanding thrust, his gaze wild and on edge.

Good, it's not just me. He pulses inside me, barely moving, but primed to resume thrusting any second, as Wyatt shifts around to get behind me.

The next thing I feel is a lube-covered finger circling my hole.

"Heath got you all warmed up, didn't he?" Wyatt murmurs in my ear as he covers my back. "You're taking this so well."

It burns, just like it did yesterday and the day before, but that softens immediately. He gives me another finger, more lube, and then his cock is there.

It's Heath who murmurs for me to relax this time. He cradles me to his chest, petting my hair, and telling me I'm a very good girl as Wyatt works his thick tip past both sphincters.

I cry out once he's inside, because I know it's not all of him, but it feels so full already.

"Let Daddy hear it," Heath says, sounding very pleased

with himself. "We're going to fuck you now, little miss. Nobody can hear you cry, so let it all out."

"It's too much," I beg.

"Shh… We know." He grips my hips, holding me still as he starts to retreat. "But soon it will be just right."

Wyatt thrusts home, and I scream. Not from pain, but from startling pleasure. "Oh God, oh God, *oh God…*"

Heath rocks forward as Wyatt retreats, nailing my G-spot, and I start to shake.

"Gonna fill you up," Wyatt groans. "You gonna milk us both at the same time? Think I'll feel Heath come inside you like this?"

I mumble something, truly helpless now. My body twists with each thrust and parry, slick fluids making it all work even though it seems impossible.

And then Wyatt wraps his arms around me, cupping my breasts as he bends me up, taking over the cradling of my body from Heath. And Heath, beneath me, finds my clit with his fingers, and pinches it gently.

I didn't realize I was so close to my orgasm, but now it's ripping through me, a shattering climax that tears me into a thousand pieces.

As I come apart in Wyatt's arms, they jerk their hips faster, harder, powering toward their own releases. And when Heath buries his cock deep inside me, the throbbing pulse and the twisted expression on his face matching clues he's gone over, Wyatt joins him.

For a long, staggering moment, they are both throbbing inside me, filling me, and every inch of my hyper-aroused sex can feel it. The spurts, the contractions. As if they're pouring their souls into me.

I twist my shaking arms up behind me, catching Wyatt's neck and holding him close. His mouth finds mine, and he kisses me through the sensitive withdrawals, and then Heath is sitting up, and I'm in his lap, kissing him, too.

All three of us tumble to the bed, our kisses as ravenous as before we got started.

Heath slips away to start the shower, and then Wyatt carries me.

For once, it may be a necessity. I'm not sure I can walk, and I don't care to try.

epilogue

Emily

one year later

THE PROPOSAL HAPPENED AT CHRISTMAS. Two rings, matching small diamond solitaires on delicate bands.

"Marry us. Be ours forever, not just here," Heath said, tapping his chest, then Wyatt's, and finally mine. "But in front of those who love us, too. Daniel and Rosie will come. Your family will, too. We can do it at the cabin."

So now we're back on Virgin Peak, exactly a year after we came together that first time.

The house is overflowing with people, and the wedding preparations are underway.

Legally, it's a little more complicated, but Heath's lawyers are on it. They're going to draw up a trust and powers of attorney that ensure that no matter what, the three of us will be able to honor every vow we make today.

The love part is locked in forever.

In sickness and in health? Absolutely.

What's mine is theirs and theirs is now, apparently, mine.

And each other's. Where other people draw up prenups to limit what one has access to, Heath's pre-nup contract is utterly generous to both Wyatt and myself. He wants us to know without a shadow of doubt that we'll always be taken care of.

I don't like to think about that too much. Not when there are wildflowers to pick and a pretty white dress to slip on.

Rosie and I climb the trail behind the cabin in the morning to find enough flowers for bouquets and bouton-nieres, and then I get dressed in my childhood room, which has now been converted to *our* room, in a pretty white sundress I found at a vintage store.

My parents weren't sure of what to make of my fiancés, until they met them. By the end of the first dinner, Heath and Wyatt had won them over.

There's a knock at the door. "Em?"

"Come on in, Mom." I smooth the front of my dress.

She peeks in, then gives me a beaming smile as she closes the door behind her. In her hand is a faded velvet jewelry box. "I found this in storage. Your dad says it was his mother's."

My hands shake as I open it up. Inside is a pearl neck-lace. I hadn't planned on wearing anything around my neck, but now… "They're beautiful."

"Your grandparents were very happy here," she whispers. "We hope you will be, too, with your men."

I blink furiously, then give in to the tears for a minute. They're happy tears, after all. That's allowed on a wedding day.

She grabs a tissue and dabs my cheeks, then hugs me fiercely. "We only want you to be happy."

I squeeze her back and promise her that I am. So very happy, always.

After we touch up my makeup, we go outside and find my father. Together, my parents walk me around to the back of the cabin, where everyone is gathered—and my men wait.

There's no aisle. No music. Just the wind in the trees and the birdsong overhead as our friends and family circle around us.

The officiant welcomes everyone, and reads a moving passage about lifelong commitment.

And then, after I pass Rosie my bouquet to hold, the three of us link hands.

"Heath, do you take Emily and Wyatt to be your forever partners?"

"I do."

"Do you bind yourself to Emily as her husband, in every sense of the word?"

"I do."

"Then repeat after me." She lowered her voice to a a whisper, so it was only Heath's voice that rang out to our friends and family gathered to watch this.

Tears threaten, and wild butterflies take off in my chest. A storm of emotions, all centered on this man. My husband. My partner. And his promises.

"Emily, today I take you, together with Wyatt, as our wife. I promise to love you and cherish you, support you and protect you, every day of my life. With everything that I am and with all that I have, this is my solemn vow."

I squeeze his hand, swaying toward him.

I love you, he mouths.

I mouth the same back, then it's Wyatt's turn.

"Wyatt, do you take Emily and Heath to be your forever partners?"

"I do." He grins, repeating it again to the next question, and then it's his turn for his vows. "Emily, today I take you, together with Heath, as our wife. I promise to love you and cherish you, support you and protect you, every day of my life. With everything that I am and with all that Heath has, this is my solemn vow."

Everyone bursts out laughing on the last line, including Heath, and Wyatt grabs him in a one-armed hug, because his other hand is holding onto me.

"Just kidding," he says, sobering up. "With everything I am, and with all that I have, this is my truly solemn vow."

I wipe away the happy tears that slide loose at his humor. Because now it's my turn.

I squeeze both of their hands as I say *I do* twice. "Heath and Wyatt, today I take you as my husbands. I promise to love, cherish, support and protect you, both of you, every day of my life. With everything I am and with all that I have, this is my solemn vow."

"In honor and recognition of these vows, it is my greatest joy to recognize you as husbands and wife. In an orderly fashion, you may both kiss the bride."

Heath grabs me first, pulling me in between them. And it's Wyatt whose mouth softly closes over mine, who kisses me first, and sweetest, before turning me to my other husband for a searing embrace to mark that I am his. Theirs. Forever.

And then Wyatt needs to meet that heat, and I'm back in his arms again, and he's dipping me all the way back.

By the time I'm standing and Rosie is giving me back my

bouquet, I'm all out of breath and my cheeks have to be fiery blazes.

I don't care. Because everyone is cheering, and my husbands both have shit-eating grins on their faces.

We did it.

And now forever can begin.

———

———

Want more of Emily, Heath, and Wyatt? Keep reading for a bonus story that shows our favorite threesome five days, five months, and five years later.

five days, five months, five years

a Cabin Mates bonus story

wyatt

Five years later

MY WIFE DOESN'T LIKE to be interrupted when she's working. Our husband also doesn't like to be interrupted while *he's* working.

And since I got off work at noon, and they're both working from home today—in their respective offices, with the doors closed—I guess the only thing left for me to do is jerk off.

And maybe record it.

Send it to them.

If they open the video in our group text chat, that's on them, right? *I* won't have interrupted their busy days.

That justification makes my dick throb, so I jump in the shower, but I don't touch myself until I'm scrubbed clean and toweled dry. Then I stretch out on the bed and slowly stroke myself, taking a few artistic video shorts to share with those who I love most.

I'm grinning when Heath appears in the doorway to our bedroom, frowning.

"I didn't stroll into your office, cock in hand," I point out cheerily. "That would have been distracting."

He peels off his t-shirt just as Emily comes running up the stairs, her little feet moving fast. She skids in the door. "I have thirty minutes until my next meeting starts."

"I *left* a meeting for this," Heath growls. He doesn't work from home that often, but he's working on a proposal for a mall or some big deal shit with Daniel.

And he's a focused man when he wants to be, so I'd bet the meeting was basically wrapped up. So now he can focus on what really matters.

I wink. "What can I say? My dick is hard to pass up."

Emily climbs on top of me, bypassing the erection in question and going straight for my mouth. "You're a naughty man," she whispers before giving me a slow, sexy open-mouth kiss. "I love it when you work half-days and we sneak in a nooner."

Heath climbs onto the bed behind her, smacking her ass before dropping his hand to cup my balls. "What did you have in mind?"

"Emily's mouth on me, and your cock in her pussy."

His eyes flash hot. "You want to watch me fuck her?"

"I'd jerk off to that for sure." I lick my lips, holding his gaze. Remembering the first time we jerked off together, at Emily's urging.

Five days after we came home from our first weekend together in Virgin Peak.

heath

Five days after Emily fell in love with us

I DON'T KNOW how we tumbled into this conversation. Emily and Wyatt came over to my house for dinner, then we fucked in the kitchen because why wouldn't we, and now… she's grilling us about porn.

"You've *never* watched porn together? Never sat side by side on the couch jerking off, arms brushing sometimes? Feeling the heat of the other guy…"

The back of my neck burns as she paints a picture I can imagine all too well. "Where are you getting that?"

She licks her lips, her gaze bright. "I might be a book-worm who never kissed anyone before a weekend in the mountains with you two dirty men, but I know how to search the internet for things that turn me on."

Wyatt leans forward, his eyes just as intense as hers. "That gets you hot? Two guys watching porn?"

She nods. "*Especially* the thought of both of you, next to each other? Whoa, that's…" She takes a big, shuddering

313

breath, and leans back, bringing her heels up to rest on the couch. The skirt of her sundress falls around her waist, and we both have a front-row seat view of her swollen, well-fucked pussy. "I'm going to sit right here and touch myself. Wyatt, pretend Heath's invited you over for a BBQ—"

"Big stretch," I mutter.

She smirks. "But when you walk into his living room, there's a video paused on the TV screen."

"Not porn," I rasp out, adding to the fantasy. "It's a video of you. Taken through your dorm window. You're touching yourself while you read."

Her breath hitches, and fuck yeah, I can play this game. "What am I reading?"

I palm my cock, rubbing the long, hard length through my jeans. "Something erotic. About a little girl and the two men who teach her everything about sex."

She traces the edges of her pussy, the lightest of caresses on her outer lips. "Wyatt, what do you do when you recognize that it's me in the video? Are you hard?"

"Fucking throbbing."

She licks her lip, her gaze intent. "When Heath wraps his arm around your shoulder and says it'll be your secret if you want to find some relief…"

Fucking hell. That's how it could have gone, I realize now. "You know us better than we know ourselves, little miss."

Wyatt glances at me and grins.

"What?"

"You gotta do it, man. She wants to see how it would play out."

I shift over until our thighs are touching, and I sling my

arm around his shoulder. His erection is obvious against his fly, and looking at it makes my mouth water. "You want to jerk off while we watch her?"

He keeps his gaze on Emily, but turns his head a little. Now I'm looking at his profile, at the way his jaw clenches, then relaxes. "You gonna stroke off, too?"

"If you are."

"Fuck, yeah."

I squeeze his shoulder. "She's beautiful, isn't she?"

"Prettiest girl I've ever seen."

"Look at her little fingers go. She's so turned on." My breath brushes against his neck as I lean in. "I'd love to see her rub that wet little cunt on your cock."

He groans and unzips, that image pushing him into a raw need to have his hand on his dick.

I follow suit, fisting myself and imagining I'm jacking him off instead.

As Emily leans back and closes her eyes, we all fall silent. The only sounds are skin-on-wet-skin contact and heavy breathing.

I keep my arm slung around his shoulder. I like his warmth, the heavy solidity of his body. Even though his hand is tugging pretty hard, the rest of him barely moves an inch.

But when I stop jerking off, and I give him my full attention—watching him stroke his long, veined length is enough to make my dick weep, no touching required—he slows, his attention sliding back and forth between me and Emily.

She grins, proud of what she's orchestrated here.

My pulse slams in my neck like a fighter eager to get put in the ring. I skate my hand over his shoulder and up his neck, sinking my fingers into his hair. It's soft, silky against my fingers, and he groans when I tug it.

"What do you need?" he mumbles, rolling his head toward mine, his gaze never leaving Emily for long, but when I have his attention, it's...heady.

She smiles knowingly.

Maybe if he'd asked *what do you want*, I'd have answered differently. But he asks what I need, and I can't lie about that.

"Your mouth," I say hoarsely.

He gives me a slow, heavy blink, then slides his tongue against his lower lip. "Where?"

My skin feels on fire. "Anywhere."

He closes the gap and presses his lips against mine. The scratch of his stubble against my chin is a new sensation that my brain record-scratches on for a second, but my body is all in, immediately.

Kissing Wyatt isn't anything like kissing Emily. He's rough and playful, his tongue plunging against mine as soon as I part my lips for him.

We break apart long enough to look at our little miss. She has her fingers buried in her glistening pussy. "Keep going," she urges. "Do whatever feels right."

I haul Wyatt sideways, stretching out on the couch as he climbs on top of me, both of us eager now. Unleashed, because as much as we were just watching her, she's now watching us. A hungry girl with the horniest fantasies.

That makes it ten times hotter that I need more of his kisses, and if our bodies line up—*yes*. Fuck, *that*.

His cock slides against mine, a heavy bar I need to grind against like my life depends on it.

We're still dressed, our cocks and bare bellies the only bit of raw contact, and God, this is going to get messy.

"Gonna come," I groan.

He grunts and pushes down my body. "You said you needed my mouth."

Fuck.

Fuck.

Fuuuuu—

I shout the profanity out loud, over and over again, as he shoves his hands under my hips, mauling my ass while his mouth latches on to the thick crown of my cock.

This isn't anything like Emily, either.

And for the first time since she sent us down this kaleidoscope of pleasure, he stops looking at her. For right now, this moment as he swallows my cock, his attention is all mine.

Out of the corner of my eye, I see Emily convulse on her perch on the ottoman, her hand buried between her legs as she comes. And then I'm coming, too, long, hot spurts down Wyatt's throat, and it's not messy at all, because he swallows every drop.

When he slides off, his mouth shiny and his smile softer than usual, I shove him back on the couch and slide off.

My turn on my knees now.

My turn to give him my undivided attention.

wyatt

Five years later, again

EMILY WIGGLES her hips at Heath, doing a very good some-kind-of-yoga pose as she licks a slow path around my cock.

But our husband isn't in any rush to fuck her—despite the thirty-minute countdown to her next meeting. He's having too much fun watching her present her sexy ass at him.

If we had more time, we could both be inside her, but making a mess in our little miss—both holes—is not conducive to her making her meeting.

And as a rising star in Conception Ridge's tech hub, Emily's work calendar needs to be respected.

Influenced heavily by jerk-off videos, but respected.

I chuckle, and she lifts her head and asks, "What's so funny?"

"I just can't wait until the end of the day."

She winks softly. "Truth is, neither can we."

Five years on, and we're still ravenous for each other. All three of us.

Our lives are fiercely private, but not any kind of secret. We still like to go to Portland every so often so we can fully cut loose. It was where Heath fucked me for the first time, after all.

emily

Five months after we fell in love

"YOU CAN'T GO OUT in public wearing that."

Heath doesn't pull the Daddy card for non-fun things, ever, so I think he's joking. But when I laugh, his frown gets deeper.

So I glance down at my adorable cat suit, then over at Wyatt. He, too, has his arms crossed over his chest. "I'm with him."

"Wait, what? You're serious?"

"Emily, your costume is *see-through*."

"Heath, *that's the point*." I'm wearing panties under it. And it's an eighteen-and-up Halloween rave in Portland, not a block party back in Conception Ridge. I adjust my kitten ears, wiggle my sparkly black-painted nose, and trail my black-painted claws over my tits. They're only slightly visible through the costume. "It's sexy."

"It's so fucking sexy." Heath growls. "That's why I want to keep it all to ourselves."

"Maybe you'll feel differently once you're in your costume." I gesture to his suitcase. "Where is it?"

He shakes his head. "I didn't bring one."

"What?" I'm…not outraged, exactly. I expected this. I have back-up options for exactly this scenario. But this feels sort of close to a fight, because what did he think we were doing when we came to Portland for a weekend of adult debauchery? "Wyatt's wearing a costume."

"Wyatt is an exhibitionist."

"And he's standing right here," our lover says dryly. "You're both right, by the way. Emily, put a bra on under that stretchy nothingness, or we're having a private party for three. And Heath, take off your shirt. You need some glitter gel on your chest."

He groans, but does as Wyatt says. I nod once he's stripped down to nothing but his jeans. He's wearing a thick leather belt, and the denim hugs every inch of his solid thighs and his nice, tight behind. "This is actually a good costume, just like this. With some glitter, of course."

Heath glances down at his hard, work-hewn body. "What am I? A middle-aged construction worker?"

I dig in my bag and pull out the perfect addition—a leather crop. "Here."

He does a double take. "Where did this come from?"

"There's a new sex store on Main Street, just down from the barbershop. I went there with Rosie last week. It's where I got the glitter gel, too."

"This is sex store glitter?" Wyatt pauses before applying an artful streak to Heath's chest. "Nice."

"What other secrets are you keeping from us, little miss?"

But Heath's bark has zero bite, because his gaze is locked on the crop.

He wants it.

The perfect counter to my extra bratty Little Miss Kitten persona.

I eye my bag. "Some handcuffs and a butt plug."

"So your plan was if I didn't bring a costume you would…"

Wyatt's grinning.

I'm grinning.

And finally Heath is grinning.

I nod. "You're my Daddy Dom tonight. The perfect costume."

An hour later, I stroll into the rave wearing a black bra under my costume, and the butt plug I shouldn't have told them about seated tightly in my back entrance. On either side of me are my burly construction workers, my Daddy Dom and my Hedonistic Sidekick.

The music pulses around us, and I drag them both onto the dance floor.

"Happy Halloween, Daddy," I murmur as I sway against Heath.

He grips me tightly and kisses me hard on the mouth.

When we break apart, two girls next to us give him the once over, then wink at me. "Hot Daddy," one of them says, making me blush. But it's okay that they heard me, too. It's wonderful that I can call him that here. "And who's your friend?"

Heath drags Wyatt into our embrace. "Our lover."

My heart explodes with happiness. And the night has just begun.

Hours later, we stumble into the hotel room, kissing each other with abandon. "I want to fuck you," Wyatt pants against my mouth. "And I want Heath to fuck me at the same time."

"What?" I turn and kiss Heath. "Did you talk about this?"

They do that sometimes, keep sexy secrets from me, so it can be a fun surprise. But Heath looks just as surprised as I'm sure I do.

Surprised, and turned on. "You sure?"

"Definitely." Wyatt pulls him in for a lingering kiss.

My heart skips a beat at the sight.

Then Heath breaks free, pushing Wyatt toward my bag. "She's probably packed some lube in there. Find it."

"Three kinds," I chirp as Daddy picks me up and tosses me on the bed.

"How attached are you to this fucking cat costume?" he growls.

"I'll never wear it again."

"Good." He rips the translucent material right down the front, revealing the tiny bra I put on for modesty. "Your sweet little body has been tempting us all night."

I arch my back as he yanks the bra cups down, baring my nipples. He latches on to one and pinches the other, his mouth hungry and his fingers clever.

His other hand yanks the tattered costume down my body, then shoves my underwear aside so he can stroke my bare flesh.

"Jesus, she's already soaked for you," he grinds out, speaking to Wyatt.

Our lover appears on my other side, and his hand joins Heath's between my legs. "Fucking wet little pussy. Can't wait to be inside you."

"I want her to come on my face first."

"I'll suck her tits, then."

Sometimes I can't believe this is my life, and it gets extra surreal in moments where they talk about me like I'm their little fuckdoll.

But then they both lift their heads and lock onto my face. "Sounds like a plan, little miss?"

And it's not surreal at all. It's perfectly *us*. I nod. "Lick me, Daddy. Get me ready for Wyatt."

They get me all the way naked, then Heath is between my thighs, his tongue slow and sure as it slides between my folds. I'm already on the edge, my clit throbbing, my whole sex swelling and soft.

Ripe and ready, that's how I feel. Primed.

So when he latches on to my clit, I go flying. "Yes, yes, *yes*," I chant, grabbing his head, my whole body curling up as he sucks my orgasm out of me. And then I collapse and he keeps licking, making hungry growls until Wyatt playfully pulls him off.

They share a kiss. Then Wyatt presses his preferred lube into Heath's hand. "I'll get inside her first."

Shaking, I pull Wyatt on top of me. He spreads his thighs wider than usual, bending me almost in half, and then he slides into me, pressing against all those sensitive nerve endings Heath just lit up.

"You okay?" he breathes when we're nose to nose.

"I think that's my question for you," I whisper back.

His eyelids flutter, his breath hitching, and I know that's Heath touching Wyatt, getting him ready.

"This is so sexy." I keep murmuring to him as he rocks into me. Everything that Heath is doing to him transferring through to where he's speared deep into my belly. "Are you going to come so fast?"

"Fucking try not to."

"First times, though…" I'm teasing, a reminder of how fast he went off *our* first time together.

Now he's an old pro who can fuck me for hours, and he sometimes does, but tonight might be fast for all three of us. Heath barely had to lick me, and I shot to the moon.

Now it's their turn. And the way Wyatt is throbbing inside me, I might go again, too.

Heath lets out a slow, controlled breath, then there's a press, a pause, and finally I feel his whole body weight rock against Wyatt.

Wyatt lets out a delicious groan, and deep inside me, his cock twitches and throbs.

I reach between us and squeeze the root of him, then glance my fingertips over my clit. Could I? Maybe.

"Fuck, you feel good," Heath growls. "So tight, Wyatt. Your ass…"

Oh yes, I could. I rub faster, my pussy fluttering around Wyatt's cock.

"She's gonna come," he grunts. "Already. Fuck, Heath, you're going to make us both come."

Heath grunts. They're both moving now, fast, bucking against each other, Wyatt riding me hard, and I hitch my legs up around his torso, finding a new angle, and *that*. *There. Yes...*

I cry out, and Wyatt groans, his whole body spasming as he fills me up. And then he's on me, so heavy, just for a second before Heath shifts his hips, bodily hauling Wyatt back against him. We lock gazes as he finishes inside Wyatt, and the electricity sparking between us could power a large city.

Love you, I mouth. *Love you both*.

He gasps and falls forward, pressing his mouth to Wyatt's shoulder.

I stroke their heads and think about what a very good idea that costume was.

wyatt

Five years later, finally

I CATCH Heath's gaze as Emily pulls me into her mouth. "Isn't our girl something?"

He grins. We both love this, talking about her while she's stuffed from both ends. Ninety percent of the time, we're wrapped around her pinky finger, but once she's naked, we're unfiltered and hot for her on every level. Loud, mouthy, perverted levels.

His eyes stay locked on me as he takes her fast and hard. It makes her gasp around my cock, her hot breath as much a turn on as her soft lips and wet tongue.

I never could have imagined all those years ago when I joined his construction crew that we'd end up here, with a girl we share, and a life we love. Together.

As Emily strokes my balls, then her clever fingers questing lower, my eyelids get heavy, but still I maintain eye contact with Heath. I want him to see what he does to both of us. What I shamelessly invited them both up here to do to me, with me. All three of us, in a tangle of flesh. Our perfect combination.

I love to be between them, but this is my favourite way to fuck, when I can see both of them stretched in front of me.

"Fuck, I'm going to come," Heath grunts.

Emily pops off my cock and swivels her head to the side. "Do it," she pants. "Then I'll climb on Wyatt."

Fuck… My balls churn at the thought.

Heath's gaze goes hot, molten hot, and his fingertips turn white on her hips as his breath goes ragged. Three grunts and a thrust later, our connection breaks as he looks down between her ass cheeks. He bites his lower lip, smacks her hip, then eases out and collapses beside me.

Shaking, she climbs on top of me.

"Messy," she whispers, her eyes sparking.

I lied. *Messy* is my favourite way to fuck.

"Gonna come for me?"

She nods.

"Good girl." I smooth my hand over her cheek, then down onto her neck. She leans into my fingers, letting me give her some pressure there as I fit my cock against her slick entrance. As I push in, some of Heath's come slides out, and fuck, that's gonna do it for me.

Heath reaches over and puts his thumb against her clit as I squeeze the side of her throat.

Panting, she meets my first thrust, then my second, but on the third, she shatters, and I take over, pounding up into her, filling her with her second deposit of come for the lunch hour.

"I think you'll be a minute late for your meeting," I mumble into her hair as she collapses between us.

A quiet giggle is her only response.

Thank you so much for reading Cabin Mates and wanting a little more! If you want to stay in touch while I write it and all the other future books set in Conception Ridge, please join my Secret Chloe Maine Book Daddy Appreciation Club on Facebook: facebook.com/groups/chloemainebooks

about the author

Chloe Maine has written other books before, but none of them as purely id-driven as Before He Was Her Headmaster. She delights in the fantasy of bending big men to the wicked desires of supposedly innocent women. When she's not writing, she's probably reading. She lives in Canada with her own big man, raising the babies they made together.

facebook.com/chloemainebooks
twitter.com/chloemainebooks
instagram.com/chloemainebooks
tiktok.com/@chloemainebooks